A Walk Through the Grapes

David Jackson

Every snail is a cheetah
In the eyes of its mother.

This book is dedicated to my loving mother who has always believed in me and supported everything I have ever done. I don't know where I would be without you.
All my eternal love.

A Walk Though the Grapes
David Jackson

Chapter 1

The train whistle's scream pierced through the silent night's cold air. The deafening quiet that everyone in town was accustomed to magnified the sound. The tracks ran straight through the small town of Willowcreek and had been in use for hundreds of years. The click clack of the pounding wheels on the unsuspecting track beneath made a somewhat therapeutic rhythm.

Jace Grazer sat in his dark blue pickup truck watching the massive locomotive steam by. This was the first time in almost two years that he was going to be back home in the small town which he loved. His mind was racing with excitement to see his family again. It was a nervous excitement which was growing with every mile that he got closer. As the last car rumbled by, his sight opened up to beautiful Main Street. Albeit the town was very old, he did not see it that way. Buildings lined both sides of the street as far as his vision could see. He loved the look of old brick structures with painted on signs which were slowly fading away. No matter where he was in the world, the thought of a town with no traffic lights brought a smile to his face. He slowly pushed the gas pedal and pulled his truck into the first open space right across from a small antique store. As his boot hit the ground, he took a deep breath and closed the door behind him. *Cool Crisp country air* he thought to himself, nothing was quite like it.

He strolled down the small sidewalk just looking around, anxious to get home to his family, yet in no hurry. He knew his mother would be making dinner for the family tonight because it was Friday, and some traditions never change. Jace wanted to surprise his mother with a bouquet of flowers before he went home. She loved to garden in her spare time and had always appreciated the gifts that nature gave her.

Three buildings down, an all windowed door flew open followed by the clanging of small bells banging onto the glass door.

"Jace!" A familiar voice rang through the air. By the time he was able to turn his head, he was met with two arms wrapped around him.

"I can't believe you are back! It is great to see you!" The young voice said. Reciprocating the hug, he looked down at the top of a blonde head with hair tied up loosely in a ponytail. He stood around 6'2 but felt much taller next to this girl.

"McKenzie? Is that really you?" By the sound of his voice she could tell he was genuinely surprised to see her.

"You look so different and grown up." He was surprised at what a woman she had grown up to be. She wore tight dark blue jeans with small holes near the knees and thighs. A short necklace with a small cross lay on top of a faded yellow t-shirt. She was three years behind him when they were in school and rode the same bus he did. They always ended up spending a lot of time together since their parents had been friends well before they were born. Her sister Ally and Jace were closer in age and friends growing up. As time went on, they became something more once they hit their late teens. The secret crush McKenzie had on Jace always made her feel jealousy toward her sister. The sad part is she loved when he came around, even if he was "taken" by her sister. He looked at McKenzie as another little sister, yet this was no longer a little girl, she was a young and beautiful woman.

"Does Ally know you are home?" She could tell her voice was high and cracking with excitement yet there was nothing she could do about it.

"I am not sure who my mom has told yet." She was the big gossiper of the family and news seem to leave her lips faster than her breath.

"I didn't leave on the best terms with her." He said looking down to his boots. Jace pointed to the door she came out of.

"You work down here?" Changing the subject as quickly as he could. The sign hanging above the door read "Creeks Cuts" and had a small pair of scissors next to it.

"I am a hairdresser now." Even through the words she spoke, she could feel that her big smile was not vacating her face.

"The pay isn't great, but I make decent tips and I really enjoy the people in town and the stories I get to hear." She was absolutely right, in a small town, any gossip was inevitably leaked at either the salon or the grocery mart. The old saying is "The nice and sometimes scary part about living in a small town, is that when you don't know what you're doing, someone else always does.

"I tend bar at 'The Ranch' usually on Thursday and Friday

nights as well." A big grin came to Jace's face.

"That must be a fun atmosphere." She could tell his words were dripping with sarcasm. The bar had a long history of being a watering hole for trouble makers. Fights were practically a nightly occurrence.

"It's not too bad there now, the food is really great and good ol' country music is mandatory. Plus, my father bought the Bar and Grill about a year ago, and it has gone through an awesome renovation." A lump formed in Jace's throat and he instantly thought about how to retract his previous statement.

"Is your Dad still a police officer as well?" Saying the first thing that came to mind, it was a good pivot.

"Yes, he is. As a matter of fact, he is a sheriff now. He manages to keep himself busy that is for sure!"

"McKenzie" A voice rang through the air from the front door of the salon. He was saved by the bell smashing against the glass door.

"Oh goodness, I have someone in my chair, I have to get back. I really would like to catch up" She said looking up at him. Her mind was racing, he looked so good and she didn't want to stop talking to him. She hugged him again and ran back to the open door.

   He continued down Main Street until he hit one of his favorite spots. A small one lane bridge that hung over the big creek. The old covered bridge which was always repainted yearly, was bright red now. There was a small walkway on the side of the bridge where he used to sit with his legs dangling over the water to think. There was a picture in his parents' home of their four children all standing in front of the bridge. Jace was around ten when the picture was taken, and he always smiled every time he saw it on the wall. He always loved to play by the creek or just hang with his friends there. There was a small park that lie right next to the water where lots of families had Sunday picnics after church. The grass was green and you couldn't beat the smell of the grills cooking up burgers and dogs. He stopped for a minute and watched the water crash over the rocks beneath the bridge. The sound of trickling water always reminded him of this exact spot.

Surprisingly, the selection of flowers was larger than he was anticipating. The lady who ran the flower stand was an older woman. She sat behind a folding table next to the sidewalk indulging in a book; not seeming to notice that Jace was even there. She looked like the type of person who would have an interest in flowers. Her apron had pictures of sunflowers on it that were fading and covered with smudges of dirt. She turned a page in her book quickly and looked up at Jace. Giving him a smile, she went back to her reading. After looking around at the many different colors and smells, he found what he was looking for and purchased a big bundle of red and pink carnations. The woman stood up from her chair and wrapped them in nice paper. Her hands worked so fast, yet she was very gentile with the delicate flowers. Thanking the woman, Jace wondered who she was and why he could not remember her. Maybe she was new to town? The fact he couldn't put her face to a name saddened him as he realized that some aspects of his hometown were going to be different than he remembered them.

As he made his way back to his truck, holding the flowers in one hand, he couldn't seem to shake the sad feeling that things may be different now. He set the bouquet in the passenger's seat ever so gently as if he was laying a baby down. Rolling his window down, he put the truck in reverse. 'The sky is always so much prettier here in the country' he thought to himself. A grin came to his face at how ridiculous that thought was, yet, he believed it completely.

Chapter 2

The small town of Willowcreek was protected well by several tall mountain ranges. Jace loved the drive down to his parents' house. They lived in a suburb of Willowcreek about ten minutes away from town. He hadn't eaten in about five and a half hours and his stomach was making ominous noises. The road to his parent's house lined the side of Finn Lake. It was a large body of water and a very desirable place to live. In the summer months, the lake was the place to be. Nightfall was getting very close and the last remaining rays of sun were glistening off the ripples of water. Jace took a right turn onto Stillwater road, the road which he grew up on. Pulling into his old driveway was an impressive sight. Trees lined both sides of the stone driveway which had a small patch of grass running up the center. The trees opened up at the end of the driveway letting you see the Grazer's large grey house which sat perched up on one of the highest points of their property. The Grazer family had owned this home for three generations. Jace's parents Robert and Marie Grazer had inherited it from Robert's father some forty years ago. They have seen their four children grow up in this home and had no plans to ever leave.

Robert had purchased neighboring land twenty-two years ago with the intention of starting a vineyard.

They owned a grand total of seventy-three acres of prime grapevine growing land. Being that a big portion of their land bordered Finn Lake, the soil was perfect for growing grapes. They also had a professional build an irrigation system onto their land. This was surprising as Robert never liked to hire "outside help" to work on his land. As progressively he had gotten older, that rule was relaxed somewhat for his own benefit. The grapevines were standing at attention in perfectly straight parallel lines. His father had started a very successful business which he loved. Hopping out of the truck and climbing the many stairs two at a time to the front door of their house, Jace knocked and waited very anxiously for an answer. As the door swung open his younger sister stood there with a surprised look on her face.

"Oh my gosh he does exist." Her words made him feel bad once again.

"Hey Jen, how have you been?" He said lowly as he stepped into the entryway.

"I missed you very much" He tried very hard to make his words sound sincere because they were, although they still came out sounding forced. Jace embraced her with a long hug and kissed her on the cheek. The smell that emitted from the kitchen was a heavenly one. It smelled of ham, potatoes and watermelon. Jace had wondered if his mother had a candle burning as watermelon was one of her favorite scents and a staple of her house.

Jace walked into the kitchen and found his mother bent over the stove temping the food inside.

"Hi Ma." Those two simple words almost brought tears to

her eyes. She hadn't seen her boy in over two years and was long overdue to be reunited. She jumped up leaving the oven door open and hugged Jace knocking the flowers out of his hands. Her hug was tight and meaningful which she held for a good thirty seconds.

"How have you been? You look so skinny. Are you hungry? You look tired. Are you tired? Was it a long drive?" Jace was flooded with questions before he could even muster a word. She rubbed both sides of his face with her two hands as if she was trying to get to know his face again.

"Geez Mom, I wish you were this excited to see your faithful daughter." Jen said with a mix of anger and jealousy.

"Give it a rest Jen." A loud booming voice came through the garage door. His father looked aged since the last time he had seen him. His hair was much lighter than it had been before. He had a beer belly started which had gotten bigger.

"Hello Son, it is good to see you again. You are looking skinny." *Oh boy its unanimous.* Jace thought to himself.

"Hello sir. It is good to see you again." His words were followed with a firm handshake. Jace and his father never saw eye to eye. His father spent eight years serving his country. He ended his time in the military being a drill sergeant for new recruits on basic military skills. He brought his military ways home and incorporated them into running a business, and sometimes, into being a father. He was a firm man who loved his family very much but had high expectations for all his children. Jace always felt that more was expected from him and that he had never lived up to what his father wanted.

Robert walked over to the sink to wash his hands. "Dinner is almost ready darling." His wife said as she leaned over and pecked his cheek.

"What about Dane and Lizzy? Are they still coming over tonight?" Dane was their oldest child and was always the "wild child." Even to this day, trouble always seemed to find him. He was also the only one who was still currently living at home. That is until tonight when Jace finally came home. Dane hardly ever slept at home as his girlfriend had her own apartment in town. He spent most of his nights there; when they were not having one of their usual argument. Lizzy was their third child and was born 11 months after Jace. Jen was the baby of the family and she took full advantage of that fact.

"They both said they are..." Her mother was cut off by a knock at the door. Jace pulled the heavy wood door open and before he could even say a word, his feet were off the ground. He was spinning in circles listening to his brother screaming his name. His feet hit the floor and he was staring into the big smile his brother was giving him.

"How have you been my man? Damn it's good to have you home!" Dane said rubbing Jace's hair back and forth on his head roughly. Lizzy had walked in and was standing aside waiting for the big show she knew Dane would put on to finally be over.

"What's up Pop?" Dane engaged into a loud conversation with his dad. Lizzy put her arms around Jace and exchanged pleasantries.

"How has school been Liz?" Jace was the only one who she

let her call "Liz." Her full name was Elizabeth but almost everyone knew her as Lizzy.

"I am hanging in there. I have several intense classes, but I plan to have my degree in a little over a year." She had always wanted to work with people so she could try to help as many as she could.

"It's ready! Come have a seat." Her mom yelled from the kitchen.

They all had seats surrounding the big dining room table that inevitably never changed. As soon as Jace sunk into his seat he felt as if all eyes were on him. Surprisingly, dinner started out very quiet. The first question was directed in Robert's direction.

"So, how's business been pop? Everyone seems pretty busy out there." Dane was referring to the four employees that work for their Father.

"It is going very well. Grapes are growing, and the harvest should be a very good one this year. I have a surprise for EVERYONE at this table." His father said with a clever smile. Marie looked at him with a surprised look.

"I am going to need your help in the morning boys." Looking confused, both boys nodded at their father. Everyone seemed to wolf down their food without hesitation. Tasting a home cooked meal again was a welcome sensation for Jace. No matter where he went or how many different restaurants he ate at, there was something about his mom's cooking that he loved. Dane and their father talked about baseball and debated who was going to win it all this year. His sisters and their mother had side conversations about many different things. Cooking, shopping, school. As soon as plates were cleared, their Father popped up out of his chair at the head of the table.

"Get your shoes, we're heading outside." Everyone obliged and they hopped in his truck, Dane and Jace climbed into the bed. The truck flew down an old dirt road that led to what they called the "back field." Three large barns stood tall full of equipment needed to run their vineyard and the property. By this time, it was pitch dark out and the only light that could be seen was small light bulbs that hung loosely above each barn door. The moon was covered by clouds which didn't help anyone's vision. The truck was pointed towards the barn but the headlights were old and dim providing minimal light. Robert slid the door open and flipped on the lights. Right before them, leaned up against the bucket of his tractor, was a huge metal sign. Engraved in big letters were the words "Grazer's Grapes." Underneath was the word "Vineyard" and some pictures of grapes on a vine. The sign was massive and was outlined with white lights.

"This is the new sign for the outside of our ranch!" Robert said proudly.

"I wanted us all to see it as a family before I hang it up. I had it custom made just for our vineyard. I hope you all like it."

"It's amazing Dad, truly." Jen chimed in.

"We will help you set it up in the morning" Dane said as he smacked Jace on the back including him in his offer.

Jen and Lizzy left about a half an hour later. They shared an apartment not far from their parent's house.

Dane was talking loudly on his cell phone from the inside of his bedroom. Jace sat on his old bed looking around his room. His mother had not changed anything from the last time he occupied the room.

"Goodnight Dane" Jace heard his mom yell from outside his room. Her footsteps were moving down the hall to his open door.

"Are you going to be okay in here tonight?" His mom asked as she sat next to him on the end of his bed.

"Absolutely! Just like old times." His answer made his mother smile.

"Do you need anything before you go to sleep? I know you have not stayed here in a while, but I promise nothing has changed." He suddenly felt like a child again but didn't mind at all.

"I am all set." There was a long pause between his words. "Thank you Mom." Jace said looking down.

"For what sweetie?"

"Just thank you." The sadness in his eyes was apparent. She kissed him on the forehead and started to head toward the door.

"Ma!" he exclaimed as his mother was shutting his door.

"Yes?"

"I love you."

"I know you do sweetheart. I love you too." A moment of silence filled eye contact made them both feel the same happiness. She closed the door gently behind her. Her footsteps were magnified on the creaky wood steps as she went downstairs. That was the price you paid for having an older home. Everything seemed to creek under your feet.

It was just more noticeable for Jace now since he had been away for so long.

Jace slid into bed and put his head on his pillow. He could see out to the dark night sky. He was absolutely exhausted from the day when he closed his eyes and tried hard to fall asleep. As his body lay limp on the fresh sheets, he could not seem to shut his mind down. His body was home, his thoughts were dispersed everywhere.

Chapter 3

The weightless feeling inside made Jace feel very unnerved. Falling, faster and faster. All he could see was blackness surrounding him. His lungs tightened making it next to impossible to breathe. A cold sweat draped over his body. At the last second, he realized what he was falling towards. He hit the water with such force it felt like his insides were bleeding. Frantically, he tried to kick his feet, but to no avail. His body was being pulled down further and further and he was powerless to stop it. The harder he seemed to struggle, the worse off it made him. One last breath filled his mouth with water...

Jace shot up in bed choking and gasping for air. Looking around the room quickly, he had forgotten where he was. As he sat there in bed trying to calm his mind down, he realized he actually had been sweating. There was an outline of sweat residing in his bed where he had been sleeping. The glow of a small light stood out in the darkness of his room. The clock radio projected the red numbers 3:47am. Standing up out of bed, Jace slipped his shirt back on and slowly headed to the door. Turning the old door knob and creaking the door open just a crack, he poked his head out to an empty hallway. Stepping as lightly as he possibly could, suddenly he was having flashbacks of when he was younger; slipping out at night trying not to get caught by his parents or his siblings. He even had every step memorized. He knew which ones creaked the most and even which part of the step made noise. He had it down to an exact science and it worked like a charm...most days. There was no need for him to sneak around now but he still felt like he should.

Jace made it down the stairs and into the kitchen without any issues. Opening the refrigerator, he noticed his mother had stocked it with orange soda, his favorite beverage. Just as he cracked the seal, a hand gently grabbed his shoulder. He whipped around and his soda flew from his hand. Hitting the floor, the orange liquid spewed from the bottle all over his father's slippers.
"Dad! You scared the crap out of me." Holding his chest, Jace was trying to recover from his sudden fright and catch his breath. His father's feet didn't move. Looking down at his feet and back up to his son's blank expression.
"I'm sorry Dad, let me get some paper towels. Did I wake you?"
"No, I was up watching some TV. I heard footsteps coming down the stairs. You must have lost your touch huh?" His father said with a sly look upon his face. Surprised his father was privy to his sneaking out, he didn't want to push the envelope any further. Jace knelt down and started to wipe the floor.
"I wanted to talk to you son." His father's voice had a mysterious tone to it. Both men moved to the counter that split the kitchen and dining room and perched on the stools next to it.
"What's up Dad?"
"I just wanted to say that I am happy you are home.

Having the whole family back together has made your mother happier then I have seen her in a long while." The blissfulness of his words let Jace feel at ease.

"What are your plans now that you are home again?" This was the question that Jace had been asking himself since he pointed his truck towards Williowcreek and didn't look back.

"I have a few ideas, but nothing is set in stone." He tried to make his answer sound as concrete as possible. Before he could expand upon his sentence his father chimed in.

"Well for now, we would like you to work here...that is if you are interested. There is a lot around here that I have plans to do and it would be just temporary until you find what you are looking for." Jace had planned to stay at their house anyway so the offer was dignified.

"Thank you, Dad. It would be great to help out around here, just until I can find employment obviously." He wanted to make sure to leave his options open, plus he didn't want to sound desperate to his father.

"Well you better get some sleep bud, morning is going to come quick." Hearing his father call him "Bud" was always a good sign. Jace climbed the stairs once again and finally felt tired enough to get some rest.

The morning breeze that blew in off the lake was always an amazing feeling to wake up to. The sound of Dane's voice from downstairs was bellowing through the house. Jace realized he had slept in longer than he wanted to. Making his way to the kitchen he could smell coffee brewing.

"What's up kid?!" Dane shouted overexcitedly in Jace's direction. He ran over to him and kissed him on the cheek. Pushing him away, Jace wiped his face and grinned.

"I see we are still being obnoxious this morning."

"You know how much your brother missed you?" His mother chimed in.

"Are you hungry this morning? Why don't you have some coffee while I whip you something up?" Both boys sat down at the table and had a cup.

"Listen Jace, I want to have a big bon fire tonight in the back field. I spoke with Dad and he said it would be cool to have some people over, you know like we used to. What do you think about that?"

"That actually sounds perfect. I'd like to get reacclimated with everyone here." Jace was secretly nervous to see some of the people from his past, but he didn't want to show it. He thought his best way to combat that feeling was to make it seem like he was excited to see everyone again.

"Who are you planning to invite?" Jace asked curiously.

"Just a few people that we used to hang out with" This was a funny statement Dane made because Jace knew there were several inaccuracies with it. First, they never really "hung out" with the same crowds, and second, everyone knew that anything Dane did was never small. If he was going to have a "few" people over for a fire; that meant you better prepare to be swamped with bodies.

Their mother placed bacon, eggs and toast on the table and they both dug in.

"Where is Dad this morning?"

"He had to run an errand. Apparently, he was having trouble getting the tractor started. He's been having an issue with it for a while, but I guess it finally gave out on him today."

Dane poured himself another cup of coffee.

"I know he wanted to put up our new sign today. I can help him with the tractor when he gets back."

"You don't have to work today Dane?" His mother sounded surprised.

"No, I took the next four days off. When I heard my little Bro was coming home, I wanted to spend some time with him." Dane grabbed Jace's head and pulled it to his chest locking him in a head lock. Squirming, Jace couldn't break free until he jabbed Dane in the side which released his constrictor-like grip. "Plus, with us working nights, I didn't want to be tired this week." Dane worked for a construction company that always had him working on different jobs. The last few weeks he had been doing general maintenance on a bridge about forty-five minutes outside of town. They needed to close two out of the three lanes of traffic underneath it; therefore, the optimal time to work was at night.

Just as they were finishing breakfast, the sound of tires crackling on the stone driveway alerted them that their father was home. Jace ran upstairs to change his clothes and brush his teeth. By the time he came down, his father was in the kitchen complaining about something.

"Good morning Dad. Did you get the part you needed?"

His father looked at him with a scowl.

"The bastards at the tractor repair place told me they had the part in stock that I needed. I get there with the part I took off my tractor, and to no surprise, it looks nothing like what they had for me. Now they need to "special order" it and it won't be in for another two weeks! I don't know what to do. This is a crucial time for our harvest." His look of anger was turning into frustrated sadness.

"Well there is something we could try Dad." Jace had an idea hoping it would go over well.

"We could look on the internet and get it shipped here faster, possibly have it overnighted." His father was an old-fashioned man and most of the modern-day technology eluded him. Passing a piece of paper to his son, Robert started to walk towards the door.

"See what you can do son. Let me know if you can find anything." With those words his father walked back outside and down the steps.

"Dad isn't eating this morning?"

"He rarely eats breakfast. Coffee is his breakfast choice each morning" His mother replied.

"You boys should get out there and see if he needs help with anything. I know he is building a fence around some of the property." Both boys nodded their heads and obliged.

Once outside, Dane shoved his brother and ran ahead with a laugh. There was a lot that appeared different from the last time Jace was home. Coming from the main barn, the distant sound of 'Dancing in the Dark' from Bruce Springsteen rang through the air. His parents loved 'The Boss' and his music always seemed to be playing at their house. The smell of old wood mixed with fresh cut grass littered the inside of the old barn. The building was an old bank barn. It was built into the side of a hill that was situated right behind their house. They had remodeled it several years back and it still looked fresh and new. His father loved the look of it and he used it mostly for his personal items. This was one of two original barns that were built around the same time as the house. Robert was standing at his bench looking down at something. Dane walked up to him and looked down at his workbench. They stood above what appeared to be some sort of plans.

"I have some lumber coming in today and I would like to get started on this." Jace finally saw what he was looking at. The plans were for a new fence to go around the front entrance to their property.

"Along with the sign I showed you both last night, I am planning on making our whole front entrance look nicer. I am hoping that will help our business and give us some new pictures for our brochures and the website."

"Wow Dad, that sounds really nice." Dane's face perked up with excitement.

"We've been having very good turnouts to our 'Fire and Wine' promotion that we host every other Friday and Saturday nights." His father's voice was in the direction of Jace.

"Fire and wine? What exactly is that?" Jace asked curiously.

"We offer a wine tasting for a discounted rate. But that is not all. We have a firepit down next to the lake where we build a fire and have some games. People enjoy sitting by the water, drinking wine and talking with each other. It has boosted our sales those nights especially now that we offer discounted rates if they were to buy multiple bottles." Dane's explanation was satisfactory as their father nodded in agreeance.

"With the wood shipment I am getting in, I plan to build several benches and tables to go around the pit. People have been playing cards and even bringing food and

snacks, so I figured we should provide them with tables."
Their father's idea was a good one. The whole night
sounded like something Jace would enjoy. Both boys stood
there as their father made a few last markings on the
plans.

"We can help with whatever you need Dad." Dane said.
"Listen, I'm not sure what time the shipment will be
arriving, are you still planning on having a fire tonight?"
"Yea, if that's cool with you sir." Dane was always so
transparent. Anytime he wanted something, he always
acted so respectful by addressing his dad as "Sir."
"Why don't you boys go to the back field, the wooded lot
has a lot of down trees that could be cleaned out and used
for firewood."

"Thanks Pop." Dane said running to grab a chainsaw. He
tossed his brother a pair of gloves and put two chainsaws
in the back of their father's John Deere Gator.

"Get in kid" Dane said to his brother. Jace had one leg in
and Dane took off. Slamming down into his seat, Jace
smacked his brother and grabbed anything he could hang
on to. The gator flew down an old dirt path that lead to
the back field. Each bump the big studded tires hit made
both men fly up in their seats. Just as they hit the back
field, the glaring sunshine stung both of their eyes at the
same time. When Jace raised his hand to shield his eyes
from the sun, Dane jerked the wheel hard to the right and
Jace flew over to him. He grabbed his brother around the
neck and held on tight. Dane kissed his brother on the
head despite the struggle Jace was making. "I missed you
man. I missed my brother!"

"I missed you too buddy" Jace responded with a smile. It
was true, deep inside seeing his family again made him

feel very dejected. He missed everybody but especially his brother. They pulled up to the edge of the trees and jumped out.

Several hours later and what felt like a hundred-degree weather, they had a huge pile of trees and were covered in sweat and wood chips. Taking a sip of water, Jace sat down in the grass leaning against the gator. "So, how was the big city hotshot?" Dane brought it up very casually yet had been contemplating this question all day.

"It was alright." Jace kept his answer short.

"That doesn't sound very reassuring" Dane responded taking a swig from his water bottle.

"It wasn't all that I had expected it to be. Things didn't work out how I had hoped they would..."

"So, you left us all for nothing basically?" The tone in Dane's voice switched sharply to anger. Looking down at the grass, Jace pulled a handful and was flicking it with his fingers. Dane didn't wait for a response.

"You know, you could have reached out to me, or anybody in the family, OR responded to one of my thousand messages I left you! You left me without a brother." Dane whipped a glove at his brother's head. Looking up at him, Jace responded with the only two words that he knew could not fix how he had made his brother, and his family feel.

"I'm sorry."

The guilt that Jace felt inside for leaving the way he had made him scared to contact his family. At the time, he would just ignore the calls and texts as this was easier than to face reality. He didn't want to tell his brother this as he felt like a coward for not having the courage to face what he had done.

Dane was breathing heavily, and it looked as if he were going to continue to yell. Instead he starred at his brother for another moment, shook his head, and with an agitated grunt, walked back into the woods. Jace stood up, grabbed his chainsaw and followed him.

"Do you think we need more?" Jace shouted to his brother.

No response.

The heavily wooded area appeared so large from inside. The trees stood tall and were a beautiful sight that nature had provided them. Old leaves and sticks cracked underneath each step the boys made. There was an old rock-filled stream that they had to jump over to get to where Dane had been working. It appeared that nobody had cleaned up this area in a while. There were a lot of down trees and the path which they had been following had diminished. Out of the corner of his eye, Jace caught a glimpse of something that looked to be tied around a tree. Stepping over several more down trees, he moved closer to it. His father never let hunters on his land, so he figured it couldn't be any sort of a marker, at least not one that his Dad knew about. Plastic bags would sometimes get caught in the tree branches when they were blowing in the wind. This did not look like a plastic bag though. When he got to the tree, it appeared to be an old cloth tied around the base of one of the mighty tree's limbs. It was very old and weathered but still clung to the tree.

"Jace, let's go!" Dane shouted from a distance. As Jace turned around to run towards the voice, he took one step and before he knew it, went sprawling face first on the ground. His head came within a few inches from smacking on a tree. Looking back at the ground he was just standing on, something appeared to be sticking up between a bushel of leaves. Cautiously moving closer to it, it appeared to be metal of some kind. He grabbed it with his right hand and indeed it was made of metal. Stepping to his feet, he pulled on it and was shocked at the discovery he had made.

It was attached to the ground.

Digging with his hands all around the metal hook-like object, he wanted to loosen it from the earth. He was about 3 inches down when he hit something hard. His first inkling was he had hit a rock, so he moved over and started to dig again in a new spot. Same result.

"What the hell are you doing?" Dane's voice startled him.

"Look at this, do you know what is back here?"

"There is nothing back here, it's probably just a piece from an old machine..." His words stopped as he pulled on the piece of metal and it did not move.

"Help me dig" Jace had urgency in his voice. On hands and knees both men started to dig. Their arms were covered with dirt by the time they were able to dig far enough to reveal what was beneath. Coming to their feet, they were looking down at an old dirt stained metal door that had not seen the light of day in some time. Looking at the door, their glances went to each other and then back at the door.

"Awesome! Let's crack this baby open." Dane said with excitement throwing caution to the wind.

"Does Dad know this is back here?" Jace always seemed to be the voice of reason between the two of them.

"It's getting late, we have so much to do to get ready for the fire." Dane acted as if he couldn't even hear his brother. Grabbing the handle once again, he pulled with all his might but to no avail.

"Hey genius it has some sort of lock attached to it." Jace said smiling at his brother's efforts.

"Damn it! It looks like it's a hundred years old." Shaking the lock frantically, Dane's frustration built.

"Wait here kid." Dane ran off towards the direction they had come into the woods from. Not five minutes later he returned with a bag full of tools.

"Good thing Dad's always prepared huh?" Dane was breathing heavily as he had just run all the way back with the heavy tool bag.

"Those were in the gator?"

Dane nodded at his brother as he pulled out a small shovel and what appeared to be some sort of cutters.

"What if this is Dad's lock?" Jace repeated himself with intent concern.

"Will you relax? What has happened to you? We always used to go on adventures when we were younger. What is the worst that could happen? Have you lost your nerve?"

"What you call 'adventures' I call getting into trouble." Shaking his head, Dane proceeded giving Jace's concerns no regard whatsoever.

SNAP.

The cutters had worked to perfection.

"That was easier than I thought" Dane exclaimed with a smile. Bending down and grabbing the shovel, he finished cleaning off the dirt and roots from the old buried door. One last thing came flying out of the tool bag and it was a small crowbar. Dane once again grabbed the metal handle and pulled with everything he had. A loud crack followed by the squeal of rusted metal and the door was propped open. The smell emitted from beneath was horrible. They both covered their faces and stepped away from the gaping hole. Looking down into the hole it was completely dark. Dane yelled down to hear his echo, the response told them both it was deep.

"We need a flashlight to see down there." Leaning over the hole, suddenly Dane's pocket began to ring. Standing up, he answered his phone. Jace could tell it was his father's voice on the other end of the phone. Hanging up, Dane closed the door and began covering it back up with dirt. Looking at his work, he stood up with a content look and made direct eye contact with his brother. He grabbed his shirt and got right into Jace's face.

"We speak of this to no one, understand?" Wiping his hands on his pants, they found the path out of the woods and started back towards the house.

Chapter 4

The person who can keep a secret may be wise, but that person is not half as wise as the person with no secrets to keep.

The sun started its routine descent over the calm lake's water. A site that was absolutely divine from the front porch. Watching the sunset from such a breathtaking place was something you could never take for granted. It was the pristine feature of this old home and the family loved spending time on it. Being a wraparound porch, there was a small table off to the side of the house where they would eat dinner on some nights. Overlooking the vineyard and the water was a picture right out of a book.

"I can't believe it is 4 o'clock already!" Panic seemed to fill Dane's voice.

"How'd you guys do in the woods? Did you get some of those trees off the ground back there? Their Father seemed happier than he had this morning.

"Yea. We got a bunch of wood cut up for the fire. There was so much back there! We could probably do that another twenty times and not run out of wood!" Jace said.

"With the winters we have, the weather always knocks a lot of trees and branches down. I just haven't had the chance to get back there this year and clean some of them up." Their father was appreciative that they had done that as any help he could get was great.

"We have to run into town to grab a few things. If anyone gets here, can you just tell them we will be right back?" Dane asked his father.

"It's only quarter after four, you think they will be getting here already?"

"I doubt it, but just in case, I wanted to give you a heads up. Thanks Dad."

Dane had gotten everything ready for the fire but still needed to get the most important part of the night...alcohol. Starting towards town, Jace had forgotten how fast his brother drove. His nerves felt tense, but he decided to try his hardest and just relax.

"How is Macie doing? You are still with her right?" Dane and Macie had been dating on and off for what seemed to be years.

"She is doing well. She works up at the hospital as an LPN."

"Ma says you guys seem to be fighting a lot recently?" Dane shrugged his shoulders as he took a corner on what felt like two wheels. Bringing the car back to the straight road ahead, Dane opened the glove compartment and pulled out a small object. "Take a look at this." Dane handed him a small jewelry box. Popping it open, Jace had a look of shock on his face. The ring which the box held inside had a large square diamond propped up perfectly for optimum sparkle.

"You're going to propose to her? That is great man I'm very happy for you! It must be pretty serious between you two then huh?"

"We have been having a few issues lately but there is nobody else I'd rather be with." Dane said in a heartfelt tone.

"Well I am excited to see her tonight..."

"She won't be there tonight." Dane interrupted his brother. "She was asked to work a double shift again. It's the third time this week!" His voice sounded agitated. Slamming on his brakes, they finally pulled onto Main Street. Being a small town, the police had nothing better to do than to catch people who had a lead foot. They loved out of towners because they didn't know the location of the speed traps they had around town. With the speed limit being twenty-five miles per hour through town, the police were usually pretty successful. And hey, they didn't mind taking out-of-towners money either!

Their truck pulled into the parking lot of Willowcreek's only small liquor store. Stepping in the door the aroma of spilled alcohol filled the air. The cashier was sitting on a stool with her feet propped up on the counter. She was reading a magazine that looked like it had seen better days. Both men split up to attack different sections of the store. Dane had put a half barrel keg of beer into his cart and had some small bottles of cheap vodka and rum propped up against it. Meeting in the back of the store, Dane scowled at his younger brother.

"What have you been doing? You have nothing in your cart." Looking surprised by this statement, Jace held up two skinny bottles of wine.

"What are you talking about, I put a lot of effort into finding this." Jace defended himself.

"Let's think about this for a minute" Dane said.

"What does our family do for a living? Do you happen to know that our parents, or Mom and Dad as you may know them by, own and operate a vineyard?" His condescending tone made Jace realize that he was right unfortunately.

Why would he buy wine from someone else and not support his own family?

Rolling his eyes, Dane pushed by his brother and started towards the front of the store. Jace slide the two bottles of wine back on a random shelf and followed his brother.

"Aww crap, I forgot this was a cash only store."

"I have some cash on me to cover this. What about mixers?" Jace asked curiously. Pausing for a moment, Dane looked down to think for a minute.

"I can swing by the apartment, I have a bunch of different drinks there that Macie won't mind if we take." A car pulled up in front of the store just as the guys were walking out. Stepping out was a tall and slender dark-haired woman. She had blonde highlights draped through her long hair that was blowing in the breeze. As soon as Jace saw her, he spun around before she made eye contact with him. Bumping into his brother, he pushed him back into the store.

"Oh my god it's Ally!" Jace whispered in a loud tone.

"What's wrong with you?" Dane said frustrated almost dropping his bag of booze.

"She caught me off guard, I just wasn't expecting to see her."

"Well she does live here." Dane's sarcasm was thick.

"Plus, I invited her and her sister to the fire tonight, so you were going to see her anyway."

"You didn't tell me that!"

"Let's just get out of here. She walked away anyway." Dane pushed him aside and left the store.

Pulling away from the shopping outlet, they headed towards the apartment.

"Wow she looked really good." Jace said looking back toward the direction of his old flame.

"Calm down there chief, I think she is with someone."

Looking surprised, Jace shrugged his shoulder and acted as if he didn't care. The funny thing was, deep inside, he did.

The apartment building was an old grey structure with white trim that had slowly been chipping away. There were two floors of apartments that were all connected by stairs and an outside balcony.

"That's Macie's car over there." Dane pointed in the direction of a small black car with a shiny license plate frame.

"I thought she was working a double tonight? That's why she wasn't coming to the fire right?" Jace's words seemed to make Dane feel uneasy.

"She told me she was." Sounding unsure of himself now, Dane quickly parked. The inevitable thought that she had lied about something ran through both of their minds.

Taking the stairs two at a time, Dane ran up them faster than Jace had seen him move in a while. Reaching the door, Dane pulled out keys from his pocket and fumbled through them until he found the right one. Watching his brother intently, Jace suddenly felt a sick feeling wash over his body. He knew what Dane was thinking and he couldn't help thinking the same thing. Turning the lock ever so slowly, he was trying to make as little noise as possible. Pushing the door open a crack with his shoulder, he slid his body through the small opening. Stopping dead in his track, Dane was looking down at the floor in distress. Once Jace found his way in the front door, he walked up and saw what he was leering at. White clothing which appeared to be nurse's clothes were wrapped up in a ball on the floor. Picking up a piece of the clothing, Dane pulled out bright pink ladies' underwear. Intertwined with the pants, they were very small and looked to be made of silk. A distant sound of laughter made both men look up at each other. Creeping down the hall towards the bedroom, a female voice was getting louder and more distinct the closer they got to the bedroom door. Finally, Dane's nerves got the best of him. Standing back from the door he yelled her name and drove his foot into the door. The force of his foot made the cheap door crack at the handle. Before Jace could get to him to try and calm him down, he was in the bedroom. A loud scream filled with panic came from the bedroom. Jace ran in after his brother prepared to grab him if anything bad was happening. To his surprise, Macie was standing there in a towel with a look of chagrin on her face.

"What the hell are you doing?' She screamed pulling her towel tighter to her body. Bending over, Macie picked up her cell phone from the floor.

"I'll have to call you back MOM." Slamming her phone down on her dresser, she glared at Dane with fire in her eyes.

"Why did you just break in my door?" She moved closer to him where she was in striking range.

"What are you doing home? I thought you were working a double today?"

"I am you idiot! I just came home to shower and change clothes before my next shift starts. I had pureed peas spilled on my arm and pants today. You know I don't like to shower at the hospital." Macie looked at Jace.

~ 37 ~

"Hey there J, it's good to see you again." Embracing him with a tight hug, Jace could feel that her hair was still wet. "Do you see what I have to put up with?" She said shooting a glance at her boyfriend.

"Well answer me! What are you doing here?"

"We just stopped by to grab some drinks for the fire tonight. Remember the ones I bought but we never used?"

"And you came here and thought I was lying to you about working a double?"

"Well I saw your car and then I come in and see your clothes on the floor..."

"Oh, so you think I am cheating on you? You think I am a liar AND a cheater?" Her tone seemed to be getting angrier by the second.

"I'm sorry okay! I lost my head. I don't think that you would cheat on me."

"My door would say otherwise. And by the way, did you need to break it in half? It wasn't even locked!" Her frustration was valid as both boys looked down feeling sorry about what had happened.

"Just get what you came for and get out. I have fifteen minutes and I have to be back. I haven't even eaten anything but a granola bar today."

"Do you want us to go get you something quick?" Jace said feeling a little scared of her.

"No that's alright. I will just grab something when I get back to the hospital. Just give me a minute to finish getting dressed."

The boys left the bedroom and grabbed what they came for out of the kitchen. As they headed towards the door, Macie was looking for her keys that she had flung in a hurry when she got home. Finding them, she jumped up and slid her shoes on. Dane leaned in to kiss her and she casually turned her head.

"Please forgive me. I am sorry I broke your door. I promise I will replace it."

Raising an eyebrow, she followed them out and locked the door behind her.

Watching her drive away, Dane dropped his head into his hands.

"You're pretty smooth man." Jace said jokingly. Looking up, he didn't look amused by these comments. The silence that filled the car on the drive home was unbearably awkward. Pulling in their driveway, the sunlight had completely departed from the sky. The bright moon was casting rays over the rolling hills of trees and vines. Their sister's car sat in the driveway next to Jace's pickup truck.

Within minutes, there were roaring flames coming from the back field. One by one, more of Dane's friends showed up. Just as Jace cracked his first beer, three shadows started to appear from the dark. Ally and McKenzie walked up to the fire with a man Jace was unfamiliar with. McKenzie ran up to him to greet him with another bear hug. Her smile and enthusiasm was infectious to everyone around here. She made seeing Ally face to face for the first time a little easier. McKenzie began making her rounds around the fire hugging everyone whose path she crossed.

"Hi Jace. It is good to see you again." Ally's voice still had the same pitch to it. Their embrace was much shorter than that of her sisters.

"It is good to see you too. You look really great Al" Jace said as he pulled away.

"This is my boyfriend Tyler." Ally reached back and grabbed the man's arm pulling him forward. Holding out his hand, Jace shook his hand giving him a quick once over. His hand shake was very firm and he met his eye contact with a nod. He was a tall man with broad shoulders and a thin face that the brim of his hat cast a shadow over. A sudden rush of jealousy washed over Jace's body. A feeling of anxiety mixed with alcohol on an empty stomach was a dangerous combination. Seeing Ally's warm eyes and her gentle smile was hard on his heart. This was his first true love and he was hoping that when he saw her again, he would be able to handle his emotions better.

As the night went on, the alcohol was flowing and the sound of drunken laughter filled the air. Jace found himself looking in Ally's direction almost the whole night. No matter who he was talking to, he kept looking around to see where she was. As weird as it sounded, he didn't want her to leave, he didn't even want her to be talking to Tyler. The thought of her with another man was too much for him to even comprehend. The thought of them kissing or worse...Jace wouldn't let his mind go there. It was easier to just pretend that it wasn't happening than face what was probably true. These feelings he was having were exactly what he didn't want to happen. There was a short break of time when Ally was standing by the fire all by herself watching the flames flicker back and forth. She held a diet soda in her hand. She was never much for drinking and this made Jace smile because it would appear that she hadn't changed...at least that element of her life anyway. Jace wasn't sure if it was possible but she looked even better than he had remembered. Her face had little to no expression on it at this moment. He didn't even

realize he was staring at her until his eyes met hers. She was looking at him with a look of surprise followed by a smile. She moved over to his side of the fire and sat down on a little wooden lawn chair next to his.

"You doing okay Jace?" She asked with concern.

"Everyone keeps asking me that, I promise I am."

"Well I only ask because you were staring at me like a creeper and you looked kind of sad." He raised an eyebrow at her. "A creeper huh?"

"I'm only kidding." She responded with a small giggle.

"I would like to talk to you if we could find the time soon. Not here with everybody around though." Jace spoke in almost a whisper to her. Before she had time to respond, McKenzie came running over and sat down in Jace's lap. She was met with a grunt from him as her drink splashed onto his face.

"What you doing sexy?" One whiff of her breath and you could tell that she was inebriated. Wiping his face with his shirt he felt a sudden rush of awkwardness and he decided to make an excuse to get out of there.

"I have to run to the restroom; will you excuse me ladies?"

"Hurry back" McKenzie responded between drunken giggles. Looking back at Ally, her expression was one of exaggerated annoyance at her sister.

Dane was hitting the bottles hard and was starting to make a fool of himself. He had attached himself to a girl that Jace didn't know. Being away for so long and having so many people around that he didn't know, he felt like an outsider even at his own home.

"What are you doing?" Jace pulled his brother's arm and his body flopped over to him. Dane was smiling at him with a glassy look in his eyes.

~ 41 ~

"Why are you flirting and touching her you idiot? What about Macie?"

"Will you relax?" Dane was slurring his words.

"She doesn't love me, she doesn't even like me. Now Savannah on the other hand is crazy about me!" Looking back at her, he winked and reached his hand out to touch her hair.

"Okay that's enough" Jace said getting irritated. He pulled his brother to his feet and put his arm around his waist.

"I apologize for my brother..."

"Don't apologize for me!" Dane yelled shoving his brother away from him. Starting to cause a scene, his loud voice was catching everyone's attention around the fire.

"Screw you man! You think you can just fall off the face of the Earth and now you want everything to be normal again?" Taking a step back, Jace looked around assessing the situation he had gotten himself into.

"You need to stop this now, you're drunk!" Jace's words had anger behind them. He grabbed his brother's arm again and this time with more force. Before he could realize what happened, Dane swung his arm and slammed his fist into Jace's cheekbone. The impact swung Jace around and he dropped to one knee. Looking back at his brother standing over him, he was taking his flannel shirt off and moving closer into striking distance again. Touching his face, he was bleeding from a cut that Dane's ring must have caused.

"Stop" Ally yelled from across the fire.

"Stay out of this bitch!" Dane screamed. His eyes never left his brother. Hearing an insult fly in Ally's direction, Jace came to his feet swinging. He hit his brother three times and bull rushed him tackling his body right next to the hot

~ 42 ~

coals that surrounded the mighty flames. As the two men rolled on the ground trying to get an advantage on the other, everyone around the fire began to yell. Hearing the commotion, Lizzy comes running out from the barn that was about fifty yards away. She gets to the fire and sees her brothers rolling around in the grass. Quickly grabbing the back of Jace's shirt, she pulled as hard as she could. "What the hell are you two doing?" She screamed in her brother's ear. Coming to his feet, Dane starred down his brother who stood there holding his cheek.

"I'm out of here." Dane made a beeline for his truck.

"Wait! You are drunk you idiot!" Lizzy screamed to him. He jumped into his truck and slammed the door hard. The engine roared as the tires spun kicking up the rocks beneath them. Lizzy watched as her brother peeled away from his own get together. Sitting on the grass with his head between his knees, Jace had a shamefaced look about him.

"What happened with you guys?" Liz was kneeling next to Jace with one hand on his shoulder. Everyone had gone back to what they were doing forgetting that a fight had even occurred.

"After that, I need another drink." Jace said holding the side of his face.

"I don't know what his problem is anyway. He got mad at me earlier too." Jace stood up and grabbed another cupful from the keg.

"Listen, he had a really hard time when you left. It happened so fast and you hardly connected with him the whole time you were gone. You were not only his brother but his best friend." Lizzy's voice was sad. You could tell by her words that she was upset about what Jace had done as well. But it was in her nature to forgive and move forward, which is clearly what she was trying to do.

Plopping down in a camp chair, Jace appeared as if he was ignoring his sister. She started back towards the barn and Ally walked up to take a look at his face. She bent down so her face was at the same level as his. She gingerly touched the open wound and wiped the blood which was running slowly down his cheek.

"I'm okay, really I am. You don't need to do that." Jace said pulling away.

"Where is Tyler?"

"He is playing pong in the barn, probably pretty drunk by now." Ally sounded irritated. She took a seat next to him and was glancing at her sister who was also intoxicated.

"I'm sorry that I left you Al." These were the words that Ally had spent many nights wondering if he felt.

"No one has called me Al since you left." She smiled at him with her eyes twinkling in the moonlight. Jace was losing his ability to think straight. He was feeling the effects of his drinks and he didn't like the sadness it was making him feel. The sudden rush of tiredness mixed with the throbbing of his cheek, Jace wished that Ally was his again. The last thing he remembered was seeing Ally's face and the mixed smell of her perfume and the fire's smoke.

A Walk Though the Grapes
David Jackson

Chapter 5

   At the end of each day, family can either focus on what is tearing them apart, or what is keeping them together.

   The next morning's sun arrived rather quickly and woke a sore and sick feeling Jace up. He felt like he had been run over by a car. His whole body hurt and he had several scrapes and sore spots he didn't even remember how he had gotten them. He walked carefully down the stairs making sure his coordination was back. Tumbling down a flight of wooden stairs is not something he wanted on top of the way he was feeling. Jace could see his mother's head through the front window. She was sitting on their front porch gazing out at what was a panoramic view of the land. Tripping over his own feet, Jace pushed the screen door open and stepped out into the beautiful morning weather.

"Did Dane leave early this morning? Jace asked the question even though he was almost positive he knew he hadn't been home.

"I haven't seen him" She said sipping her coffee. "He probably went back to Macie's for the night."

Smiling to himself, he was positive that wasn't where he was. Sitting down next to his Mom on the swing, he tried his best to keep the side of his face hidden. His mother was curled up with a blanket glancing back and forth between the view and her morning paper when she surprised Jace with her question.

"What happened to your face last night?"

Jace looked to his other side as if he were checking for a mirror that she might have caught a glimpse of it in. She always seemed to find things out no matter how hard any of her children tried to hide them from her. Not that trying to hide a major gash in his face was going to be possible for too long.

"Nothing happened. There was a misunderstanding last night and I just got mixed up in it." He was trying to make it seem as innocent as possible.

"How did you see it from there anyway? Do you have x-ray vision?"

"I'm your mother, I know everything remember?" Winking at her son, she felt satisfaction that she knew what he was trying to hide.

Jace just rolled his eyes.

"I saw you last night after your friends brought you into bed. I poked my head in your room to see if you were still awake, but you were sound asleep snoring like your father." She took another sip from her coffee cup and set it down on the small metal table next to the swing.

"I noticed your face was very red and then I saw a little blood on your pillowcase. I dabbed your face with a cold cloth and cleaned it as best I could. You were sleeping pretty deeply because you didn't even move once."

"Yea it was a long day yesterday, I was tired." Jace knew that his mom was aware he had been intoxicated but he appreciated that she didn't rub it in his face.

The wind seemed to be blowing a little harder than normal. His mother's chimes sang from the corner of the front porch where they hung. The ripples in the water were crashing against the rocks with more force. It was the perfect setup for a storm. There was a small birdfeeder in their front garden that appeared to have liquid in it. Looking closer, Jace noticed there were two small birds which appeared to be hummingbirds by the speed of their wings. Their long snouts were poking the end of the feeder as they seemed to be fighting the strong gusts of wind as well.

"So, you are having trouble adjusting to being back home I see?" His mother finally made eye contact with his cut.

A long pause of uncomfortable silence filled the air. His mom jumped in before he could muster up any words.

"I would really like to know about what has happened with you. I feel like I don't even know you anymore." Her words were heartfelt and filled with sadness.

"I want to start by saying I apologize for not keeping in touch with you and Dad. You were right, I have made several poor decisions in my life and I am truly sorry for the negative effects they have had."

"You took a shot for yourself, you don't need to apologize for that." His mother was always understanding of her kids even if she didn't agree with the decisions they made.

"I do however blame you for not keeping in touch! What did I do that pushed you so far away from me?"

"Nothing! It was my fault. Can we please just try to move forward with everything? I am back here to stay."

Jace looked down at the wood floor boards that were

uneven in certain spots under his feet. The feelings that filled his body weren't ones of anger or sadness, he felt ashamed and embarrassed of his actions. Looking up to his mother's eyes and then back to the floor, a long pause really made him feel uncomfortable.

"Can I ask you one question?" His mother's voice had turned soft.

"How are you doing financially speaking?"

"I have a little bit of money. Enough to be able to get by for the time being. But certainly not where I thought I would be at this point in my life." A disappointed look came to Jace's face.

"I definitely thought things were going to go differently for me than they have. I have just made so many…"

"It is okay Jace." His mom cut him off with an insuring tone in her voice.

"You made your choices and that is that. You don't have to explain yourself." His mom smiled at him and touched his shoulder. The comforting forgiveness she was displaying towards him was received with mixed emotions. In a way, it made him feel better about what he had done. In another way, he felt even more guilt that he needed to be forgiven in the first place.

"We love you and always will my son."

Just as she said those words, a loud clap of thunder followed by the pitter patter of rain drops on the metal porch roof caused them both to jump. The hummingbirds had vacated the feeder and the wind was blowing with wicked force. Jace grabbed his mother's coffee cup and ran to the door holding it open for her. Jen was just coming down the stairs looking as if she had just gone through the middle of a hurricane. Her hair was propped up on the top of her head and she wore baggy sweatpants and an old sweater with the words New York in big bold letters on it.

"You're looking radiant this morning" Jace said with a smile as he went to sit on the couch.

"Shut up Jace... Mom are we out of Advil?" Rubbing her temples, she plopped next to her brother on the couch. She had also drank too much the night before and was paying for it now. Marie handed her daughter the medication and set a glass of water down on the end table next to the couch.

"Where is Dane this morning? I didn't see him in his room." Jen asked after taking a big gulp of her water. Marie responded with the same answer she had given Jace when he inquired. "Probably stayed over at Macie's place." There was a silent pause as Jen made eye contact with Jace with a raised eyebrow. Jace's eyes got big and he subtly shook his head as if to say, 'don't tell her anything.' He stood up and started up the stairs. He needed to get away from the house for a little while and clear his mind. He had always enjoyed his time alone and used it to think and relax. Putting his bright orange sneakers on and his cutoff shirt, he started towards the front door.

"I'm going for a run, be back in a little while." Closing the door behind him he stepped out on the porch looking at the rain which continued to fall. Shrugging his shoulders, he stepped out from the protection of the roof and let the rain fall upon his face. He looked around at his surroundings and started jogging down the stairs and heading for the road. The therapeutic sound of his shoes against the pavement made him feel good. He ran through puddles of water splashing his legs, yet he didn't care. When he got to the railroad tracks, he stopped to catch his breath. He loved to run and when he was in high school, these were the tracks that he always ran on. The cross ties were about ten inches apart and he would take them two at a time, perfect distance for his running stride. The clouds started to part as he made his way down the seemingly endless tracks. He made his way to the next road that crossed the tracks and started walking. Even though he had been gone for a while he still knew the way around this town like the back of his hand. Ally's house had been down a side street near where he found himself. He wanted to go see her again after he didn't really say goodbye to her. Whether he wanted to admit it to himself or not, he still had very strong feelings for her. With his hands on his hips, he moved onto the side of the street and kept walking in the direction of her house. The first glimpse he had at her house seemed to make him feel very nervous and anxious. He couldn't understand why his palms were sweaty and he had the urge to turn around and run the other direction.

Loud sirens screaming from the distance made him pause just as he was about to knock on the door. To his surprise, a police car pulled into her stone driveway at a faster pace than it should have. Out stepped officer Rick Harper...Ally's father. Stepping down his front stairs, he greeted me with a firm handshake.

"Good afternoon son." His expression was not one of joy to see Jace and his words were cold and straight forward.

"It is good to see you Mr. Harper." I smiled at him and the thought crossed my mind that he may not be as nice to me due to the past. Unfortunately, to my surprise, that was not the case.

"Ally, McKenzie! I need you out here right now." His voice was loud and he was yelling their names as he walked to the front door of his house. Before he even reached to unlock the lock, the door swung open and there stood McKenzie in what appeared to be pajama bottoms and a bright yellow spaghetti strap tank top.

"What's wrong Dad?" Her voice was low and inquisitive. He was a very large man with broad shoulders, so broad that Jace didn't even know if she had noticed him standing behind her father. The screen door creaked open and slammed shut again as she stepped out of the house.

"Jace!" she yelled with her usual excitement. She went to give him a hug and her father caught her arm and stopped her.

"I need to speak with you right now! Where is your sister? Tell her to come out here as well." His tone was making Jace nervous and he wasn't even his dad!

"She is at work dad. She picked up an extra shift this morning. What's the matter?" She looked up at him with concern and then his attention turned to Jace.

"You need to hear this as well." He said as he signaled for Jace to step over to him. After a long pause, his words finally broke the tense silence.

"Last night Leo Johnson was killed. He was hit by what we

think is a truck due to the tire's skid marks we found at the scene. There was broken glass and what appeared to be shards of a vehicle left behind. His son Oliver was hit as well but was only knocked unconscious...well, I shouldn't say 'only' because he Is in bad shape. We are hoping that when he comes out of it he will be able to give some identification of the truck that hit them or possibly if he saw who was driving." Officer Harper was now looking down as he told the grim news.

"Where did this happen?" McKenzie's voice beat Jace to the punch.

"At the end of your street." Her dad turned and nodded his head towards Jace.

"So, what I need is to know what happened last night. I got word that you were having a party and some people said that things got a bit out of hand" pointing to Jace's cuts on his face, he made his point pretty well. Jace turned his head as if he was trying to hide what was already in plain sight. Before either of them could answer, the radio inside the officer's car was calling with a loud voice. He returned to his car and sat in the driver's seat with one leg still outside of the car. His voice was inaudible to them as he responded to the call.

"I can't believe old man Johnson is gone!" She whispered to Jace in a low voice. He wasn't sure exactly why she was whispering to him.

"Oliver is the same age as I am, we went to school together. I hope that he is going to be alright." He responded in a voice a little louder than a whisper. The sky was beginning to clear up and the dark clouds seem to be replaced with whiter ones that were less threatening. Walking back to where they were standing, officer Harper no longer looked sad.

"I need you both to come down to the station with me. We have to talk." They both looked at each other with a puzzled stare and obliged with the request. Jace had never been in the back seat of a police car and it was a strange place to be. A cage between the front and rear seats protected the officer from whoever had the pleasure of riding in the back seat. The windows were accompanied by thick grey metal bars, for what Jace assumed was to protect the windows from angry criminals. The ride seemed to be a long one and the car was filled with deafening silence. Jace wished that her dad would at least turn the radio on or something. Feeling like he needed to say something, Jace couldn't find the right words for the situation they were in. Soft skin touched the back of his hand as he glanced down and saw McKenzie's hand over his. She smiled at him with an innocent expression as if to say, 'everything will be alright, we didn't do anything wrong.' Pulling into the police station, he saw a familiar truck parked in front, it was his dad's. Climbing out, the officer opened the back door of the cruiser and let them both out. Jace wasn't sure exactly what was going on. The confusion mixed with what he assumed was still a little bit of a hangover made him feel uneasy. Stepping into the building, his father was already inside and had a stone-faced look. His eyes never left Jace. The look of anger was very evident even with his body's posture. Several other officers were moving around the station and the lady sitting at the front desk was typing something very fast. The clicking of her nails on the keyboard made him wonder how she learned to type that fast. Her hair was up in what looked like a loose bun and she smelled of perfume that reminded Jace of 'older people.'

The three of them were led into an empty room with a round metal table. The walls were white and had nothing on them whatsoever. Jace sat between his father and McKenzie on a flimsy folding chair. Officer Harper proceeded to walk into the room about five minutes later with another man who was not wearing a police officer's uniform. Instead he was wearing a shirt and tie, and had a noticeable weapon holstered by his side.

"What are we doing here Dad?" McKenzie said almost yelling at him. She knew that she had done nothing wrong, but these circumstances were making her feel uncomfortable and her mind was racing with thoughts. She had seen far too many shows where they brought people into the interrogation room and things turned ugly. She knew it was ridiculous but couldn't stop her mind from wandering.

"First off I'd like to apologize Robert." The officer spoke directly to Jace's father.

"I hate having to call you down here, but we need to figure some things out. Last night there was a party on your property is that correct?"

"My Dad had nothing to do with it!" Jace cut in sharply.

"Please, I am speaking to your father."

"Yes, the boys had some friends over and they had a fire out in my back lot. All of their friends are older, so I assure you there was no underage drinking Rick." Being that both of their fathers had been friends for a long time, there was no doubt that the officers believed him. Then, the words that were spoken next shot through Jace like a sharp knife. "Where is your other son Dane right now? We can't seem to find him."

Suddenly the vision of Dane driving off in the dark angry came to Jace's mind. He felt a large knot in the pit of his stomach. Without another word being spoken, both Jace and McKenzie finally knew why they were here.

Chapter 6

A general rule of thumb is that when you invite trouble into your life, it usually accepts without hesitation. There are certain moments in life where you actually wonder... why is this happening to me? Even though self-pity is always frowned upon, and many people may not show that they have it, when bad things happen, it is usually resorted to.

In Jace's case, he could not believe that this was happening to his family. After what seemed to be hours on end, they finally let Jace go from the police station. Having asked him many questions, he really had no information to give them. Being completely intoxicated the night before, he couldn't be completely positive about his story. He told them about the fight he had with his brother, but that was it. Unsure what McKenzie or anybody else for that matter would say, there was nothing he could do about that anyway. Stepping up into his father's big black pickup truck, he was nervous about what his father might say to him. The ride home started with silence which surprised Jace. His dad must have been thinking about what he wanted to say. Being a man of few words, this kind of silence made the ride more uncomfortable than normal. Once they got home, Robert put his truck in park and turned off the loud engine. He kept looking forward out the front windshield as if he were still driving.

"Do you know where your brother is?" His voice was low and monotone. His body language was laced with discouragement and exhaustion.

"I'm not sure." Jace's voice responded with a slight crackle. Taking a deep breath, Robert looked at his son with piercing eyes. Expecting a response, he looked back at his dad like a frightened dog looks at their owner after they had done something wrong. No response came. Sliding down out of the truck, Robert slammed the door and walked towards their front door. Stepping out himself, he heard a loud noise coming up the driveway. A black car came flying down the driveway and hit the brakes sending stones and dirt flying through the air. Out stepped Macie with a combined look of panic and anger. Walking towards him, she was not at a loss for words.

"What the hell is going on Jace? Where is Dane and why did the police show up at the hospital wanting to question me?" Her eyes looked droopy and her hair was up in a messy knot. Her tired look and strong words made him feel bad for her.

"I don't have any idea where he is. We got into a fight last night and he drove off angry." His mom had stepped out of the house and was standing on the front porch looking down at them.

"Both of you come inside, I made dinner and it is getting cold." They both did as his mother told them to. Even though he had not eaten at all today, Jace did not feel hungry. He picked at his food but his mind wouldn't rest. Halfway through dinner, there was a loud knock on the door. Robert stood up and opened the big wooden door slowly. Outside stood Ally who appeared to have been crying.

"Come in darling." His father's voice was soft and warm to her.

"I need to speak with Jace please." She sounded sad as she looked in Jace's direction. They both stepped outside and spoke about what happened the night before. Their interaction lasted for several minutes before her words hit Jace with what she had done.

"I told the officers everything about the night before. About Dane being angry and recalling what he said. Plus, I told them that he had been drinking heavily and drove off drunk. I didn't mean to hurt anybody, but I had to tell them what I know." Her lip was quivering as if she was about to cry again. Embracing her with a hug, he told her everything will be alright even though he had no idea how this whole thing would turn out. Trying to comfort her was his only option at this time. Stepping back from her, he looked her up and down. Her eyes met his and he was reminded of all the good times they had together. It is strange when things in life can go so poorly yet his mind could not resist her and what she still meant to him. Ally wiped her eyes with the corner of her sleeve and gave Jace a smile through her sniffles. Feeling somewhat composed, she leaned towards him and gave him a peck on the cheek.

"Get some sleep J. You can always call me if you need anything." Her being so nice to him after all they had been through didn't help him as he tried his hardest not to still have feelings for her. Ally walked down the front steps and drove away slowly into the dark night. Jace watched her taillights until he could no longer see the two red dots in the distance. For the rest of the night, it seemed like the whole family was in a fog. Macie stayed for a little while after dinner and conversed with what she had hoped for some time now would someday be her family. When it was time to go to sleep, again Jace was kept awake due to his many thoughts. As he lay in bed, he couldn't help but think that this was his fault and he shouldn't have fought with his brother the night before.

Maybe he had made a mistake coming back home.

Finally, he closed his eyes and prayed that he could just fall asleep and forget this day had happened.

The next morning came quickly as the beams of sun screamed in through the panes of glass. Jace couldn't believe it was morning already. He had tossed and turned almost all night and did not feel rested. Jumping in the shower, the warm water made his muscles relax and the tension that was building up in his shoulders seemed to dissipate…if only just for a moment. His parents were both out of the house by the time he made it downstairs. Even though he didn't want to, Jace felt as though he should go and see Oliver to see how he was doing. Oliver had been a friend of Jace's and his siblings ever since they were younger. Being neighbors, they stood at the same bus stop together. Jace felt like going to see him was the right thing to do. He did feel bad for him as well. The potential guilt that Jace had for his role in what had happened scared him. That is if what Jace thought happened was in fact true. There was a chance that the accident had nothing to do with him or any of his family. Even though the longer

Dane is not seen, the chances of being innocent get slimmer and slimmer.

Going to hospitals was never enjoyable for him...but then again, who actually likes going to a hospital? Hopping in his truck, he made his way down the street and towards town. The water was running down the side of the street looking for an open drain mouth. It was a foggy day and the mugginess was the aftermath of the previous day's rain. Mixing with the heat, this weather made Jace's shirt stick to his skin.

"And I'm free! Free fallin!" Tom Petty's voice screamed from the radio speakers. The upbeat tone mixed with him knowing the words made him sing along.

"Damn song, I can never get it out of my head once it is imbedded in there!" Feeling good for the first time in what seemed to be days, he pulled his truck onto Main Street. The good feeling was soon put on hold as his truck dashboard was beeping loudly to attract his attention. Looking down at his dashboard full of gauges, his fuel light had come on and the little needle was almost resting on the 'E'. Reaching into his pocket, he only had about six singles which would not do him any good. The bank in the town of Willowcreek was a small one and carried odd hours. They were open Tuesday through Saturday from 1:00pm to 9:00pm. The town had gotten together and decided that these hours would work better due to most people being at work during the day. Luckily, there was an ATM available for anyone needing cash immediately. Jace hated going to any ATM when you had to pay a fee to access your own money. Left with the choice of paying a small fee or walking home once his truck is by the side of the road thirsty for fuel, the fee sounded like the less irritating option. There was a little hut that had the ATM underneath it accompanied by two vending machines. Being that he hadn't eaten this morning and the sick feeling which prevented him from indulging completely in last night's dinner, he was hungry. Deciding food was more essential at this very moment, he pulled out his money clip again. The dollars that it had protected were all folded in different directions. Using the scummiest one that had a tear down the side of it, he inserted it into the machine hoping that the promise of Doritos on the other side of the glass would soon come true. Rejected. Putting the dollar on his knee and trying to flatten it out, he tried again. Rejected.

"Come on!"

"Need some help?" A friendly voice said.

"No, I have more dollars, thank you though." Not looking at the female voice, he didn't even recognize who it was. Suddenly there were small fingers running through his hair.

"You could use a trim Jace." McKenzie stood behind him still holding a fresh-looking dollar in her hand. Before he could answer, she spoke again.

"Even though I hate cutting beautiful hair like this." She said with a smile and a wink. Jace was suddenly glad he just took a shower this morning.

"Beautiful huh? Maybe I will charge you for the privilege of cutting it" He said jokingly.

"I'll give you a freebie today." She responded with a come-hither look.

"Thanks, but I really have to be somewhere today." He said trying not to give out too much information. Grabbing his wrist, she slapped her dollar in his hand completely ignoring his previous statement.

"It won't take long I promise. Now I would like Fritos and a can of pop please. Thanks babe." She started moving away and turned back towards him still walking backwards.

"See you in five?" She spun back around and left out of sight before he could answer. She knew that leaving her money with him, he would have to come back to see her at the salon. Trying his own dollar one more time...rejected. He was suddenly in a jovial mood and didn't care anymore. Quickly getting forty from the ATM, he grabbed the two items she requested plus his own bag of chips and started towards the salon. The bell clanged loudly as he opened and shut the glass door. Salons always have an interesting smell to them. This one smelled like a mix of hair color and cleaning product, more specifically, bleach.

"Have a seat" she said spinning a black and white striped chair around. Her foot pressing on the metal bar beneath making the chair rise to his level. Handing her what he presumed to be her lunch, he obeyed her orders. She ripped open the bag and a loud crunch quickly followed. "Ugh I have been starving all day. I've had nothing but appointments this morning. I'm not complaining trust me, I could use the money, I just haven't had a minute to stop and eat." She was so vivacious that he found himself enjoying the time he was spending with her. He didn't plan on a haircut today yet here he was. He had other plans that were more important yet here he was. She reminded him a lot of her sister Ally, which he knew in the back of his mind he still cared for. Thinking to himself about how taboo it would be to have dated sisters, his mind was quickly running away with him.

Suddenly a burst of water sprayed on the back of his head making him jump.

"That's cold!" He exclaimed trying to make his startled jump seem like the fault of cold water instead of his blank stare and wandering mind distracting him.

"Just relax, it's fine." Rolling her eyes playfully, she sprayed him again.

"Jace Grazer!" The sound of his own name had somehow become fearful to him. He turned and looked at the female voice that was standing there looking at him.

"I heard you were back in town." Smiling in her direction, he was flipping through his 'book of names' in his head trying to remember her name. The panic on his face must have triggered McKenzie because she stepped up to the plate and saved him.

"Mary Sherwood, you have owned this salon since before I can remember...you know Jace came home because he couldn't live without me!" Winking at him, she went back to fumbling with her tools on what looked to be a stainless-steel tray. Mary was an unusually tall woman who was skinny as can be. Her voice was deep due to the years of tobacco consumption. She had a pretty severe cough to put the icing on what looked to be an unhealthy cake.

"Yea, I am sure it was all for you Kinzy." She was shuffling a broom across the floor picking up what appeared to be whitish or gray hair. She began to cough hard to the point where it sounded as if she was wheezing.

"Where is my damn coffee?" She scowled leaning the broom against her chair and looking around for her cup.

"You are looking well." Jace said with a smile. She grunted looking back at him with two bloodshot eyes. She snatched her coffee from the stand next to her chair and grabbed a pack of cigarettes.

"I'm taking a break, be back soon." Stepping outside Jace could hear the coughing continue.

"Well she is a barrel of laughs, isn't she?" Smirking, McKenzie plugged in her razor and began to trim. The softness of her hands on the back of his neck made the tiny hairs on his arm stand up. He wondered if she was doing this on purpose. As he sat in the chair, he wondered what this feeling was that was coming over him. With all the troubles going on in his life, it seemed like everything else was on the back burner and he was enjoying himself. A feeling which sadly he was not accustomed to. As the razor clicked off, the scissors were the next choice of weapon in her hand. As his hair dropped from above and softly landed on the floor, McKenzie was gently humming a song under her breath.

"And I'm free…. Free fallin."

"Are you kidding me?" Jace blurted out. "That song is stuck in my head too!" He almost sounded happy about it.

"Yea, we had the radio on earlier. We were jamming. Now please sit up straight and close your eyes. I just have the bangs left to do." Each tug on the scissors and slice of the two blades coming together, he could feel the tenderness in each stroke and the care she took in doing her job well. Listening intently to each breath she took, he could feel her soft exhale on his forehead. Why was she turning him on so much? Never had a haircut felt more erotic than this one had.

"You're all done. See if you like it." Relieved by these words, he stood up and looked in the wall sized mirror across the shop. She had done a good job and he was pleased. The week after a haircut he felt was always when it looked its best.

I have to get going. Thank you very much for the haircut." Jace said pulling a twenty out of his pocket and dropping it on the counter next to where McKenzie was standing. Looking back at him, she grabbed the bill and quickly jammed it back into his side pocket.

"I told you it was on me." She said winking at him as she pulled her hand from his pocket giving it a little tug.

"Where are you off to now?" She asked trying to pry information on what his plans for the day were. Jace paused for a moment trying to think of a good response. For some reason, he did not want to tell her that he was planning on going to see Oliver. He didn't want her to ask him questions about why he was going. So, he said the first thing that came to his mind.

"I have to go look for my brother." Jace said looking nervously around as if other people were going to hear him. McKenzie instantly stopped cleaning and looked back at him. It was as if someone had pushed a pause button and time was standing still.

"I have an idea where he could be, but I'm not positive."
The elephant in the room finally came to fruition. Jace was
surprised that she had not brought this up sooner. Her
expression looked more serious than it had all day.

"I'll come with you." She said continuing to clean up the
hair from where he was just sitting.

"You really don't have to do that McKenzie."

"Are you saying you don't want me to go with you?" She
asked sharply. This was a trap question, there was really
no way out of it.

"Of course, I would like you to come, but I..."

"Then it's settled." She interjected before he could finish
his sentence.

"Just give me five minutes to finish cleaning up and change
and I'll be ready."

"Aren't you working now?" he asked in an obvious tone.

"Perks of renting out a chair, I can make my own hours
within reason and leave if and when I want to. Besides,
Mary is here in case we get any walk-ins." Disappearing
into the back room, the sound of an old locker door clicked
open and banged shut. Visiting Oliver was going to have to
take a back seat now as he was unable to get out of her
coming with him. McKenzie came running out still pulling
her shirt down over her stomach. They both walked slowly
toward the truck and got in.

"So where are we going Jace?"

"You will have to wait and see when we get there." He
gave her a generic answer as he did not want to answer
any more questions that might lead to even more

questions from her.

Pulling into the only gasoline station that was still in business on main street, he put the twenty bucks that she had given back to him in and it moved the needle a little passed a quarter of a tank. Unhappy with this result, he let out a dissatisfied sigh and put the truck into gear. Just as the wheels bumped over the railroad tracks, McKenzie's phone made a loud beeping sound. As she looked into the bright light that her phone was projecting, she began to scroll down which was followed by what appeared to be the world's fastest texting. Her fingers were flying at what seemed to be a mile a minute!

"Is everything alright?" Jace asked cautiously.

"Yes, Ally just asked me about yesterday at my dad's station. I haven't even seen her since your party. I told her I would talk with her later because I didn't want to text it. Plus, I told her I was riding with you to go get Dane."

A lump formed in Jace's throat. He suddenly felt guilty like he had done something wrong. Why did he feel this way? Ally was no longer his girlfriend and he was free to do whatever he liked. Even with that being the case, he hasn't done anything with McKenzie except get his hair cut! Was he not supposed to ever communicate with another woman again? And it is not as if Ally wanted to be with him again, she had her own boyfriend. This was the rationalization that was flying through his head. The truck was starting to veer to the right and his tires began to hit the rumble strips they put on the side of the road to get your attention.

"Oh man." He said quickly correcting the steering wheel

and getting them back to the center of the lane. McKenzie had a puzzled look on her face.

"Are you alright?"

Smiling back at her he nodded and kept looking out the front windshield. About fifteen minutes went by and McKenzie was not at a loss for words. She was so talkative and there were some points where Jace didn't even know what she was talking about. He nodded his head as if he did and kept on driving. She was in mid-sentence before she blurted out...

"Wait!" McKenzie's elevated voice scared him.

"Look over there!" Her finger was pointed in the direction of a farmer's field. This field must have been harvested recently as it consisted of nothing but dirt rows. There was a small figure in the distance that appeared to be either a car or a truck. Quickly turning the wheel, they pulled onto an old dirt road which led down the side of the field. This was not where Jace had thought he might find Dane, but his interest got the best of him. He wasn't even sure who's land this was. As they got closer the image became clearer. It was a truck.

It sat lifeless in the middle of the field. As they slowly got closer, Jace realized what McKenzie had seen in the distance.

It was Dane's truck!

Jace accelerated his truck to a speed which dirt roads did not like. Each bump they took hit the truck hard and made them fly out of their seats. Slamming on the brakes, the dirt kicked up into a cloud of dust.

"Dane!" Jace jumped out of his truck leaving the door

open and ran towards what he hoped was his brother. Opening the door to the truck, his brother was not in it. It was certainly his truck though.

"Hey, come look at this." McKenzie was standing in front of the truck looking towards the ground.

"There is no damage here." She said with a surprised grin. She was right! The front of his truck looked completely intact. It was a little dirty but there was nothing wrong with it. Both of his headlights were unbroken and there was no sign of an accident whatsoever. Where was he then? This was not like him to just leave his truck here, even if he was drunk. Both searched through his cab for any clues but there was nothing.

"Something is not right here. Come on, let's go find my father." Jace's voice was covered with worry. Getting back into his truck, the feeling of hot sweats was almost unbearable.

"What is that?" Again, Jace followed her finger. Off in the distance, there appeared to be a man standing in the middle of the field. He looked to be wearing all black and was not moving.

"Come on, come on!" McKenzie screamed.

"Go see who that is!"

"I can't get passed Dane's truck!" He yelled back.

"The field is too soft to go off the road, I will sink!" Putting the truck in reverse, he slammed the gas and they both went flying backwards creating another shield of dust. When they hit pavement, the tires squealed and the truck's rear end seem to be fishtailing. They turned the corner at the nearest street to go down closer to see who it was. When they pulled up, they were both surprised at what they found.

Nothing.

There was no one there.

Chapter 7

Looking and seeing can be two very different things.

I'm not going crazy! Jace thought as frustration filled his head. After finding Dane's truck, Jace decided he didn't want to go any further and he was nervously anxious to tell his family what he had found. He had no idea what the next steps would be, but he did have a big clue to the puzzle. Dane's truck and the fact that it was damage free! The ride home was unbearably long. This time, McKenzie was not making a peep. That made Jace feel even more unnerved.

By the time they got back to town it was starting to get dark.

"The nights here are starting to get colder" She said continuing to look out the open window. Her hand was going up and down catching the wind as it hung out of the side of the truck.

"It is almost time to harvest the grapes. I wonder if Dane will be helping this year." The morbid statement he made instantly made him feel regret for saying it. Turning onto the street where McKenzie lives, the truck slowly pulled into her driveway.

"Thank you for coming with me. It is nice to have a friend that isn't mad at me for something." Smiling in her direction, she pulled the center console of the truck up and slid over next to him. Her embrace was warm as she hugged him. Her arms were around him so tight he could feel her breasts against his chest. They were nice. He liked it. Her death like grip began to loosen and she kissed him on the cheek. Pulling back, she brushed his shoulder with her hand as he still had remnants of his haircut left on his shirt.

"Don't worry about your brother. He has always been wild and I'm sure he will turn up soon with a hangover and a severe headache." A sincere smile was on her face followed by a subtle wink. These comments made Jace smile as a hangover and a severe headache were exactly what he was blessed with when he awoke this morning.

"Call me soon?" Her inquisitive yet purposeful tone surprised him.

"You want me to call you?" *Stupid question* he thought in his head.

She raised an eyebrow at him and slid back over to her seat. Cracking the door open she hopped out and shut the door behind her.

"I guess you will have to find out." Pleased with her answer, she made her way up and into her big house. Feeling butterflies in his stomach, he drove home feeling mixed emotions about his brother and her.

Once he made it back to his parent's house, he walked in and found both his parents in the living room watching a bright flickering television. His mother was on the couch sewing what looked to be a pair of pants that had seen better days.

"Hi sweetie!" Her voice was surprisingly cheerful.

"Come join us. We are watching our favorite program."
Looking over to where his Dad was sitting, he had his feet
up and the chair was completely reclined back. His father
was breathing deeply and his eyes were shut.

"Dad looks like he is enjoying it, he is sleeping!"

"Oh, you know your father. Once he sits down we lose him
if he is not eating or watching a game." There was a
popping sound which was coming from the kitchen.

"You cooking something Ma?" He wanted the answer to
be yes due to his own hunger.

"I am making popcorn" A loud voice from behind him
made him lurch forward in surprise.

"Damn you! Do you have to scare me like that!" His voice
was loud with anger and he was suddenly taking deep
breaths. He could feel his accelerated heartbeat in his
neck. Jen stood behind him with a proud grin on her face.

"What is all the ruckus about!?" Their dad sat up in his
chair and clicked the reclining legs down. He was making
grunts like a bear coming out of hibernation.

"Your kids are home." Their mom chimed in sarcastically.
As the popping noise subsided, Jen ran back into the
kitchen and popped the microwave door open.

"Whose idea was it to have all these noisy kids?" The bear
grunted angrily.

"Well if I wasn't so damn good lookin', you would have
been able to keep your hands off me." Their mother was
always quick with her wit.

"I seem to remember a young woman who couldn't resist
my chiseled muscles and manly ways. You were always
ready to jump on the roller coaster…" His father's words

were cut short.

"Oh good, it is always wonderful to think about your parents love life." Jace's mockery of this made his mom smile bigger. Walking in with a big bowl of popcorn, Jen must have been eavesdropping because she started right in on the conversation.

"Yea it is always nice to hear about your parents having sex. Don't you guys know that you shouldn't be doing that anymore at your age! Ugh yuck. You should be too tired!" Pulling the handle on his chair, his feet once again went jerking up and the recliner eased back into a laying down position.

"Yup darling, according to these kids, we are dead. They should just bury us now and call it a day because we are too old." His sarcastic words met his wife's ears and she nodded in agreement.

"You are lucky I like your father Jen, being that you are the fourth, we could have stopped after three."

"This conversation is making me wish you did!" Jen replied tossing a piece of popcorn in her mouth.

"I have to speak with you guys about Dane." Jace's voice was low.

"You don't need to worry about that right now son." His father was reassuring. His quick answer meant that he was prepared to handle the Dane situation and that everything was under control.

"He has done this several times before. He goes off because he is either mad at us or something in his life."

"I wanted to tell you that I found his truck though, and there was not a scratch on it!"

"We know Jace. His truck ended up on our friend's property and they called us about it. Being that there was no damage, I'm fairly certain he couldn't have been the one to hit farmer Johnson and his son. At least not in his truck and I don't know how he would have gotten another vehicle at that time of night... especially being as 'drunk' as he was." His dad made air quotes around the word 'drunk' as if to imply that Dane had not really been that intoxicated. Feeling a sense of relief, he was surprised his parents were acting so cavalier about this whole situation. "I have spoken with officer Harper and we will be going out to retrieve his truck in the morning. When I know more then that, I will certainly let you know. For right now, don't let it stress you." Jace looked over at his mom and she was looking down continuing to sew. The happiness her body language was giving off when he had gotten there had faded. He could tell that this subject was bothering her.

"Are you alright Mom?"

"She is just worried about Dane. She is always worried about you kids even when you are safe." His father jumped in to answer before she could. He always tried to protect her no matter what.

"Listen, I have something important I want to ask you." His voice perked up as he was trying to change the subject off his clearly ailing wife.

"Jace, we have a group of potential investors coming up tomorrow for a wine sampling and to see our facilities. I would appreciate if you could provide them with the information they request and of course let them sample as much as they would like." His father's eyes were wide open now and looking in his direction.

"Investors Dad?"

"Yes, they are from several different companies that will potentially be buying our products and distributing them to their own clients or whoever they choose to. It is a wonderful opportunity because if they like what they see, they usually buy in mass quantities."

"Yes, Dad. I would be happy to." The feeling of nerves came over him as his father was entrusting him with these *important* people.

"You should read our brochures again and brush up on all the different types of grape we have to offer, our facility here in general, and the programs and specials that we offer. Also, please make sure the sampling counter is clean and stocked. I have closed it to the public tomorrow, so you will only have to worry about them."

"I will absolutely do that. Thank you, Dad." Grabbing the big brochure with the words 'Grazer's Grapes' written in cursive across the top of it, he made his way up to his room. This was his chance to hopefully get back on his parent's good graces. The excitement of this opportunity mixed with his parents' calm and collected mannerisms regarding his brother made him forget about the situation...if only for one night.

The screaming of an alarm jerked Jace's head off his pillow. Reaching over to the end table to try and silence his phone, he ended up knocking it onto the floor. It flopped face down covering the speaker which muffled the sound some. He got in the shower as fast as he could.

He wanted to be ready early and brush up one last time. He already knew most of the information being around it for most of his life, but a little refresher never hurt. When he got out of the shower, there was a purple shirt hanging on his doorknob that looked fresh and ironed. A small crest on the chest of the shirt read 'Grazer's Grapes' and underneath it was his name embroidered as well. For some reason, this made him happy. The feeling he had as an outsider in his own family was fresh in his head as it was a recurring thought playing on repeat since the day he had returned. The simple gesture of his name on the shirt with his family's company made him feel like part of the team.

His mother was in the kitchen cleaning the countertops with a very potent smelling cleaner.

"Good morning Ma. Are these people coming into our house too?" This sarcastic question was directed to the fact she was cleaning with such intent.

"No, I don't believe so. It is just the day I like to clean the kitchen. After all, other than the bathrooms, this is the room in house that always seems to get the dirtiest." Her response made a lot of obvious sense as she completely disregarded his sarcasm.

"You look handsome today Jace. Something is different. New haircut?"

"Yea, just a trim. McKenzie talked me into it."

"It looks nice. She did a good job. I have been trying to get your father to go to her for some time now, but he is stuck in his old ways. Same old hairdresser, same old hairstyle, same old crooked bangs." Her comedic tone made herself chuckle.

"I should be heading down to the sampling room. I want to make sure everything is all set." As he reached out for the knob on the side door, his mother caught his arm.

"You know, your father is happy you are home. He wouldn't have asked you to do this if he was upset with you. He really loves you and someday soon you should sit down with him and have a talk about everything that has happened." A surprised and gracious look came to his face.

"I will Mom. I have thought about it since I left. It will happen when the time is right." Opening the door and stepping out, he turned around before he closed it.

"Oh, and I hope he knows that I love him too." A short pause and his mother's eyes met his. Her eyes glistened in the sunlight and a soft look of happiness came to her face. "He knows."

With those simple yet meaningful words, he shut the door and headed for the store.

Having a winery the size of theirs was a lot of work and making sure they turned out good products was very important to the whole family including everyone who worked for them. After all, everyone's livelihoods depended upon it. The store sat across the driveway next to the barn. A small parking lot had formed that used to be just grass. Over the years, customers parked their cars there so his father put down some leftover crushed up stones he had. The stones were scarce and grass would tend to grow up between them, but it still served the purpose. Opening the front doors, you were met with a heavenly aroma of different fruits and berries. There were wooden shelves around the perimeter walls that would hold many different shapes and sizes of bottles. In the middle of the store sat an island consisting of four wooden countertops that came together to make a complete square. Barstools accompanied the outside edges of each countertop. The middle of the square was large and had several refrigerators and freezers to hold the wine that was to be sampled. There was a small piece of the countertop that was on hinges and would lift to let the workers enter the middle where they could provide the customers with tastings. A stainless-steel sink sat just below where the counter was. That came in handy for quick dishwashing and rinsing of the glasses. Built in drawers underneath the counters would pull out and held within them several essential items. Bottle openers, wine lists, crackers, popcorn, dark chocolate miniature bites, towels and a few other tools. The drawers were pretty much full, and the store looked exceptionally clean already. Knowing his mother, she took pride in keeping the store as clean as she did her house. She had already begun to decorate for the upcoming season with several pumpkins varying in size and shape scattered throughout the store. Bundles of calico corn which ranged from three to five ears tied together had been placed strategically on the sampling counters. These were a seasonal decoration that worked well in almost any setting due to their variety of colors. A small cash register sat at one of the corners of the island. An attachment at its side that allowed for credit card purchases. For a long time, they were a cash only establishment but keeping up with the times is essential for a business to succeed. It made sense since people sometimes spend more when it is just a swipe of a credit card. The feeling of 'I'll just pay this off later and forget about it now' is one that people enjoy. Casinos use bright colored chips because if people had to sit at a card table and fork over twenty dollar bills every time they wanted to play, they would stop playing a lot sooner. This way you don't actually see yourself losing money. Even if you know you are, your eyes don't see it.

A crackling sound coming from the stone driveway caught Jace's attention. His father was driving Dane's truck. The first thing he thought was how was he driving it without the keys? He must have hotwired it or something. Stepping out of the truck, he was making his way to the store.

"Hey Dad." Jace's greeting met his father as he stepped inside.

"Do you need anything?" With only these words and his clearly agitated body language, he could instantly tell his Dad was in a bad mood.

"I am all set Dad. We are completely stocked up and ready to go." Wanting to ask about Dane's truck, he resisted the urge to because he didn't want to add to the anger his father was displaying.

"If you need anything I will have my phone in the tractor with me. I am going to begin harvesting today."

"Alright Dad. I can come out and help you later if you would like me to?" He figured this question was safe as offering to help was not adding to his problems.

"Just focus on getting the job done in here." He was

wrong. Obviously, no question was safe at this time. Walking back out the door, he disappeared into the barn.

About an hour later, three cars pulled in next to the store. The first two cars held a man and a woman, both pairs seemed to be middle aged. The third car held two ladies, one seemed very young, probably Jace's age. The other woman was dressed nicely and looked like she could have been her mother. They all knew each other obviously as they greeted one another and headed slowly for the front door of his store. The chatter was loud and followed with laughter as they walked in.

"Wow this is nice in here." He heard the man from car number two say to the lady that rode in with him.

"Welcome to Grazer's Grapes!" It may have been forced excitement in his voice, but his nerves were getting the best of him and everyone responded to him with smiles and greetings of their own.

"My name is Jace and I will be happy to help with anything you may need or want this afternoon." Stepping out from behind the counter, he shook their hands and offered for them to have a seat at the counter. The man from the first car who introduced himself as Gary began the conversation.

"You guys have a beautiful location here. Finn lake is stunning this time of year!" Starting off with a compliment was always a good way to begin a business meeting.

"Yes, it is kind of like living in a vacation spot year-round! Plus, this area provides us with some of the best land to do what we do best...grow wonderful tasting grapes!" Jace Smiled at the ladies sitting closest to him. He made sure to make eye contact with everyone.

"I bet it does. Would it be possible to get a little more information on your establishment and possibly a tour?" Jace could see that Gary was clearly the "leader" of this bunch.

"Absolutely! If you will allow me to, I'd be happy to tell you about Grazer's Grapes." Smiling at Gary, he nodded and pulled a pen and notebook out from the inside pocket of his jacket. Jace passed out the brochures that were printed in bright colors.

"Before we get started, is Robert here today?" Gary asked. "I spoke to him earlier in the week and he told me that he is the owner and runs the day-to-day operations here."

"Yes, he is. We will be meeting up with him later." Jace was unsure why he said that as there were no plans in place for them to meet his father.

"I am his son and I run the operations of the store and sales." There was lie number two. Was it nerves? What was the point of doing that? The thought in his head was that he wanted to sound credible and make it seem as if they were meeting with someone important, not just an employee of the store. In fact, he was hardly even that! "Oh, you are his son? Alright sounds great. We would all love to hear about your products." Gary said flipping a page in the brochure. Apparently, being his son gave him enough credibility for them to be satisfied.

Jace cleared his throat and began.

"We began operation some twenty-two years ago. We are situated on just over seventy-three acres of prime grape growing soil. As some of you may know, there are over ten thousand different varieties of wine grapes in the world. People have long been experimenting with different grapes to find or create the taste that their individual palate enjoys." Holding up the brochure, he pointed to the list of different types of wine they had to offer.

"We offer a wide variety of various selections of wine in the following categories...dry, semi-dry, semi-sweet, sweet and of course, dessert wines. Merlot and Riesling are our most popular. I am partial to sweet wine myself even though our region tends to lean towards the drier wines we offer. At least that is what our sales indicate." Here was another fact he wasn't a hundred percent sure about but he has heard it many times from his Father.

"I have a question." The young girl who introduced herself as Madison was half raising her hand and half waving at Jace.

"Yes, please go ahead."

"Do you have an average number of how much wine you produce here? Number of bottles?" She tried to adjust her question, but he knew what she was getting at.

"Well each grape varies in size and how many we actually have growing. The vineyard is set up in rows and each row needs to be around nine feet apart. Then the vines can be planted anywhere from 6-10 feet apart in each row. I will show you this when we take our tour." He looked around and all six of them had eye contact and genuinely looked interested in what he was telling them.

"Now for your original question. Let me ask this first, does anyone know on average how many grapes it take to make one bottle of wine?" Looking at each other, they shrugged their shoulders and Madison responded.

"I have no idea. 100 maybe?" She laughed after she said this because she knew her guess was probably way off.

"That's not a bad guess. It is actually between six hundred to nine hundred grapes to get a full bottle of wine. As you probably know, grapes grow in clusters, so it can range anywhere from five to eight to ten clusters needed to make a bottle depending on their sizes. Next, we measure each acre of land by how many tons of grapes are produced. An acre of land can produce one ton of grapes or it can produce up to ten or twelve tons of grapes. Last year we were very lucky and we produced around eight tons per acre. Each acre is not exactly the same. Some yield lower numbers and some yield higher but we averaged out at eight. Now I am going to do a little math with you." Jace smiled and looked down at the brochure even though he was not reading off it.

"Now keep in mind these number can fluctuate, but one ton of grapes can produce around two barrels of wine. Each barrel contains sixty gallons. Everybody with me so far?" looking back up, Gary nodded to him.

"So that means that that one ton of grapes can make around 700 bottles of wine. Like I mentioned, last year we were able to get eight tons per acre which equates to roughly 5,600 bottles per acre. Now we have 73 acres here but we only use around 70 to grow grapes. Last year's total was right around 392,000 bottles of wine that our farm produced. This year we are hoping to break the 400,000-bottle mark." He paused for effect.

"Wow! That is impressive." Gary's approval of these

numbers was obviously a good thing.

"Our operation here has expanded over the years as we have brought in additional barrels to handle the load. The process which I can show you in a few minutes is very simple. The harvest where the grapes are picked is the first step. Knowing when to Harvest the grape is pivotal to the whole process. The rotten or under ripe grapes are sorted and removed so it will not negatively affect the flavor of the wine. Only pristine grapes are moved to the next stage. Then, they are ready to be de-stemmed and crushed. The fermentation process is next which can last anywhere from ten days to a month. Then the clarification process begins where the wine is basically filtered to remove different things such as dead yeast cells. This is also the time where the wine will be put into either wooden barrels or steel tanks to store. The final stage which is my favorite is aging and bottling because you get to finally start to see the process come full circle. The choice is up to each farmer whether to bottle the wine right away or let it age further in the tanks or even once it is bottled." He felt like he hadn't taken a breath in minutes!

"I know that was a lot of information, but does anyone have any questions?" Everyone was staring up at him shaking their heads as if they understood everything he had said.

"Would we like to try some samples now?" These words made everyone perk up as if he had just offered them free money. Jace was feeling good about what he had presented to them and he felt that this meeting was going very positively. Just as he pulled out the first bottle to sample, a car pulled up next to the store. To his surprise, Ally stepped out and was walking fast toward the house. "Maybe we could see your facilities and then come have a tasting?" Gary's words caught Jace by surprise. He had lost his attention when he saw her drive up. The others Gary was with seemed to silently protest this idea as they wanted a sample of what Jace had just explained to them. "Yes, we can do that." Jace said smiling at them and putting the bottle back into the refrigerator. As Jace came out from behind the counter, Ally had opened the store's front door and was walking his way.

"Hey Al, I kind of am in the middle of something..."

"I don't give a shit!" Cutting him off, her ferocious tone accompanied by the swearing made him panic. His heart instantly began to race and Jace could feel his face getting warmer from the inside.

"Is everything okay?" Gary asked standing up from his barstool.

"YES! Everything is fine." Jace assured him and started to direct him to the front door when Ally caught his arm with a very firm grip.

"You want to date my sister now?! Are you really that much of a dirt bag?"

"Maybe we should go wait outside?" Gary told the others that were starting to stand as well.

"Please don't! Ally you have this all wrong!" His voice was climbing even though he was trying to stay calm and collected. Trying to answer both his clients and Ally proved to be a difficult task.

"I have a meeting right now. I can't talk about this." Jace pulled his arm away from her grip and began to walk away to lead his father's clients outside. Suddenly, a wine cork came flying at him hitting him in the ear. Looking back at Ally, her next throw had a handful of corks that flew in his direction. Out of instinct, Jace ducked out of the way as the corks flew over his head hitting Gary and two of the other ladies. Jace was stunned and horrified. How could this be happening to him? As Ally reached down to grab what Jace assumed was another handful of corks, the three that had just been hit flew towards the doors as if she was reloading a gun for another shot.

"Alright that is enough, we are leaving now." Instant anger came from Gary's voice. He couldn't have been pleased that a cork had hit him in the face nearly missing the corner of his eye.

"No! Please don't go! Please let me show you around." Jace pleaded with them to no avail. They each got back into their cars quickly and began to pull away.

"Wait, please don't go." He continued to shout and wave his arms at the cars for them to wait. As they pulled out onto the street, Jace stood outside in the middle of the driveway in shock. He looked back to see where Ally was now to protect himself from further objects being projected at his head. She was still in the store waiting for him to come back in he assumed. He hung his head still in disbelief that they had left. He couldn't blame them though; would he want to go to a vineyard to have things thrown at him? Turning back around slowly as if he had been shot, he looked up. In the distance he saw his father standing there in the middle of a row of trees with a death stare directed right into Jace's eyes.

Chapter 8

The sudden fear and anxiety Jace felt looking at his father in the distance was astronomically high. Disappointing his family, especially his father, might have been Jace's greatest fear, not just at this point in time, but for his whole life! Throughout his life, people always told him not to worry about what others think, and don't worry about what they say or if they are judging you. He was good at this with almost everybody else in his life...but his father was different. He cared about what he thought. He cared about what he thought about him. Disappointing him and not living up to his standards was an unbearable thought. He wanted to make his dad proud and in his eyes, failure was not an option.

Looking up at the house, he could see his mother looking out the window at him. He just wanted to die right there and then. Looking back to where his father was, he had turned around and started walking towards his tractor. He had only one place to go and the thought of what was waiting for him was spine-chilling. Opening the door slowly as if he was leading a funeral precession into the store, he looked at the face that he once loved sitting on a barstool.

"Glad you could make time for me!" The exasperated tone was calm now. The calm before the obvious storm that was coming.

"You couldn't have waited until I was done with them? How did you even know I was in the store?"

"I went up to the house and your mom told me that you were down here giving wine tastings or something."

"Or something? Those people were very important to our business!"

"Yea, well it gets a little cloudy who and what is important to you ever since you ran off and left everyone who loves you!"

"That's a different issue that you have no idea about!" His voice sounded shaky.

"Oh, I don't have any idea?!" It was beginning to escalate quickly.

"The man that I loved and was hoping to marry someday just up and leaves me! And for what? To chase a stupid dream that everyone told him would not work out!" Her face was beat red and her eyes were fierce with rage.

"I told you many times that I was sorry..."

"Well sometimes sorry isn't good enough! Let me guess, you are sorry that you are going after my sister now?"

"Now wait a minute..." Not letting him explain, she cut him off, "She told me that you are going to call her now. That you spent that day together and she is hoping more will happen!"

"She told you that?" His eyebrow raised as he tried to calm the situation down.

"Yes, she came to me to ask if it would be alright with me if you and her might someday be something."

"Nothing has happened. I swear to you this wasn't my idea." "Idea for what? You are blaming my sister?"

"No of course not." Jace felt like he was backed into a corner and was unsure how he got there. He hadn't done anything wrong in his mind. He hadn't even pursued McKenzie at all. What could he say to calm Ally down? "You both expect me to be okay with this? After everything that you and I have been through together? All those years! You never even began to think about the repercussions of dating MY sister?"

"What is the difference now? You are with Taylor now."

"His name is Tyler you ass. And the only reason I was forced to move on was because the love of my life left me!" The toughness in her voice was beginning to sound shaky as well. Jace could sense that tears were inevitably going to follow soon.

"I'm sorry. But you have to believe me that I have not gone after your sister at all. Nothing has happened." A long pause between words and Ally was wiping her left eye.

"Is something going to happen?" As if Jace couldn't tell already, the softness in her question confirmed that severe sadness was behind this anger.

How was Jace going to answer this? He loved Ally and she clearly still had feelings for him. She had moved on though and it didn't matter what they had before. Their lives were going in different directions now and the love he had for her must be suppressed.

"I don't know." Those three words seemed to be an end to their screaming match. Ally stood up from the chair and moved over to where he stood.

"You are not half the man I once knew!" Her arm swung back and her hand slapped his face with a loud pop. His head turned from the impact and he kept it off to the side looking down.

"I'm sorry."

"You disgust me." She walked passed him and out the door.

Jace did not want to leave the store ever again. He did not want to face his mother or his father. Or any of his siblings for that matter. Why could he seem to do nothing right in his life? Another car pulled into their driveway, this time he knew who it was. As the white and black police car came to a stop, Officer Harper stepped out and looked at him.

"Good afternoon son. Is your father around."

"Hello Mr. Harper, yes he is, let me take...ugh...I'll show you where he is." Not wanting to face his father just yet, he pointed in the direction of the field where the tractor was. The officer walked down that way and Jace's curiosity got the best of him. Was he going to give his dad information about Dane? Or the accident? Or was he here to talk about the fact that he has turmoil in his own family because his daughters both have feelings for Jace? He doubted the latter was the case but you never know. Being that his father and officer Harper were good friends, maybe it wasn't anything bad at all. The growing desire to know what was going on consumed his thoughts. Suddenly he became a slave to his impulse and began to slowly run down toward the field. He kept low enough so his head was not over the tops of the trees. He stayed two rows away from where the two men came together. The tractor's roaring engine was cut off and the silence became very loud. Jace put his hand over his mouth to keep his inhaling and exhaling as hushed as possible. Some of what they were saying was inaudible. He had to move closer. The trees and vines were very thick complicating his ability to see through them.

"I don't like what is going on." He caught his father's voice clearly for a moment. Sliding between two trees, he was still a little bit of distance away from them. On his hands and knees, he began to army crawl closer to them. Their voices were becoming inevitably clearer with the increased danger of being caught.

"How do you not know where he is or have any contact with him?" The officer sounded agitated.

"Listen, you have known me since we were young, If I knew, don't you think I would tell you?" He had not heard his father's voice sound this way in a long time. Normally he is calm and collected. Now he sounded like a boy on trial for murder.

"There are just too many holes in this story and the Johnson family wants answers to what happened. I don't blame them, I would too if someone killed a person in my family."

"I understand completely. How is Oliver doing? Marie and I are planning on going up to see him. I also reached out to Leo's family to give my condolences. Leo and I were neighborly...I wouldn't say friendly, but we tolerated each other. When I called, I inquired about a funeral date, but she said that it was a private ceremony." Being in a very tight knit farming community, when someone passes away, lots of people from the area show up to give support to the family.

"Oliver is awake and recovering. He has a little bit of memory loss, but he remembers things that happened from long ago in his life. It is just the short term that is a little foggy for him. We all hope he will be out of the hospital soon and back to his family who really need him."

"I hope so too." He could hear his father plucking clusters of grapes off the vines and tossing them into the large bucket.

"By the way Robert, I noticed Dane's truck in the driveway, where is yours?" A lump formed in Jace's throat and his heart felt like it was going to pump out of his chest. *Where was his truck?* Jace thought in his head. It always seemed like the police asked questions as if you were already guilty or had something to hide.

"My daughter Elizabeth has it. She needed it to move some furniture. She bought a new couch and needed to drop off her old one. Her little puddle jumper that she drives could barely carry two people, let alone a couch!" A nervous laughter followed his own joke.

"She didn't need you or Jace to help her with it? I saw him coming out of the store just now."

"She told me some of her friends were planning to help her with it. I offered to help, but she told me she had it covered."

"Alright, well if you hear from Dane or have any other information, please call me."

"I will Rick." He said tapping the officer on the shoulder.

"We need to get in a few more fishing days before the season is over." The officer's tone was light and friendly now.

"Well I would love to if I could get my boys out here to help me harvest these grapes. We will find time don't worry." Jace began to move backward as he could tell the conversation was about to end. Officer Harper walked to the end of the row and turned back towards his father. "Oh, and tell Jace he better watch himself with my daughter. He apparently is after my youngest now."

"Jace is perusing McKenzie?" Jace froze upon hearing his name come from his father's mouth.

"Apparently he is. You know...this is not the only gun I own." Officer Harper smirked and tapped his four fingers over the pistol at his side.

"I'll see you later Robert." With that, he walked back up to the house and Jace could hear his car pull away. Getting to his knees, he looked down at his shirt that was covered in grass and several burdocks which were a pain to get off. The burrs pricked your fingers and if you don't have the right type of glove, they either go through the glove and poke you or get stuck to the glove instead of your clothes. Deciding to avoid this all together, he took off the purple shirt and turned it inside out so he could hold it without getting pricked. The wind gave a sudden whip of cold air as if nature was disapproving of what he was doing. Jace lay in waiting for the loud bellow of the tractor engine to fire up again so he could get away easier. Instead, he heard small beeps of a cell phone's buttons being pushed. A couple seconds went by, which thanks to the chilly breeze against his bare skin, felt like the longest seconds of time ever recorded!

"Hello Elizabeth, how are you doing?" Jace could not hear who he presumed to be his sister on the other end of the phone.

"Listen, I need you to do something for me. If anybody asks you, I need you to tell them that you borrowed my truck to move an old couch out of your place because you bought a new one." A couple more seconds passed.

"Because I need you to alright? It is very crucial that you listen to me okay?" Jace couldn't believe what he was hearing his father say!

"Yes, everything is fine. We are just in a sticky situation with your brother and we need an alibi. This shouldn't come as a surprise, this is just like last time."

Last time? There was a last time his family has lied to the law? All of a sudden, burdocks being caught in his shirt were the last thing on his mind.

"Yes, your mother knows about it. Now say it back to me." Jace could hear the sounds coming from his cell phone and they didn't sound like a voice who was cooperating without a fight.

"That is good, perfect." His father said pleased with her answer finally.

"I'll give you a call later. Please keep this between us...alright I love you too." With that, the cell phone clicked shut and within seconds, the tractor began to roar again as his father began his work. Jace could not remember the last time he had heard his father say he loved anybody, including his mother! Fast running and hunched over, he made it out of the rows and back up to the house.

"Ma, where are you going?" His Mother had her coat on with her small handbag of a purse over her shoulder that looked as if it wasn't even big enough to carry a dollar bill. She was heading towards her car in a carefree manner.

"I am going to the supermarket. Would you like anything specific?" It was clear she knew what had happened in the store but either decided to ignore it all together and pretend she didn't see it, or, let his father deal with it which inevitably he would either way.

"No Ma, I'm all set." Closing the door, she started the engine and backed up to where he was standing. She slowly rolled down her non-electric windows and looked at her shirtless son.

"It is getting cold, why did you take your shirt off?" A common-sense question that was going to require a quickly developed answer.

"I-uh...the tag was bugging me so when everyone left, I took it off."

Giving her boy a peculiar look, she didn't seem like she wanted to press the issue any further.

"Alright then. Just one thing, be careful getting those burdocks out. The burrs will poke you." She said this with a devious smile as she hit the gas pedal and peeled away. Before he could respond, she was down the driveway and out onto the road. Had she seen him? How did she know about the burdocks on his shirt? It was inside out. Did she know he was spying on his dad? If she did know, why didn't she come out to stop him? She always used to tell him that mothers know everything, but could that really be true or was she just a great detective also known as a spy?

Several hours passed with Jace lying on his bed trying to figure out what to tell his dad and how to fix the problems which he inadvertently seemed to have caused with Ally. The television screen was making his eyes hurt. There was nothing on but an infomercial about supposedly the most unique and wonderful mini oven that you cannot live without.

'Set it and forget it.'

This must have been said a hundred times over the last half hour! Their household only had one cable hookup and that was to the television in the living room. Honestly, he was lucky to even have a TV in his room that could pick up any channels. If he wanted to watch anything other than cable, he had a stack of the same four DVDs that he had seen probably a thousand times each! Looking out his window over the vast land that had yet to be harvested, nightfall was coming and the tractor's lights were burning brightly providing just enough beams of light for his father to continue to work. He had been out there for hours and Jace wondered how long he was going to work into the night. There was an aroma of some kind of seasoned meat or chicken filling the house that made his mouth water. Meandering down the stairs and into the kitchen, his two sisters were sitting at the table. Lizzy was chopping up what looked like onions and carrots. Jen was peeling potatoes when she looked up and saw him enter the room.

"Hey hotshot! Want to help me peel these potatoes? Oh wait...I don't want to give you an easy job that you will just find a way to screw up."

"Jennifer!" Their mom yelled from the dining room. Scolding her daughter with just her name. Jen looked back down at the potato in her hand with a grin. She could always be counted on to make a bad or awkward situation worse.

"Don't worry about it Jace. Everything will be fine." Lizzy said with a smile. She was always the sensitive and compassionate one. Hence her choice of degree and career.

"Where is Dad?" Asking a question which he already knew the answer helped the uneasy feeling he was having. Plus, it was all he could think to say.

"He is still working. I told him to come in and eat but he said to go ahead and start. I will warm his up later when he gets done."

"He has a really good work ethic doesn't he Mom?" The intent of these words was another subtle attack towards her brother. Jen's snarky attitude was getting on Jace's nerves.

"Will you just shut up for a few minutes and give us all some peace!?" Lashing out at her to defend himself felt good, yet inevitably, would be followed by remorse.

"Wow! Someone ate their Wheaties this morning." Surprise in her voice was clear as Jace was not the type to speak up even if he was being wronged. Dane and Jen were the loud ones and usually always had plenty to say. The bookends of the children seem to end up with the 'type A' personality. More aggressive and outspoken than most.

"Why don't you wash up and have a seat sweetie?" His mom spoke to him with her head in the oven.

"Yea, come join us. Do you think you can sit down without breaking the chair?" This was the last straw. Jace spun around and charged towards the front door. Pushing it open, he could hear Lizzy's voice again scolding Jen which was followed by a yell in his direction to come back. Slamming the front door to make the point that he was upset, he headed down the stairs and hopped in his truck. He was going to confront his father, tell him what had happened and deal with the consequences. This waiting all day was slow torture and he was about to make it end!

Jamming the truck into gear, he spun the tires kicking up stones and leaving two deep tire marks right down to the dirt underneath. The thought crossed his mind that it had rained heavily the past few days and that his truck might sink in the grass pathway. He didn't care. Not slowing down, his truck roared into the back fields. The headlights were no match for the overwhelming darkness of night. Bumping up and down, the truck squeaked and cracked with displeasure. It was old and not up for this kind of treatment anymore. Coming to a stop at the end of the row his father's tractor was currently sitting in, he stepped out leaving the truck running and his door open. The bell from the open door kept dinging as he raced down the row on foot. The ruts caused by the big tractor were not as deep as he thought they may be.

"Dad!" he yelled over the loud engine.

"Hey Dad, we have to talk." Jace was breathing heavily and his anxiety was kicking in. Hopping onto the tractor's steps, he looked inside the cockpit to see if he was behind the wheel. Empty.

Jumping down, he landed in squishy soft mud, which now covered his shoes. Pulling his leg out, he tried to rub his shoes on some clean grass which didn't seem to be helping. Looking up and down both sides of the row of trees, he could not spot his father anywhere. He had to be close by. It was not like his dad to leave the tractor running and not be using it. Diesel fuel was not exactly cheap and letting it run for no reason was not something he would do. In fact, that would be exactly something that he himself would do and get yelled at for.

Suddenly, a loud bang rang through the air. It sounded as if it had come from either the next field over or the barn which sat between the two sprawling fields. It was loud enough that he could hear it clearly over the tractor engine. It sounded like a gunshot. Running back to his truck, he slid into the open door and punched the gas. The engine whined as the rear wheel spun frantically in place. Reverse. Now they spun the opposite direction kicking mud up towards his door. The rear end tried to fishtail loose from the dense mud but there was not enough weight over the rear wheels to get traction. Reaching down to the small shifter on the floor, Jace shifted into four-wheel low. Waiting a few seconds for the truck to adjust, finally, it jerked forward and backwards trying to get loose. Looking down at the tires, he could see he was just burying the truck even deeper. His frustration was building. Slamming the truck door, he began to proceed on foot. He ran towards the old barn. His lungs were already desperately trying to fill with any oxygen they could get. He could feel his heartbeat in his neck. His panting was getting louder and he had to stop for a minute. He could hear his old high school football coach screaming "Arms above your head! Stand straight up and don't bend over! It opens up your lungs to let more oxygen in."

As Jace stood there bent over trying to catch his breath, he thought of this and stood up gingerly. Before he knew it, he was running again. Hard running up a mild slope to where the barn sat. The lights were on as his legs fumbled his body inside the building. Coughing between lungfuls of much needed air, the thought hit him that he was obviously not in as good of shape as he thought he was. He now put his hands behind his head and moved slowly toward the back of the barn. It was filled with lots of different tools and machines, some of which he wasn't even sure of what they were used for. His father's classic car...a 1969 z28 Chevrolet Camaro was nestled in the back-left corner of the barn. It was cherry red with black racing stripes down the center. Even in the dim lighting that was provided by the old barn lights, the old car still had a proud glow to it. His dad loved this car almost more than life itself. Walking up to it, there was something not right about this. The barn door was wide open and his father's prized car just sitting there. Then it hit him, why did the car not have its cover on? He knew that his father had been working all day and was almost positive that he had not left. The large and strong engine that the Camaro was equipped with was thundering loud. If it was to be started and moved, you could hear it from inside the house or the store. Another thought entered his mind, this was not the normal place where he kept the car. It had its very own single garage on the side of the barn. His dad had added this some years ago when he used to store the car in the barn as it is now. Jace could still remember the day when he and his brother were playing hockey in the driveway and it began to rain. Not wanting to stop, it seemed like a good idea to move their games into the barn where their father's prized car happened to be resting. Not five minutes in, Dane takes a hard slapshot that ricochet off Jace's stick and hit a pile of boards that were standing upright leaning against the side of the barn. Of course, they proceeded to fall into the Camaro and luckily did no serious damage. They did knock his side mirror clean off the car and made a nice scratch down the side of the door. This was the single time in both their lives they were afraid that their father was going to actually end their lives. From that moment forward, they were not allowed to play in the barn at all and their dad built an addition to the barn that could only fit his car and nothing else. Smiling to himself, this memory was one where he could only laugh at because of how stupid they had been. It had been years since it had happened and to this day, nobody brought up it up. He may have been able to chuckle at it now, but he was almost positive his father was not at that point, nor would he ever be.

Looking back at the open barn door, his original and still unanswered question weighed on his mind. He made his way out of the big doors and there was still no sign of his father anywhere. Jace walked around the outside of the barn, his panting was starting to desist, and his curiosity was peaking. The small add-on garage faced the opposite direction of the front large doors of the barn. It was hidden from plain sight which is just how his father had planned it. There was a side door to the garage which allowed access to the car without opening the big garage door. This door was always locked and did not have a window to see inside. The main door was without windows as well. This kind of protection made his dad relax and feel safe that nothing else would happen to his car. Going back to check the side door, he pulled on the small round handle but had no success. He figured it was locked but why not give it a try. An owl's screech in the distance caused a sudden rush of fear through his body. The night was still cold and the moon was behind some thick clouds. It was the perfect scene for a scary Halloween film. All he needed now was for Mike Myers to jump out with his mask and knife and completely put him over the edge.

Stopping cold in his tracks, Jace heard a car door slam shut and voices which he could make out as his sister's. Her car started and drove away to let the silence recapture the night. For some reason or another, Jace could not let this go. He wanted to figure out why the cars had been moved around, why the tractor was still running, and where was his dad? The main garage door was emitting a tiny amount of light where the bottom of the door touched the ground. Dropping down flat on his stomach, Jace put his eyeball as close to the door as he could, trying hard to see inside. No luck. He stuck his fingers under the door to see if he could move it up just the slightest so he could get a peek inside. To his amazement, the door slid up like the rails were covered in butter. Freezing in place, he wondered if his dad might be inside and would catch him snooping around. At this point, it was too late. The door had been slid about a foot off the ground and if there was anybody inside, they already knew someone was opening the door. Getting to his feet, he grabbed the handle and pulled the door all the way up. It settled above with a squeak and a bang. Now that the door was open, Jace had a clear view into the small garage. He must have been in shock at what he was looking at because he didn't move. His feet felt like they were stuck in cement that he couldn't get loose from. His mouth had inadvertently dropped open and his eyes were as wide as saucers. Before him sat his father's big truck. It barely fit into this space and you would have to turn to the side if you wanted to get around it. The truck was fronted in so all he could see was the tailgate. Something must be in the air tonight. He thought this because his father was a creature of habit and he never pulled any of his cars into the garages or barns head first. He backed everything in so he could get out easily. He figured now that he was in here, if his father did catch him, he could just say he was looking for him to talk about earlier. Moving to the driver's side, he turned sideways and sidestepped on the balls of his feet down the side of the truck. Ducking down below the side mirror, he popped up at the side of the hood just as he tripped forward over a piece of large metal. Catching himself before he fell, he glimpsed at what he had just tripped over. It looked like a part of a bumper...and then he saw it. The front end of the truck was completely smashed in. The headlights were broken and there were parts hanging off the front of the truck. Covering his still open mouth with his hand in shock, he couldn't even begin to fathom what had happened. He wanted out of this garage before he was seen! Then, without warning, the lights went off and the garage door abruptly came slamming down followed by the sound of the lock clicking.

Chapter 9

The most beautiful curve on a woman's body is a smile. Ally had a smile that drove Jace crazy! He loved her voice and the way she was always so upbeat and positive. Even when they were fighting, a simple smile on her face could melt him into a puddle and make him give into whatever she wanted. One of those rare women who had elegant beauty in all different kinds of ways.

"You are so gorgeous." Jace said releasing their lips from each other and resting his forehead on hers. Her eyes were a dark shade of brown and glistened in the moonlight.

"You're not too bad yourself." She responded with a wink and a longer kiss of approval for his previous compliment.

"Let's go inside." Ally said this catching her breath from the long exchange.

"Is anybody in your dorm right now?" Jace said this sounding cautious but really, more nervous than anything.

"No, my two roommates have class now, it will just be us." Once again, that smile she flashed him always seemed to work like a charm.

"Are you sure?" Jace asked again.

Grabbing his hand, she responded confidently. "Yes! Come on let's go quickly." Stumbling up the stairs and into her room, there were clothes which looked to be thrown everywhere.

"Sorry about the mess. I have to do laundry soon." Ally apologized even though Jace said nothing about it. She giggled and kicked what looked to be a small pair of shorts off the couch and sat down.

"Want to watch a movie?" Ally suggested. The thought of this eased his mind. Jace wasn't sure why he was so nervous. Even though the two of them had not had sex yet, he had been with others before. He liked her a lot and in the back of his mind couldn't really figure out why she liked him. Plopping down on the well broken in sofa, he kicked his shoes off. Ally was bent over in front of the TV trying to get the DVD player to work. Her shirt slid up as she bent down and the top of her pants opened ever so slightly. Jace badly wanted to get a better look but stayed put on the couch. He didn't want her to catch him and think he was some kind of pervert or something.

"There we go!" She said happily satisfied that she was able to get the movie playing.

"Want something to drink Jace?

"No, I'm fine. Thank you though." He was too anxious to think about food or drinks.

"I'll be right back, I am going to put on some comfier clothes." Disappearing into her bedroom, she was gone for what seemed to be an hour! In actuality, it was about three minutes. He quickly jumped down to the floor and banged out twenty pushups to 'prepare' himself for whatever might happen. Opening her bedroom door, Ally came out with light pink pajama-looking bottoms and a white t-shirt with her college's logo on it. Stepping up to where Jace was sitting, she put one leg on one side of him and swung the other around mounting him. She looked incredible and she smelled like a bed of roses. She clearly had freshened up when she changed her clothes. Her lips met his and he could feel his heart pumping harder. Her tongue brushed his lips gently looking for an opening to enter. Grabbing Jace's hand, she placed them on her breast as she continued to polish his tongue with hers. Her hair fell over his face and she flipped it back with one hand as she sat up. Pulling her back to him, he grabbed her ear with his teeth and gently caressed it with his lips. Her moaning assured him that she was enjoying what he was doing.

"Arms up." She whispered in his ear as she tug at his tight form-fitting shirt. Releasing both arms, she pulled the shirt up and it got caught over Jace's face. Jace's arms flopped to his side with his shirt still covering his face and Ally's laughter seem to make it worth it.

"Leave it on" She whispered between giggles. Kissing his chest, he ran his fingers through her soft hair. She could feel him, hard, and wanting her. Her hand rubbed him over his loose jeans. Her tongue met his nipple and made him jump.

"That tickles." He said covering his nipple with one hand.

"Oh yea?" Her smirk was followed by her grabbing the bottom of her shirt and in one motion, pulling her own shirt clean off. She was wearing a white bra with small bows on it. Lace lined the top of it where her cleavage would have shown. Reaching both hands behind her back, he saw her bra loosen at the straps. She proceeded to pull it off and spin it above her head in a lasso motion before she threw it across the room.

"Well I'm not ticklish at all." Looking at her bare breasts and devious smile, the invitation he was given was taken quickly. He wasn't sure how this was possible, but her nipple tasted good to him. He tried to calm down the thoughts running through his mind, but he couldn't seem to shut his brain off. She pushed on his shoulders and forced him to sit back. Pulling his shirt all the way off, she looked into his beady blue eyes.

"Are you ready for me?" The way she looked and moved was so sexy. Even her words were adding to his excitement. He wanted to come up with something clever but honestly, having a topless woman straddling him really made his wit go out the window.

"You should find out." He responded back trying to keep up with her sexiness. It sounded weird to him as soon as he said it. Sliding her legs back, she went to her knees on the floor. Pulling at his jeans button, it finally released and the zipper followed. Pulling his pants down, he was wearing black boxers and his excitement was definitely showing now! The throbbing he felt was made worse when she ran her lips over his boxers and pulled them down with her teeth. Surveying what she had to work with, she smiled up at him and licked her lips. Her tongue about to meet him and send him into ecstasy...

BANG, BANG, BANG!

"Ally! What was that?" She didn't move.

"Ally?"

BANG, BANG, BANG!

Rolling over, Jace felt himself still excited. Trying to force himself to go back to sleep, his dream was over. That always seemed to happen to him. When he was having a dream he liked or wanted to continue, he would wake up. This time though, he was awoken by loud noises. Opening his eyes, he could see nothing but darkness. Then he realized he was still in the garage. He had fallen asleep in the bed of his dad's truck. He had gotten locked in and couldn't get out...he had tried hard but was unsuccessful.

"Is someone in there?" His father's voice bellowed from outside the door. What choice did Jace have now but to answer him?

"Dad! I'm in here." He shouted.

"Well come on out then." His father said sarcastically as if he could just wander out of there any time he wanted to.

"I am locked in here. Someone closed me in and locked it from the outside."

"Well I just tried to get in there and it is padlocked from the inside or I could get in." His father's words were making sense but how could it have been locked from the inside too? Jumping out from the bed of the truck, he looked at the big door. The door had been slammed so hard that several of the wheels had fallen off the tracks and jammed the door stuck in place. Trying hard to get the wheels back into the track, they hardly budged at all.

"I can't get them back in." He sounded like a helpless puppy stuck in a crate.

"Try getting the side door lock unlocked. The key should be in the center console of my truck." Listening closely, he made his way to the driver's door of the truck and popped it open. The opening for him to enter the truck was very slim. He sucked his breath in and was able to pop his hips by the door and in. Looking where his dad told him to, he found a small silver key with nothing else attached to it. Adjusting himself, he found he was still showing signs of being in the mood. Grunting as he slid back out of the truck and over to the door, the lock clicked open and the padlock hasp was released. Being that the door opened inward, it too only opened a small amount. Climbing down out of the bed of the truck, he felt like a snake with his body being contorted in different directions to get out of this tight space. Finally breaking free and out the door, he stumbled and caught his balance before going down.

"What on earth were you doing in there? How did you get locked in?" His father went on the attack with his questions first.

"I was looking for you!" Frustration came out in his words. Breathing in the cold night's fresh air, Jace began to cough.

"Looking for me? I was in the fields working! You knew that." The 'matter of fact' attitude his father had made Jace feel angry. He knew what he had seen. He looked for his dad and found nothing. He felt like he was in an episode of the Twilight Zone. Everything was different and he was the odd one out. Before he could muster a response, his dad continued...

"I see you got your truck stuck out back. Why would you even try to drive back there? You know it has rained and it gets soft back there." Plus, I see you have buried the damn thing even further in the mud and tore up the path." Now Jace was being scolded when he felt it was his dad that should be on trial!

"I WAS LOOKING FOR YOU!" He shouted at his father. "What the hell is going on here? I looked everywhere for you last night and you were nowhere to be found. Then I see you have moved the Camaro into the garage to make room for your truck...which is all smashed up. What happened with that?" Jace was having word vomit but he couldn't stop himself. The old door in the back woods was still hanging in the back of his mind. Questions galore filled his head and the door suddenly reminded him of his biggest inquiry... his brother.

"And on top of it all, where is Dane? You guys don't even seem concerned about it!"

"Listen here boy, I don't need you to yell at me nor do I need to answer any of your questions." His stern voice was calm and forceful. Jace looked at the ground kicking a small stone from underneath his shoe. Seeing the concern in his son's actions, he wanted to ease his mind a little.

"I got into a little fender bender a few days ago and I didn't want anybody to know about it. You know your mother, she would just worry. I am planning on fixing it when I get the chance." A little fender bender? The whole damn fender has fallen off and the front end is crunched. Thinking this and wanting to say it, he kept it to himself. If he had gotten in this accident a few days ago, how was Elizabeth supposed to be borrowing the truck to move furniture? He again wanted to say this, but he remembered that he wasn't supposed to know about that. If he said anything, how would he explain how he knew. He couldn't tell his father he had been spying on him.

The sun was starting its usual ascent into the air

and the light it provided was starting to overtake the darkness of night.

"It is morning already?" Sounding shocked, his dad smiled.

"Yes, it is 5:30 in the morning. You must have been sleeping for a while."

"Yea, I don't know why they call the bed of a truck the 'bed,' it certainly is not as comfortable as an actual bed!

Snickering at this, Robert walked down towards the store as two cars pulled in. They parked next to the house on the grass. Three men stepped out and greeted his father with a handshake and a smile. They were all dressed in worn jeans and different colored shirts and hoodies. Walking with his dad up to the fields, his body language showed Jace that he was giving instructions and pointing things out. These must have been the extra help that he brings in come harvest time.

"Jace!" His father yelled for him and motioned to join them.

"This is my son Jace." If you need anything or have questions, find him if you can't find me." He introduced himself to the men and just like that, they were off to the barn to grab what they needed to begin work. Grabbing his shoulder and squeezing, Robert looked at his son.

"I see it didn't go too well yesterday huh?" He was being uncharacteristically calm about it.

"Yea, I disseminated all of the information about our winery, it just went south at the end..."

"You mean when Ally showed up?"

"Yes."

"Yea, your mother called me on my cell phone and told me

she was here and very upset. I was going to come down and help you, but you have to fly on your own sometimes. The problems we create for ourselves are ones that we have to deal with and live with if they become big enough problems."

"But I didn't even do..."

"Let me stop you right there boy." Abruptly interrupted before he could explain.

"Like I said, they are your problems, you have to deal with them. You can't just run away from everything in life."

"What about the important business people? You could have come to get them. They obviously meant something to you and the business." Jace was pleading with his father and he wasn't sure why. This had already happened and he couldn't go back in time.

"Their business was important to me. That is why I called them later in the day, apologized for anything that may have happened, and gave them a discounted price on a couple of cases. Business requires you to know how to work with people. In the end, they want good product and I want to sell the good product that I have. It is a match made in heaven. And yes, they could have gone elsewhere, but have you tasted some of our choices this year? I know I am partial to our wine because we make it, but it has a very solid taste. I don't know anyone who wouldn't take a deal that gives them some money off just for being hit in the head with a cork." Chuckling at this, Jace realized how wise his father was and his business savvy ways were really something to be admired. He always knew this about his dad, but every time he saw it, it made him appreciate it a little bit more.

"I won't let that happen again Dad. I am sorry they got hit, the cork was aimed for me. I ducked" Jace felt cowardly saying this out loud.

"Oh, the tangled webs we weave." His father said shaking his head.

"I am going to go help the guys in the field, I need you to run into town to get a few things. There is a list on my tool bench in the barn of what I need and where you can get it." Beginning to walk away, Jace stopped him.

"Hey wait! My truck is stuck in the field."

"Well the tractor is already hooked up to the trailer and I can't pull it out right now. Go and see if you can use your mother's car." Turning back around, he made his way towards the fields and Jace looked over at the house. There were no cars in the driveway. His mother must have gone out. What was he supposed to do? Walk? Not wanting to go disturb him again, Jace called his father's cell phone.

"Hello?" He could hear the background noise of the tractor was very close to him.

"Mom is gone. I have no way to get there." All he heard on the other end of the phone was a frustrated grunt and the phone was hung up. About ten minutes later he could see a figure walking up to the porch where he sat overlooking the water. The loud boots that slammed on the wooden floor of the porch startled him. His dad stood there with keys in his hand. Grabbing the back of Jace's neck, he looked into his eyes and pulled his son's neck and head closer to his. His body inadvertently followed.

"Listen here, I can't get away from the fields right now with the guys here, I need those things for later today." Letting go of his neck and grabbing his hand, he slammed the keys into his open palm.

"I need you to be as careful as you have ever been!" He was kind of scaring Jace for a minute. He wasn't sure about what his dad was telling him. Taking a step back, he opened his hand and saw two older looking keys with a small faded keychain that read *Camaro*.

What had just happened? Did he really just give him the keys to his prized car?

"If I didn't need those things so badly, I would just wait, trust me on that! I need you to be very careful with it. Drive slowly and watch for other drivers."

What seemed like many years ago, his father had once taught him how to drive. "You need to drive defensively! There are too many bad drivers out there and I want you to be a cautious but a good driver, and unfortunately, that means driving for others as well." This was the phrase that he could recite backwards and forwards because it is what his father had instilled in all his children.

"I will be very cautious Dad." His words were sincere. Almost in a state of shock, he couldn't believe that his dad was letting him take his car!

"Come right home after. DO NOT go anywhere else with it. Do you understand me Jace?"

"Yes sir, I do."

With that, his father was down the stairs and out of sight. He sat back down on the old swing and remained there for a few minutes. Swinging gently with the breeze, he couldn't help himself but to wonder why his dad gave him the keys. It may not seem like much in the grand scheme of things, but this was a huge gesture of trust by his father. That is what he couldn't figure out. After he just messed up the important meeting, got stuck in the garage and was able to manage to get his truck stuck in the back field, he did not look like the most responsible candidate to entrust with something this big. The only other reason Jace could think of was desperation. Robert had no other choice but to trust his son.

Collecting his thoughts, he walked down to the barn and the cherry red color stood out like a sore thumb. Opening the door slowly, he had hyped this up so much in his head he wasn't even sure if he remembered how to drive a stick shift. Inserting the key into the ignition, he felt as if he was opening a treasure chest that was all his. Turning the key, the car jerked violently as the ferocious engine turned over and caught. The tailpipes sang a beautiful tune that any true car person would enjoy. Releasing the clutch, the car began to roll. He had only gone up and down the driveway with this car once. It was on his birthday and his dad sat next to him watching his every move. The front of the car finally broke out of the barn and the sunlight danced off the shiny chrome. Jace was just about to hit the gas when he remembered he had forgotten something. The list! Pulling the parking brake up, he made sure it was set and jumped out of the car as it sat there idling. Grabbing the list, he got back into the rumbling car and eased his way down the driveway. Jace sat at the end of their driveway looking back and forth several times before he turned out. He made sure there were no cars coming either way and he punched the pedal. The rear wheels spun violently as rocks kicked up into the air.

"Oops." He said out loud hoping that his dad wasn't watching him. Flying down the road in a car this cherry, literally, was an amazing feeling. He had always loved this car since he was a boy and being in full control of it was better than he had imagined. You barely had to touch the gas pedal and the car responded quickly. Every time a car passed going in the opposite direction he let off the gas a little. He wasn't sure why he did this, but it made him feel a little safer. The air was crisp coming through the open window and it blew his hair in random bursts. For the first time he could truly see why his dad loved this car. It may have just been a bunch of metal to a lot of people, but to his father, and now to him, it was something special. The trees seemed to whip by and Jace looked down at his speedometer. He was going steady at forty-two miles per hour. The speed limit on this road which bordered the lake was forty-five in some spots and twenty-five when you would hit the densely populated areas and the schools. Looking back up from the gauges, a police car passed by going in the opposite direction. Police vehicles made him uncomfortable. Even though he had never been in trouble with the law, he did not like to be followed by one when he was driving. He would even go out of his way and turn down random streets to get away from a following police vehicle. He always figured that if they were behind him long enough, they could find something to stop him for or something that he may have done wrong.

Sure enough, he looked in his rearview mirror and saw the black and white police vehicle pull off to the side of the road and hang a big U-turn. Now he really let off the gas even though he was clearly not speeding. Continuing to make his way down the road, the police cruiser was now closing in on him. His vision kept alternating from the road to his rear-view mirror for several more minutes. He would have turned off, but you can't turn into the lake and there were no side roads readily available for him at this exact location. He held his breath as if that was going to prevent him from getting pulled over. Why was he even worrying about this? He had done nothing wrong and the police don't just pull over innocent people.
Wrong again.

Within seconds of having this calm thought, the cruiser's lights flashed on. Red and blue flashing bright lights in crazy directions. No siren though. Jace pulled the car to the side of the road and the feeling of tears felt like they were pushing on the back of his eyeballs. What else could go wrong? How could he have messed this up and how could he explain getting a ticket less than a mile from his house? Having no idea what was coming, he was shocked when he found out what it was.

Chapter 10

Life is unpredictable. Either things will happen that please you or disappoint you. If you are not prepared for the disappointment, the pain it will cause can be scarring. If it would provide you comfort, expect the worst and hope that you are wrong. That way, you are never disappointed.

As Jace sat in his father's car, he put his head down on the steering wheel, and for a brief moment, felt sorry for himself. The car continued to idle as the wind whipped into one side of the car and out the other.

"License and registration please." A deep voice came from behind his door. Jace did not look back as he handed the officer the requested documents.

"You were going kind of fast, weren't you?" This voice was strange. It sounded like either a female voice which had become deep from smoking or was an odd sounding male voice. The next thing Jace knew, his license was tossed back into the car and he got a soft smack on the side of his head.

"Hey!" He exclaimed whipping his head around.

"I got you!" Outside his window, McKenzie stood laughing at her words.

"What the hell?" The confusion he felt made his words sound angry.

"What are you doing driving this car?" Officer Harper

walked up behind McKenzie and looked down into his window.

"I have known your father for over twenty years and I have NEVER seen him let anybody else drive this car, not even your mother."

"My dad asked me to run to the store. We are harvesting now, and he needs these things urgently." Even though he was telling the complete truth, Jace wasn't sure why it came out sounding like a lie. Raising an eyebrow at him, he made a noise that told Jace he was thinking about what he said and didn't believe him.

"I swear! You can call him if you would like to."

"I already have. He didn't answer his cell." A car passed by making the officer grab his hat to prevent the wind from blowing it off.

"Something just doesn't seem right here. Can you understand my confusion Jace?"

"Oh Dad, I am sure he is just doing what he said. Look, this is the list." Snatching the paper out of Jace's hand, she put it up to her dad's face so he could see it. She must have been reading the list that was in his hand because he hadn't even shown it to them yet.

"What made you pull me over? Have I done something wrong sir?" Even though his question was directed at the officer, McKenzie was excited to answer instead.

"My dad was giving me a ride home and we saw this hot car and when we passed you, I told my dad I thought it was YOU driving!" Her voice was high with excitement.

"I asked my dad if we could pull you over as a joke but then he wanted to see if it was really you or your dad. Isn't that right Pop?"

Shaking his head, he gave a non-verbal response and looked back down at his phone.

"I am going to let you go Jace. I can't reach your father and I wouldn't be privy to this situation if I wasn't a close friend of his."

"Thank you, sir. I promise I am telling the truth. No disrespect to you at all, but if I wasn't, my father would do much worse to me than you are probably allowed to do." The humor in this statement seem to ease the officer's mind a bit.

"I am sure you are right about that." Agreeing with Jace, he clicked his cell phone back onto his belt holder at his waist.

"Wait, can I go for a ride with you Jace?"

"I don't think that is such a good idea." Her father stepped in before Jace could answer.

"It will be fine dad, he is a good driver, don't worry." She made this claim when she had only ridden with him once and really had no idea how he drove.

"Well, alright. I guess if she goes with you, that will alleviate my worry that you are taking the car and running away." The officer said this as he winked at Jace.

"Please be careful! I know how much power this car has. Don't do anything stupid...ESPECIALLY now that my daughter is with you." As he said these words to him, he couldn't figure out why everyone was speaking to him like a kid again. Being that he was in his mid-twenties, he felt he deserved to be looked at as an adult. Then again, he would always be his parent's child and the officer was only trying to protect him and his own daughter. Deciding not to respond wisely, he was respectful to the officer.

"I will sir."

With those words, the officer walked back to his car, turned off the lights and pulled away. Jace was relieved that the questioning was over. How would he have explained that his truck was stuck. Then why he couldn't have taken his father's truck? Or his mother's car? Or why couldn't he have waited until his truck was pulled out of the mud?

McKenzie ran around to the passenger's side of the car like an excited child runs down the stairs at Christmas. Reaching over, Jace pulled the lock button up and released the door to be opened.

"This is so nice! I love this car!" Her excited words were followed by her reaching her head over and kissing him on the cheek.

"What's the deal? You were supposed to call me, remember?" Releasing the clutch, the car pulled back out into the road and up to speed.

"It has only been a couple of days! I was planning on calling." He was unsure if this was true, but what could he say now that he was with her. He hadn't given it much thought, but he did see how her sister reacted to the idea.

"I even spoke to Ally about it." She said this as if it was a positive thing.

"Yea I know!" He said sarcastically.

"She came over to talk to me...well...I guess you could call it talking."

"I knew she would be fine with it." Adjusting herself into

the bucket seats, she pulled her seatbelt over her lap. Her shorts squeaked as they rubbed against the leather seats.

"Fine with what exactly?" Jace asked.

"And I am almost positive she is not *fine* with it." He said before she could answer.

"It is what it is." McKenzie said with a grin. Looking back at the road, Jace repeated what he had just heard.

"It is what it is huh?"

That was a lazy answer he thought to himself. The car rumbled onto main street. McKenzie waved frantically at the salon where she worked but she didn't think anybody saw her. The water was high and running fast underneath them as they passed over the one lane wood bridge. This made sense as it had been raining for several days before.

Stopping in the big Home Depot parking lot, he decided to park as far away from other cars as he could. McKenzie put her hands up to her face mimicking looking through binoculars.

"Hmm, Is there a store over there? I think I can see it. That tiny dot over there."

"Yea yea, I don't want to take any chances with the car. It is better to be safe than sorry. How is that for a saying?" He looked at her with a pleased grin.

"Geez, we are almost parked at the diner across the street." She pointer her finger at the old diner which actually was closer than the store was.

"Maybe if we go to the diner later, we could park at the store? What do you think?" Her sarcasm made him chuckle.

"Maybe. We will have to see. Come on, let's go." Locking

the door from the outside with a key, McKenzie looked at him like he had three heads.

"Just press the button. I don't know anybody that locks their car with the key anymore. Looking up at her in disbelief, he couldn't believe what she had just said. Wanting to give a snide answer, he didn't want to hurt her feelings.

"You do know that this car was made in 1969, right?" The look on his face must have been one of shock because she looked down as she answered.

"No, I had no idea. I just see a nice car, I don't know the details." Defending herself, she began to head towards the store. Jace felt guilty over making her feel stupid in any way and he was glad that he hadn't laid it on thicker. Walking at a pace that seemed to be a slow run, they made it inside and split up the list. Meeting back in the front of the big store, there was only one thing they couldn't find. Asking about it, there were none in stock and the closest other store that carried it was out too.

As they walked through the parking lot back to the car, McKenzie had something on her mind for quite some time and couldn't find the right time or the right words to say it.

"I like you Jace" She said these words very softly almost under her breath. After all her deliberation on how to tell him this, she could only come up with these four words? Jace stopped walking and looked over at her. She was still looking down.

"What did you say? I couldn't hear you."

Suddenly a burst of embarrassment came over her and she

could feel her cheeks getting rosy.

"It is nothing, never mind." Trying to back out wasn't helping her feeling of insecurity.

"No, tell me what you said." Jace was insistent as he thought he knew what she had said to him, but he wasn't positive.

"No, let's just go. I'm an idiot." She said forcing herself to chuckle over her statement. Not moving from his spot, Jace kept his eyes glued on her.

"McKenzie."

Looking up at him, she finally gave in.

"I like you okay!" She blurted out. Looking around to see if there was anybody else around, she realized as soon as she said it how loudly it came out.

"I guess you already could figure that out though, couldn't you?" She responded not giving him time to process what he had just heard.

"It's alright if you don't feel the same. I know you were with my sister and that could be weird for the two of you." She couldn't stop herself now.

"I just was so happy to see that you were back in town and I have always kind of had a crush on you. Now I am going out on a limb and feeling vulnerable." Jace looked at her and took a deep breath ready to respond.

"But like I said, if you don't feel the same way, I still want to be friends and hang out with you!" Exhaling, he could see he wasn't going to get to say much until she was done talking...which may have been never! She couldn't control it. She was suffering from word vomit caused by insecurity and embarrassment.

"I could tell by your face you don't feel the same. Right? Do you feel the same? Maybe we could talk about it and..."

"Okay stop!" He blurted out.

She had stopped walking before she got to the car door.

"Let's just get in the car and we can talk."

"Wait, I thought we were going to go to the diner?" Her voice perked up.

"When did we agree to do that?" Puzzled by this, he tried to remember if he had agreed to that. He was pretty sure that he hadn't.

"When we pulled up. Remember?" Her confidence in recollecting what had happened just a few minutes ago was undeniable.

"I have to get this stuff back home though. My dad needs it." Looking down again, he could tell she was feeling rejected and this was not at all what he had tried to do. Plus, in the back of his mind, he could hear his father telling him not to go anywhere but the store in his car. Then again, if they crossed the street on foot, he wouldn't have technically gone anywhere but the store with the actual car!

"Come on. Let's get some lunch." Tossing the items he had just purchased in the back seat, he closed the door and locked it once again. The old diner had been renovated recently but it still looked like they had stepped back into the 50's. Sitting down in a booth, they both ordered.

"I like you too." Jace broke the silence that was inevitable once the waitress had left with their orders. Excitement gleamed from McKenzie's face.

"I feel like we are back in High School again saying who

likes who." Jace said.

"So, I think you should take me on a date." McKenzie's confidence had come back.

"What would you call what we are doing here exactly?"

"This is just lunch. Let's go out. We can go to dinner and maybe some dancing? You know my dad's bar and grill has a live band this weekend. I think you should take me." Smiling, she took a sip from her iced tea the waitress just brought her.

"Okay, it is a date." Jace felt good about this even though he was trying to forget about Ally's objections to it. Suddenly, Ally's face flashed in his mind and he remembered the sex dream that he had just had about her the night before. Not having a great feeling in the pit of his stomach, he tried to repress his thoughts and focus on McKenzie.

Finishing their food and talking more about their potential date, they both made their way back to the car. McKenzie had a half of a cheeseburger and some fries in a leftover Styrofoam take home container. Sadly, Jace's first thought was that it was going to make the inside of the car smell like deep fried food. What could he do now though? Tell the girl who he just made a date with that she couldn't bring her food with her because his daddy might yell at him?

Not an option.

They made it to McKenzie's house very quickly. At least it seemed that way. *This girl has a lot to say.* Jace thought to himself. She had talked the whole way home, but he didn't mind. This was her normal vibrant personality.

"Thank you for letting me ride with you." Her smile was soft and sincere.

"I am glad you enjoyed the car." He responded.

"That's not all I enjoyed." Putting her hand on the center console and lifting herself out of her seat and over to him. Looking at his lips, she moved in slowly and met his lips with hers. Hers were soft and small. They fit with his well. She gave a little tug on his bottom lip and pulled back as she eased her way back down into her seat.

"Wow, that does not usually happen before the third date!" She sounded surprised at herself. For some reason, this made Jace feel special. He assumed that was the reason she said it.

"Call me or text me soon? This time, actually do it!" Nodding with obedience, she closed her door and bent down looking in to the passenger's side window.

"Give me your hand." She said reaching her own hand out to him. When he grabbed her hand, she squeezed it and pulled his watch that he was wearing off. Jace winced as the tug of metal grabbed the hair on his arms. It was a large silver watch that was clearly a knock-off.

"Hey! What do you think you are doing?" Jace said with a playful grin.

"This ensures me that you will call me." The cleverness of this move took Jace a moment to let it waft over him. With a quick wink, she was gone in her house like a flash.

The silence on the drive home was palpable. He wanted to turn the radio on but didn't want to mess with any extra buttons that he didn't have to. The sun was at its peak in the sky and provided mild warmth on a cool day. Jace tried his best to avoid any potholes he could and especially any puddles. He didn't want to bring the car back dirty. When he made it home, his mother's and Jen's cars were both parked next to the house. He kind of wanted his sister to see that he was driving their dad's car. The sibling rivalry that they had their whole lives, Jace usually would come out on the bottom. Now, he had been given the keys to his father's precious car. This would have been a great opportunity to show up his sister. He didn't see Jen or his mom at all though. Jace parked the car outside of the barn doors as he wasn't sure where his dad would want it. There were very few clouds in the sky today which probably meant no rain. There were several other cars in the store's parking lot and he assumed they were there for tastings. He felt he should go down and see if they needed some assistance, but mother nature was calling. Half jogging into the house, he was glad to see that the restroom on the main floor was vacant.

"Jace!" His father's voice rang through the house.

"Dad, I'm in the bathroom!" He shouted back.

"I will be right out!" He could hear his Dad's footsteps moving though the house getting closer to where he was. Washing his hand quickly, he jerked the door open and found his Father standing in the kitchen looking at him.

"Did everything go alright?"

Jace wondered if he was talking about the car or getting everything on his list.

"Of course, it went well Pop. I am very trustworthy." He patted his dad on the shoulder and smiled at him. He wanted his father to agree with this statement, but he was granted no such thing.

"Nothing happened with the car?" Why was his father pushing this issue with him? He obviously saw the car when he pulled in and now he had walked back up to the house to confront him. Going through the possible scenarios, he didn't want to tell his dad that he had gone to lunch or given McKenzie a ride, yet he also did not want to lie to him. His father was giving him a chance to lie, but how could he have known anything?

"Well..." He stopped his words before they came out.

"Well what?" His father's look Intensified. Jace was committed now.

Just tell him that you went to lunch quick and that was it. He thought to himself.

"I was hungry, so I grabbed a bite to eat after I picked up everything from the store." Looking at him like he should continue, his father didn't seem satisfied.

"That is all I promise." Jace assured his dad.

"Hmm." His Father grunted purposefully.

"No run ins with the law?"

Oh crap. Busted. Jace thought to himself. He had forgotten that he was pulled over and the officer had alerted him of it.

"Oh, well yea, but I know you already knew about that." Jace figured the best way to play it off was to make it seem like it was nothing and that he had already known that his father was called by the officer.

"Officer Harper pulled me over because I was driving your car. He told me he had called you to make sure it was alright that I was driving it." He felt like he was on strong ground now as this had actually happened.

"You took McKenzie with you? You think that was a smart idea?" This confirmed the officer and his dad had spoken.

"She asked to go for a ride and I didn't think it was a big deal. Don't worry, I was still very careful."

"You are creating a big mess boy. I hope you know that." His father always spoke with wisdom and even though he may not have always liked it, he was usually right. It was not like his dad to mettle in his kids personal lives, that was usually a job that his mother took on as she enjoyed it.

"I know Dad. I am being cautious. I was able to get everything on your list but one thing." Quickly trying to change the subject, he showed his dad the list with all but one of the items crossed off. Taking the paper from his hand, he reviewed what he had written down.

"I figured this might have been difficult to get." Jace was very happy with this response as the blame was not placed on him for not being able to find it.

"I am going to make a call and see what I can do. Thank you Jace." With that, his father was off and out the door.

Watching as his dad made his way back to the fields, Jace walked down to help in the store. He noticed that Dane's truck had been moved and was now sitting in the store's small parking lot. Curiosity still filled his mind. His nerves about this whole situation were getting the best of him. Trying his best not to be seen by anybody in the store, he walked around the back of the building where there were no windows to be seen from. The truck sat there innocently and tempted him to search some more. He had looked through it when he and McKenzie found it in the field, but he did not feel he had done a thorough enough job. Quietly, he pulled the handle of the passenger side door and much to his surprise, the door popped open. The old hinges let out a painful squeak which triggered him to look around to see if he had been spotted.

The coast was still clear.

He slowly looked from the center console, to the glove compartment and even underneath the seats. An old McDonalds french fry was pulled out from underneath the driver's seat. It was hard as a brick, yet still looked just like it would when you first buy it after it had been deep fried. This made Jace wonder what they put into these fries to preserve it like this. Who knows how long this had been under the seat. If it had been a regular potato it would have rotted and smelled awful! Once again, his random thoughts had distracted him from his original mission.

Not finding anything, he was about to give up when he saw a small lump in the driver side floormat. Reaching over, he pulled up the corner of the floormat which was loaded with dried mud and stones. As the mat was pulled back, it revealed a small black object. Grabbing it quickly like it was on fire, it was a cell phone...Dane's cell phone! It was a small flip phone which had a cracked screen. The phone looked like it had seen better days but there was a big sticker over the back with a construction company logo on it. Obviously, this must have been where Dane was working. Jace flipped it open and held the button to try to turn it on.

It was dead.

Slipping it into his pocket next to his own cell phone, he laid the floormat back down in the exact spot he had found it and rearranged the stones again so it looked like it had not been tampered with.

Jace was positive that his dad had probably gone through the truck at least a few times but he must have missed this. He wanted to run back into the house to put the phone on a charger, but he decided it would be better to be subtle and help in the store as if everything were normal. He would put the phone on the charger later at night when he could make sure he was the only one who saw it.

"Hey Jace! Come on over!" His mother was behind the counter and was very excited to see him.

"We are celebrating a birthday today with some wine and chocolate!" His mom was as excited as all the people at the counter. Looking at them, there was a young-looking lady who was wearing a party hat that had two big numbers on it. 21. The whole group seemed to be right on the border of carefree and tipsy. Everyone seemed to be having a good time. Greeted with a hug from the birthday girl, they all shouted with happiness. He did not recognize any of them and when you are from a small town, you generally have an idea of who everyone is. His mom continued to pour into each one of their stemless wine glasses.

"How much have they had?" Jace whispered in his mother's ear.

"They reserved this time and paid to sample a bunch of

our selections. If they like the taste, they are getting a full glass." His mother smiled in a unique way which told Jace that they were making out well with this group.

"What about when they leave? They can't drive." The worry in his voice was evident. Pointing to the lounge area of the store, there were three men sitting in the chairs watching the big screen tv that was projecting what looked to be a hockey game.

"I'm back!" Jen yelled walking in the front door with two bottles of wine in her hands. A loud cheer from the happy semi-intoxicated people filled the air.

"Hey Jace." Jen smiled at her brother. She slid passed him and set the bottles down on the countertop.

"Wait until you try these ones! They are my favorites and I can't get enough of them!" The excitement in her voice made all the women cheer again.

Thunderstruck from AC/DC began to play from Jace's pocket. The loud song made everyone stop to look at him as he pulled his cell phone out and answered it. Walking towards the front door to get away from the loud commotion, he heard a woman's voice on the line that he couldn't make out.

"Jace! Can you hear me? Jace?"

"Yes, I can hear you. Who is this?"

"It's Lizzie. How do you not know my voice?" She questioned her brother.

"I'm sorry! It's loud in here and you are not coming up on my caller ID."

"Yea It's because I am calling from my roommate's phone, I had a little accident with mine." She didn't want to tell him what had happened to it.

"Accident? Did you break it or something?" Jace was always a curious person and he was going to question her anyway.

"We will go with 'or something' alright?"

"Just tell me Liz." Now he wanted to know since she was clearly embarrassed about it.

"I dropped it in the toilet okay?" She said forcefully hoping that there were no more questions to follow.

"The toilet? How did you do that?" He wasn't going to let her off the hook.

"It just happened. Now can I tell you why I am calling you?" Hoping to pivot off this subject.

"Did it slide between your legs when you were wiping or something?" Jace burst out with laughter at the thought of this.

"Just shut up." She snarled at him.

"What can I do for you?" He asked her this as if she were a customer.

"Can we meet somewhere that is not at home? I want it to be just you and me." Jace's laughter had subsided and his tone turned more serious.

"Yes, of course we can. Is everything alright?"

"Everything is fine. Tomorrow night come pick me up around six o'clock and we can speak then."

"Sounds like a date." His jovial tune had returned.

"You're stupid. Don't be late. Goodbye Jace."

"Bye Liz." He put his phone back into his pocket and walked back into the store. Getting back behind the counter again, he began to wash some of the used wine glasses. Jen began to help him as they had started to pile up. Not even a minute later his phone rang again with the same obnoxiously loud ringtone.

"Why don't you just shut that off for a few minutes." His sister sounded frustrated with him receiving phone calls, but he wasn't sure why. He was going to help with whatever needed to be done before the end of the day anyway. Wiping his hands dry, the phone from in his pocket kept screaming for his attention.

"Let me just take this, I will be very quick." He pulled the phone out of his pocket and flipped it open.

"Hello? Is anyone there?" A long pause of silence before Jace heard it. The ringtone continued from his pocket after he had answered it.

"Oh my god!" It was not of a voice on the phone, it was Jen.

"That is Dane's Phone!" She was pointing to the phone at his ear in what looked to be shock. Looking down at the small black phone with the construction sticker on it, he realized he had pulled the wrong phone from his pocket. The next thing Jace knew, his mother had ripped it away from him glaring at him.

"Where did you get this?"

Chapter 11

Keeping something a secret can sometimes turn into more work and headaches than the secret may actually be worth. I have found that some of the happiest people in the world are the ones who don't carry the burden of secrets and do not have any for anybody else to know. As Benjamin Franklin once said...Three people may keep a secret, but only if two of them are dead.

As Jace stood there looking at his empty and sweaty palm, he was in disbelief that he had made such a stupid mistake. It felt like time was standing still. As his mother stood there firing off angry questions, he went deaf. He could see her lips moving and the anger in her face that he had been keeping this from her. Jen had gone back to rinsing the last few wine glasses at the sink. She was clearly trying to remain calm to not alarm the women who were still having a good time on the other side of the counter. His mother grabbed his shoulder and was shaking him like an apple tree hoping apples would fall off him.

Finally, as if he actually were asleep standing up, he popped back awake.

"Just wait a minute. Let me explain." By this time, the whole group of ladies was silent and looking at him. The raised voices of both his mother and sister had alerted them that something was awry.

"Let's hear it then." Jace was getting a little tired of Jen's snarky remarks to him. His mind was once again racing. He wanted to get out of this situation, but, how could he? Deciding not to think any longer, in one fell swoop, he lunged at his mother's hand snatching the phone from it like an eagle snaps up its prey. He did a spin move right out of a pro football game and was out from behind the counter. Darting in and out of the ladies who stood nearby, he made it to the front door and out. Panicking, he ran towards the house with the plan of jumping in his truck and taking off. Looking around frantically, he remembered his truck was stuck. Was this phone really worth it? Could there be some clue on there where his brother had gone or possibly what may have happened to him? He desperately wanted to find out!

Looking over his shoulder, he could see his mother calmly making her way to the door. He needed to get away and find out what was going on. At this point, he wasn't sure who was in on what and what secrets that the family may be keeping from him. He reached into his other pockets and pulled out his father's car keys to the Camaro which he was still in possession of. Making a quick decision, Jace made a beeline towards the car that was still sitting where he had left it. He could hear his mother in the background yelling for him, but he pretended like he didn't hear her. The car roared to a start and he fishtailed the rear end around so he was facing the road at the end of their driveway. He stomped on the gas pedal and the stones flew from underneath the spinning tires. Flying by his Mother who had now been joined by his sister, he heard her voice one last time as he whipped by them.

Once on the road, he was in shock at what he had just done. Would they consider this stealing a car even though it was his dad's car and he had given permission earlier? He didn't have time to think of all the possible ramifications. He needed help but at this point, who could he trust. The one thing he decided he needed the most was to find a place to charge his brother's phone. His phone began to ring again and he struggled to pull it out of his pocket which was squeezed tightly in the seat. Finally getting it to release, it flew from his hand and onto the passenger's side floormat. Looking up ahead at the road in front of him, there was nobody coming in the opposite direction or no one in front of him. Quickly, he unbuckled his seatbelt and reached over the center console. His outstretched hand almost had it when the car began to rumble violently. He had begun to drift and was now hitting the rumble strips. Jerking his head up he realized he was only feet away from the guard rail now. Correcting the steering wheel in a smooth motion, Jace took a deep breath and realized how close he just came to the end of his life. Not because he would have gotten into an accident, because his father would have killed him due to the accident! The phone's vibrating came to a halt. A small ding alerting him that whoever had just called left him a voicemail.

The car came to a stop at a three-way intersection that had flashing red lights for all directions. Not taking any chances, this time he put the car in park and was able to retrieve his phone. Sitting back down in his seat, he fastened his seatbelt and scrolled though his phone. His mother had called him and he suddenly felt a burst of panic run through his veins. He could feel the little hairs on his neck were standing straight up. Not wanting to listen to her message, he was afraid of what she had said to him. He was just now realizing the magnitude of the situation that he had created.

"Just go back and everything will be fine." This is what Jace kept repeating to himself. He wasn't even sure of where he was driving himself to. He was going ten miles per hour below the speed limit because his mind was in a fog of potential outcomes for what he was doing. Making it to main street, the cell phone began to ring again! This time Jace answered it.

"Liz! Oh, thank God it's you! I need your help!" Pleading with his sister, her response was not what he had expected.

"Jace, you need to turn around right now and go back home. This is very serious!" Her voice was stern and almost angry with him.

"How did you find out what's going on?" He assumed that his parents reached out to her and told her to make this call, but he wanted confirmation of this.

"That doesn't matter Jace. You need to go back home. We need that cell phone."

A long silent pause between them as Jace tried to process what he had just heard.

"WE need that cell phone? Why did you say 'WE?' What is going on here!?"

Pulling the car to the side of the road, he wanted to scream into the phone with frustration.

"WE have to find him! Don't you agree? That phone could help us do that!" Trying to make Jace sound like he was part of the team, he did not feel that way. He felt that his family was a team and he was an outsider that was causing turmoil.

"What's going on Liz? I have so many questions and never get any answers! I am going to charge this phone and see if there are any clues in there before I go back home!"

"NO!" She yelled into her end of the phone.

"Bring it home now so we can look at it together!"

"Calm down! What is the difference Liz? I'm going to get some answers myself so I can be in on whatever the hell is happening with this family!" Jace found himself yelling into the phone now too. This was very strange for Liz and for Jace as he rarely raised his voice to anybody...let alone the sister he was closest to.

"Please Jace, Dad told me you took his car and they are going to call the police if you don't bring it home NOW."

"Listen Liz, I appreciate you calling I really do, but I think you are more worried about me finding out what is going on than you actually are of protecting me!" Just as he finished his sentence, church bells began to ring in the background. Willowcreek had a grand church that was built in the 1920's. The bells could be heard from all around town as they rang proudly.

"He's in town." Liz whispered putting her hand over the transmitter to not alert Jace of what she had said.

"I heard that!" He screamed back into the phone. He pulled it away from his ear and looked at it. Before he hung it up, the last words he heard were that of Liz warning him that the police in fact were coming to get him!

What was his next move? Who could Jace call now to help him? Now that the police were going to be after him, he had nobody to rely on. His father always told him growing up that the problem with living outside the law and being a rule breaker is that when the time comes and you need it, you lose the protection of the law as well. He had never been in trouble before. He was not a law breaker and had never had any run-ins with the law in his life! He suddenly had flashes of Frank and Jesse James being chased by lawmen and them robbing trains and laughing about it. Maybe he was the modern-day Frank and Jesse James now! Ah, who was he kidding? He had taken his father's car for a ride and that was it. It's not exactly like he is dangling off the side of an old steam engine train that is going sixty miles per hour trying to rob it. He did have a distinct disadvantage though. Back in the day, robbers could get away on a horse very quietly. He was in one of the best and brightest cherry red cars he had ever seen! Not to mention every time he touched the gas pedal it would roar louder than a male lion who was pissed off!

Trying to be as gentle as possible, Jace eased the car through town barely hitting the accelerator. He purposely slid down in his seat so he could just barely see out the front windshield. Once he had made it past the main part of town and over the bridge, Jace sat back up in his seat and took off. The thought of going to Ally and McKenzie's house crossed his mind but being that their father was an officer, he thought better of it. It is kind of funny because if he was ever in trouble in his life, he could always count on his brother to get him out of it or even sometimes would take the fall for him.

There was another town about fifteen miles over from his and he thought maybe he could hook up the phone at a store there. It was the best idea that he could come up with at the moment. As the old car carried him towards the neighboring town, his phone began to ring once more. The thought crossed his mind to open the window and just whip it out like you would see in the movies. The part you don't see in the movies is when the characters must go back to the phone store and pay big bucks to get a replacement phone. Looking down at the flashing screen, it was his father this time calling from his cell phone. He couldn't keep this up not talking to them and he was going to do things his way before his parents or sisters could interfere again, so there was no reason not to answer. Pulling the flip phone open with his teeth, He put it on speaker as he wanted to tell his dad not to worry and he had both of his hands on the steering wheel. Jace went to set the phone down in the cupholder next to him which caused his hand to hit the knob on the shifter accidentally. The car made a sudden revving sound and was jerking insanely back and forth. Trying to put the strong car back into gear, he had inadvertently drifted into the oncoming lane. As luck would have it, he was not so lucky this time as what appeared to be the front end of an eighteen-wheeler was coming right for him with their lights flashing and horn blowing. Pulling the wheel as hard

~ 145 ~

as he could back towards his original lane, he missed the brake pedal and hit the clutch instead. The last thing Jace saw was the car heading right for the guardrail.

The impact was fierce! The sudden turn of the steering wheel projected the car off its wheels and into the air. Flying over and over the car continued to flip until it came to a rest on its roof. The spinning thrusted pieces of the car all over the road. Shattered glass covered the interior. The front wheels of the car kept spinning as it lay lifeless upside down. Jace was being held into his seat by his unforgiving seatbelt. It had cut through his shoulder and he touched his head softly which was bleeding profusely. His vision was blurred and the last thing he remembered seeing was a puddle of fluid collecting next to the car. It was growing bigger and bigger as the smell of gasoline fumes and exhaust filled the air. His eyes flickered and closed slowly as blood tickled down his cheek.

Chapter 12

It is said that there is no such thing as an accident. Just carelessness or the failure to plan ahead. Accidents are similar to success in that way. Success doesn't generally just fall into your lap. You must work hard, do the right things and success will inevitably follow. Many people complain about success or their lack thereof. That generally means they are not doing something correctly or perhaps, their definition of personal success needs to be altered. Just the same as anyone who is involved in five car accidents in a year. They may believe that they are a great driver, but their defensive driver skills may need to be improved on.

Ally stood there in disbelief at what she was hearing. She had yet to have her heart broken in her short life. I guess you could say she was lucky in that sense. Jace had tried to plan out what he wanted to say for several weeks and now that the time came, he couldn't seem to get any of his words right.

"Why on earth would you leave now? We have so much ahead of us!" Ally was fighting back tears as hard as she could, but the shakiness of her voice was not helping.

"This is an incredible opportunity for me. Jobs of this nature don't come along very often!" He had been contemplating whether or not to take the job every minute of every day since it was offered to him. Jace's whole life, people had asked him what does he want to be when he grows up. Even when he was in high school, everyone, including his parents, wanted to know which direction he wanted his life to go. Jace never had an answer for this question. He always thought in the back of his mind that there would be more time. I guess you always feel that there is more time. The problem is, you inevitably run out of time and then comes the wondering to yourself where the time has gone? His father naturally wanted him to stay home and work with him and the Vineyard. Lord knows there was plenty of work to be done there. His father had hoped that one of his children would be interested in taking over when the day comes for him to move on, but as luck would have it, none of his four children displayed the slightest interest in it.

Jace had gotten in touch with a talent agency who offered him several roles to be an extra in a couple of movies with the possibility of some stage acting. He had no experience except for a few plays and the drama class that he had taken in high school. Jace was always nervous on stage but once he got going, he loved it. Having sent several emails to different companies who said they were looking, one had responded back. They asked him to send a couple of photos of himself to see if he had the desired look they were searching for. The talent company responded back in a little less than a week and offered him a small part in a movie that was being made. Plus, they explained to him several other opportunities he would have to audition for. The dream of being a star and being famous always lingered in the back of his mind. He knew it was crazy, but he felt he would regret it if he didn't at least try.

Having to explain this decision to everyone in his life was not going to be easy and he had braced himself for the ridicule he was going to receive.

"New York City? You are going to pack up and move to New York City?" Ally was going to be the hardest one to explain this to. He felt he had two options, break it off with her now and have it be quick like ripping off a band-aid. Or, stay together and have a long-distance relationship that would probably cause many fights and be dragged out until they couldn't stand each other anymore.

He made the decision that he knew would crush her but in the long run, he hoped she would be better off.

"Yes, New York City. Please try to understand. I know we have been dating for a while, but I have to do this." Ally's tears had begun to run down her cheeks. Pulling up the corner of her sleeve with her hand, she wiped the corner of the eye producing the most tears.

"I just can't believe you!" She screamed. The look in his face was one of hurt as well. He knew he was being selfish and that he was about to hurt every single person who he was close to. He thought he was still young and wanted to make his own choices and learn from his own mistakes. Jace felt the whole world was in front of him and he intended on taking full advantage of that.

"Have a nice life Jace." Opening the door to his old beat up clunker that he drove back and forth to school, she slammed the door so hard the window slid back down and got stuck.

"Wait! You can't get out here, where are you going to go?" They had been sitting at the public dock on Finn lake where they used to come to fish or feed the ducks. Sometimes, they went there just to have some private time together.

"I'll walk home before I go anywhere with you!" Her tears were now flowing and she was speed walking towards the road. Not knowing what to do, Jace sat there for a minute until she was out of sight. He slowly pulled up to the road to try and see if she was really walking home but she was nowhere to be found. Pulling out in the direction of her house, he drove further than she could have walked in that short amount of time and she was nowhere to be seen. His guilt was getting the best of him and he contemplated if he had done the right thing or not. Someone who was that passionate about you might not have been the best person to break up with. He had several women who he had dated in High School that had broken up with him or they just stopped going together. Of all of those instances, no woman that he had ever dated responded this passionately.

Later that day, the dinner table was full of freshly prepared food. Even though his family was big with three siblings and two parents, they always made time to sit down and eat dinner together. As the years went on, they all had extracurricular activities and sporting events to go to which made dinner a little more complicated. Sometimes, it would be a half dozen burgers from McDonalds at nine o'clock at night, but they were still together. Nervously mixing small peas into his mashed potatoes, Jace tried not to make direct eye contact with anyone at the table. His mom would ask everyone how their days went and his sisters monopolized the conversations with problems they had or people they didn't care for. Dane and his father would sometimes talk about sports or work or what was going on with the vineyard. Waiting for the right moment to jump in between conversations proved to be exceedingly difficult.

Finally, he dropped his fork on his porcelain plate which made a loud clang.

"Whoops." He said as if it were an accident.

"Easy there boy. These are your mother's finest dinnerware." His dad always protected his mother and her feelings, even over plates!

"I'm sorry. Fork got away from me." He didn't want to lose this pause that he had just made in the conversations now that everyone was paying attention to him.

"I have to tell everybody something." He picked his fork back up and began to play with his food again.

"What is it Jace?" His mom's soft and happy tone was not helping him with the bombshell he was about to drop.

"I have accepted a job opportunity and I am very excited about it!" He figured he would start off this way to see how happy everyone would be for him. His dad was pushing him to get a job now that he was out of High School...especially since he really didn't want to work at the vineyard.

"That is terrific news son! I am happy for you. Where will you be working?" His father smacked him on the shoulder with jubilation as he said this.

"Well…" He wanted this good feeling to last as long as possible.

"It is a good job. Something I have been wanting to try for some time now." A smile came to his face to display the happiness he had just told them about.

"Well, what is it Jace?" His mother asked impatiently.

"You are going into the adult industry, aren't you? You are going to make some porno, right?"

"Jennifer Grazer! We don't speak like that at the dinner table!" Their mother scolded her before Jace had a chance to say a wise remark back.

"Jeez, I was just making a joke." Jen said irritated that she had been yelled at.

"Even though that's about all he is qualified to do." Saying this under her breath, she made a point to say it loud enough so that it could be heard by all.

"That is it! Leave the table right now young lady!" Their father stood up in his chair and pointed towards the stairs leading to her bedroom. His voice was loud and booming even though he wasn't actually yelling. Standing up fast, she pushed her chair out with the back of her knees. The extra force she used to make the point she was angry caused the chair to fall over. Storming up the stairs, she stomped on each wooden step making her father grimace each time. He moved his chair back and began to move angrily towards his insubordinate daughter who was almost at the top of the stairs. Grabbing his arm, their mother stopped him from pursuing this any further.

"Just let her go to her room Robert. It is not worth the argument. Besides, this is about Jace and his good news!"

Being level headed was one of their mom's best attributes. A final slam of her bedroom door put the cherry on top of her outburst.

"She is almost fifteen years old. She is too damn old to be throwing these tantrums. And that mouth of hers is going to get her in serious trouble if she doesn't start watching what she says!" Clearly upset, Marie stood up and patted her husband on the shoulder.

"Just relax darlin. I will speak with her later. Would you like some more milk?" Grabbing his almost empty glass, she answered her own question as she took her glass and his in the kitchen to refill them. Sitting back down in his chair, Robert took a deep breath and looked at his three other children sitting quietly at the table.

"So, spill the beans Jace. What will you be doing?" Lizzie broke the uneasy feeling that they all were inevitably feeling.

"Guess what I made?" Their mother spun into the room singing these words in a high pitch tone. She set Robert's milk glass down on the table and gently placed a freshly made pie down in the center of the table.

"I made a concord grape pie with grapes that we have just picked!" Marie loved to bake, and she incorporated grapes into as many recipes as she could. Even though not all of them came out as hits with her family.

"Don't pick off the crust!" Their mother said quickly swatting Dane's hand away as he grabbed some of the outer rim of the pie that was about to fall onto the table. Popping it in his mouth, he smiled and winked at Jace.

"As I was saying, this is a great opportunity for me to

spread my wings and try something new." Jace tried to get back on track before he lost his nerve. Cutting a piece of pie and scooping it onto Jace's plate, a drop fell onto the table from the stainless-steel pie serving utensil that his mother held. She quickly wiped it up as if it were going to cause a stain on her wooden table.

"I don't want you guys to get mad at me when I tell you. Can we agree on that?" Everyone at the table looked up at him like they had all just heard a loud noise at the same time.

"Why would we be mad at you for getting a job?" His mom looked at him like he had three heads.

"It's in New York City."

Silence filled the room.

Nobody moved. They all seem to be struggling to process what they had just heard. It was almost as he had said something in a different language.

"What did you say?" Dane had heard him the first time, but he wanted him to repeat it due to his disbelief at what he had just been told.

"I am taking a job in New York City."

"Doing what?" His father snapped this question at him. Jace could see that he was already upset with Jen and this certainly wasn't the mood he wanted him to be in when he told him.

"I have been in contact with an agency and I am going to try some acting." Looking down very fast, he felt his face go numb.

"Acting? Are you kidding me with this?" Robert slammed his hand on the table making the glass dinnerware clang together. He apparently didn't care about his wife's dinnerware now that he's upset. Jace wanted to say this but instantly thought better of it.

"No, I am not kidding. I want to try this and they already have a gig lined up for me to start with." Trying to be strong proved difficult for Jace as he knew nobody would be on his side about this.

"A gig? Are you planning to be in some kind of rock band?" Dane's sarcasm was easier to handle than his father's clear anger.

"Yes. That is what they are called. Gigs. The pay isn't half bad and I have already found a very small apartment in New Jersey where I am going to stay. I am sure you all probably know how expensive it is to live in New York City, so I'm just going to commute." His confidence was building as he showed them that he had done his research and had a plan.

"Get out of here! You are not going anywhere. You're just messing with us, right?" The fear Dane felt was clear and he tried to conceal it with jokes.

"I am one hundred percent serious Dane." His brother's face turned pale white. The joking mood he was putting forth subsided. Standing up in his chair, he walked into the other room the whole time keeping his eyes set on Jace. His mother had not said a word yet and sat there calmly eating small pieces of pie at a time.

"Maybe this will be a great opportunity for you Jace!" Lizzie chimed in trying to recover any optimism that was left for Jace.

"Don't be a damn fool! You are going to move away from

everything you have here to go to try something that is more likely than not going to fall through?"

"What do I have here? Please tell me what is stopping me from pursuing my goals!" Jace raised his voice and found himself yelling at his father.

Standing up from his chair slowly, he looked down at his son who had never felt so small as he did in this very moment. He could not make eye contact with his dad. He shot a glance over at Lizzie whose mouth was inadvertently open from shock.

"What do you have here?!" His father began to shout.

"Robert! Calm down." Now his mother's tone began to get louder with concern. Jace wanted to get out of there but couldn't muster the energy to move his legs. The old grandfather clock that resided between the dining and living room began to ring. The old chimes had a deep sound that sounded like church bells.

"You are not going to New York City or anywhere so you can screw up your life! And that is final!" Slamming his chair against the table, Robert stormed passed his wife and made his way down to the basement.

Sitting at the table, the feeling of hopelessness came over him and he had an urge to just give up. How could doing something you wanted to do upset so many people? He was always told to live his life and make his own choices. Now that it was time to, he apparently wasn't allowed to make the choices he wanted. Only the choices that others around him wanted were acceptable for him to make. Lizzie remained at the table. Their mother began to clear the plates.

"When do you plan on going?" Lizzie asked.

"Who knows now? Maybe I will just sneak away." He made a quick grunt to assure his sister that he was kidding. Standing up from the table, he went into the kitchen where his mother stood. The water was running into the sink but her hands weren't moving. She stood staring out the back window over the sprawling vineyard. The moonlight was bright and provided enough light to see the vast trees they had on their land. Walking up to his mom, she did not turn around. He touched her shoulder and rested his hand there. She softly touched his hand with hers.

"I'm sorry Mom. I'm sorry I have upset everyone." Removing her hand from his, she continued to look out the window.

"I love you Jace. More than you will probably ever know. I want the best for all my children. More importantly than that, I want them to be happy. If you believe this will make you happy, I will not stand in your way." A short gasp of air told Jace she was right on the brink of tears. He always knew the hardest person to tell bad news was his mother. He would have done anything to prevent his mom from feeling pain. Now ironically, he was causing her a massive amount of it.

"I love you too Mom. I love everyone here and that will never change!" A small tear formed in the corner of his eye. Closing his eyelids, the tear ran down his face and onto his shirt. Sniffling, his mother turned around and hugged him tightly.

"Fly Jace. Fly as high as you can." Releasing him from the

hug, she smiled and wiped the wet spot on Jace's face. "You should go on up to bed. Maybe we can talk to your dad another time when he has calmed down. He loves you Jace. His kids are his whole world. Sometimes, he just has a hard time showing it.

"I know Mom." Walking out of the kitchen, Jace waved to Lizzie who was helping clean the table now as well.

Later that night, he could hear voices coming through the floor. It was hard to make out what was being said, but he could tell from the tone that his parents were arguing about something. Jace pressed his ear against the wooden floor boards to try and make out the words being said. It was extremely rare that his parents would fight and if they did, it was usually never in front of the kids. Even now that they were all older, they still worked out their issues in private. None of the four kids knew where they would fight but it was obvious that they hadn't been married all these years and never had some sort of disagreement with each other.

His mother's words were muffled and drowned out by his dad. He was clearly the louder of the two of them. He heard a curse word fly through the air which was also an abnormality. Next, he heard his father screaming about something and then his name came out loudly from his dad's mouth.

They were fighting about him!

He should have known this. Sitting there listening to his parents argue over him was a horrible feeling. Was him deciding to move away truly causing this much turmoil in the family? Just as he thought the fight was dying down, his bedroom door burst open and startled him. Jace jumped up from the floor as his heart was pumping fast from the fear that he had been caught.

"Oh, I see your eaves dropping on Mom and Dad's fight huh?" Dane's shadow blocked the bright lights coming from the hallway.

"They are fighting because of you. You do understand that right?" Jace was taking quick breaths trying to calm his nerves down.

"Obviously I do. Did you come in here to lecture me too? I've had just about enough of everyone telling me how stupid I am and that I am making a horrible decision!" Jace threw the magazine he had been reading at his headboard.

"Maybe because the decision you are making is affecting others too. You are getting all mad because you have people who care about you? You know how stupid THAT sounds?"

"Just stop. I don't want to hear this anymore."

"Fine. Be a blockhead. I always thought that we have been more than brothers. I thought we were best friends too. But what kind of friend makes this decision and doesn't even let him in on it. Thanks for letting me know where I stand." Dane turned around and headed for the open door.

"Go ahead and be dramatic then!" Jace yelled as Dane closed the door.

Lying in bed that night, Jace could not even think about sleeping. A stress ball that was bright yellow and had a smiley face on it was the object he was trying to take his aggression out on. Squeeze after squeeze. It did not seem to be helping. Sweat gathered on his lower back as the temperature in the house was stifling. The house had settled down. The commotion and turmoil had subsided...at least for the night. Jace wondered if his mother was asleep yet or if she was lying in her bed awake like he was. He did not want to hurt his family with his decision any more than he already had. Thinking this to himself, he sat up in bed and tossed the stress ball onto the nightstand next to him. The ball proceeded to bounce to the ground and roll underneath his bed. Clicking the table lamp on next to him, he made a swift decision. He was going to leave tonight while everybody was asleep. His room was full of his things that he knew he would not be able to take with him if he was to leave tonight. He only had one small suitcase and a duffle bag which was not going to carry much. Packing as many clothes as he could, he filled the suitcase until it was difficult to get it zippered. Pressing down as hard as he could, the zipper finally popped free and closed his suitcase. Grabbing a few pictures off his nightstand, he loaded a few more things and was ready to go. Getting out of the house while five other people slept was going to be the hard part. Looking out his window, he contemplated if he would be able to jump or if he would hurt himself. Deciding against jumping from the second floor, he had to go slowly down the stairs and out the front door. Being that each step squeaked, and he was carrying a big load that would make it hard for him to be limber, this was going to prove to be an even more difficult task. Each step he took, he counted under his breath.

"One, two, three…"

He made it all the way until nine when the old house decided to stop cooperating with him. The floorboards under his feet let out a loud moan and Jace froze in place hoping he had not woken anyone up. He could hear his father snoring from their bedroom. He was a notoriously loud snorer and when he would fall asleep by the television, you were screwed if you wanted to hear the show you had been watching anymore.

Slowly, he continued down until he made it to the bottom step. His keys were in his hand ready for a quick getaway. Closing the front door behind him, he clicked the lock ever so carefully and was down the steps to freedom. Tossing his bags into his rust bucket of a car, he sat in the driver's seat looking back at the house which he had spent his whole life in. A rush of sadness came over him and he almost decided to go back inside. He couldn't. If he truly wanted to do this, he needed to fight through his emotions. Turning the key, the engine fired up and he glanced at his gauges. His fuel level had less than a quarter of a tank left. Pulling out his wallet, there were only twenty-seven dollars starring back at him. This was not nearly enough to get him to where he needed to go. He had planned to ask his parents to loan him some money that he would promise to pay back. That idea went out the window when he decided to sneak out in the middle of the night.

Just about to put the car in gear, an idea entered his mind. Jace pulled the keys out of the ignition and ran up the front steps two at a time. He was pleased to find that everyone in the house was still asleep and had not been alerted to him leaving. Their house was old and had a basement that showed the age of the house. Part of the floor was cement with settlement cracks all over it. The other part was dirt and the ceiling was just low enough that you had to duck when you went down. Jace grabbed a pen and a small piece of paper from the junk drawer in the kitchen and made his way down to the dingy basement. There were two free standing freezers in the basement that his mother always filled when she went grocery shopping. She was a deal hunter and having to feed six people each day was not a cheap thing to do. In the back of the fridge was an old Chock Full o' Nuts coffee can with a yellow top that sealed it shut. His parents always had a unique way of hiding money throughout the house in case there was ever a "rainy day." He had found this can a while back and never told anybody that he had. Reaching to the back of the ice-cold freezer, a bag of Oreida French fries slid out and smacked onto the floor. Jace pulled the can out carefully and he hoped that there was still money left in it.

There was.

He stood there pulling out the big wad of bills and he closed the freezer door for a minute. Dropping to his knee, he propped the piece of paper up against the door of the fridge and began to write.

> *I, Jace Grazer, promise to reimburse you every penny of this money that I am borrowing. I truly*

hope you understand why I am taking this without
your permission. I Love you all very much!
Love, Jace.

Folding this short note carefully, he placed it inside the can and clicked the top back on. Grabbing the bag of fries from the floor, he carefully opened the door, put the can back where he found it, and stuffed the fries in. They began to slide back down again so he quickly slammed the door shut to keep them in. They were the next person's problem now.

About to climb the basement stairs, he heard the refrigerator door open in the kitchen. Freezing with panic, he covered his mouth to muffle the sound of his breathing. A loud cough alerted him that is was his brother. He must have been getting a drink or something from the fridge. Jace prayed in his head hoping that he would just make his way back up to his room and not linger around the kitchen. God must have been listening to him that day as he heard the creak of footsteps going up the second-floor stairs. Moving as fast as he could while still being silent, he made it out of the house again with no trouble as far as he knew. Maybe this was a sign that he was destined to leave. Jace wanted to count and see how much money was in his pocket now but he thought that it would be better if he did that when he wasn't sitting in his driveway in plain sight asking to get caught. Taking one last look at the house, he shifted the car into reverse and began backing up. At the last second, something caught his eye. The light in his bedroom was on! He must have woken somebody up or someone must have wanted to talk with him. Fear shot through his veins. Fearing that someone was about to catch him, he raced to shift into the right gear. Getting to the end of the driveway, he stopped to look both ways before entering the road. One more glance in his rearview mirror and it revealed a sight that he will never forget. A figure stood in the middle of the driveway standing still looking at his truck. The moon's light created an eerie feeling as the figure didn't move, it just stood still in the spot his truck was just parked. Putting the truck in park, he stepped out and looked back.

It was Dane.

The two boys looked at each other for over a minute. They stood too far away to communicate. Jace raised his arm to wave at his brother who looked more distraught than he had ever seen him. Without acknowledging Jace's gesture, Dane turned back towards the house and slowly walked inside. Jace got back into his car, shut the engine off and cried. He kept telling himself that this was a selfish move and that it was his choice to leave this way, but that didn't provide him any comfort. Ten minutes later, he wiped his blurry eyes, and pulled away from the only life he had ever known.

Chapter 13

The phrase "you don't know what you don't know" has always baffled me. Obviously if you don't know something then you don't know that you don't know it! Similar to when you lose something and someone will tell you that it will be in the last place you look. Everything lost is always in the last place you look because once you find it, you stop looking! In any case, if you have lost something and you don't know you have lost it, I guess you are really "up a creek without a paddle" as they say.

Loud voices filled the small room with background noise. Jace's mother sat with a tissue clinched tightly between her fingers. Tears filled her eyes and the small tissue was beginning to have no dry spots left on it. Robert sat next to his wife with his arm around her. Her head rested on his chest as he held her close. A blank stare off in the distance was interrupted by the occasional kiss on her forehead.

"Get the nurse! Quickly! He is moving!" Marie shouted to no one in particular. Lizzie jumped up and ran out of the small hospital room. Curtains served as protection and privacy from the chaos of the hospital. She ripped them open and the tiny wheels which held it to the ceiling screeched along their tracks.

"Jace. Jace. Can you hear me Jace?"

Opening his eyes slowly, he could see nothing but blurred

figures standing over him.

"Macie?" His lips moved, but no voice accompanied them. His legs began to move trying to release themselves from the cocoon of blankets which entrapped them.

"Just relax Jace." Macie said putting her hands on his shoulders.

"We need you to stay calm and try to relax your body." Her voice was strong yet calm with no panic at all.

Looking around the room, Jace could not figure out what was going on. Where was he? How had he gotten there? He was feeling very cold even though his body was sweating. His stomach felt queasy and upset. The urge to vomit had Jace feeling very poorly. There was a small pink pan that was shaped like a neck pillow sitting on the table next to his bed.

"What is going on?" His voice was a whisper. His parents stood at the side of his bed. Jace reached to scratch an itch on his head but he was stopped by the bandage that was wrapped around his head.

A tall figure walked into the room wearing a long white doctor-looking coat. He had a shirt and tie underneath his coat that you could see exposed by his neck. Macie began to speak to him. Jace wiped his eyes again and his right eye was gaining more clarity. He could now see his parents who stood next to him, but he couldn't make out anything too much further away than they were. His left eye felt sore and was not cooperating.

"What is going on?" Jace asked again. This time, he forced his voice out, but it still sounded froggy.

"You were in an accident sweetie." His mom said softly

touching his hand. He could see that she had been crying from the puffiness of her eyes. Tubes were hanging out of his right arm and a monitor that kept beeping showed very high numbers on it.

"I can't remember anything. How did I get here?" His father took a step back and ran his fingers through his hair.

"Hello Jace. I am glad to see you are awake." The tall man's voice projected well across the room.

"What happened?" Jace said weakly. He was suddenly feeling tired again.

"You were in a very serious automobile accident. Do you feel up to answering a few questions for me?

"Who are you again?" Jace said this as if he knew who he was but had forgotten.

"I am Doctor Anderson. I am currently monitoring your status and making sure that we will get you back to full health." The doctor's optimistic tone made his mother feel somewhat better than she had in a while.

"Go ahead and ask me Doc." Jace laid his head back down on the pillow and closed both of his eyes tightly.

"Can you tell me your name?"

"Jace."

"Your full name please?"

"Jace Raymond Grazer." Picking up a clipboard, the doctor marked something down and continued.

"Do you know the reason you are here?"

"You just told me I was in a car accident! Remember?"

"Good." The Doctor's short response puzzled Jace.

"Do you remember who was driving?" This question seemed to cause Jace to think as he took a moment before he responded.

"I can't remember. It couldn't have been one of my parent's because they are both standing right here and they look fine." He said pointing at them.

"Do you remember where the accident happened?"

"Ummm...No." The Doctor looked deeply into his eyes as if to insinuate that he was lying.

"Do you remember where you live?" Jace could remember the house perfectly but he couldn't seem to jog his memory enough to come up with the numbers in his address.

"I live on a vineyard at my parent's house." Jace thought this was a clever answer until the Doctor asked his next question.

"Do you know the exact address?" Smirking at the Doctor, he did not look like he was in a jovial mood.

"It is right on my license...wherever that got to."

"So, you can't remember off the top of your head?"

"No." Jace's response caused his mother to whimper a bit.

"One more question, can you tell me what your last memory is? What is the last thing you can remember?" This again made him pause. He turned his head to the side to indicate he was thinking. He was not sure why he did that.

"I remember leaving the house at night. My brother Dane was standing in the driveway behind me. I was leaving to move away." This was his last memory that he could remember.

"Oh my God! He has forgotten everything!" His mother shrieked and sat back down in her chair dabbing her eyes once again.

"Alright. I am going to check back on you in a little while. I understand you know nurse Macie. She will be taking care of you and if you need anything, let her know." He tapped Jace's hand which was laying on the bed and went to sit next to his mother. The doctor and his parents were speaking for a few minutes, but he could not make out what they were saying. They must have purposefully been speaking at a low tone so they could not be heard.

Several hours went by and Jace had fallen back asleep. When he woke up again there was no one in his room. The lights were still on and the obnoxious beeping from the machine next to him continued. A gurgle in his stomach told him that he must have been hungry even though he did not feel hungry one bit. Sitting there for a few moments, he was trying to think back to the questions the doctor had asked him. What had he forgotten? His mother was so upset and said he had forgotten everything. Why did she say that? His head was pounding. He decided to press the button on his remote to call the nurse in to see if she could do something about his headache.

"It's about time. I only called you fifteen minutes ago." Jace said wisely as the nurse entered the room. It was not Macie who answered his call this time. This nurse was older and she had a tired look on her face.

"It was fifty-seven seconds young man." She said holding up her phone. He did not know that they tracked when he called for them.

"Well I'm sorry, but I have a splitting headache and it felt

~ 169 ~

like fifteen minutes. Is there anything you could give me to ease the pain?" He tried to be nice to her now that he knew he needed her help to get any sort of relief from this head throbbing pain. Looking at what he assumed was a chart on him, she closed the folder and looked down at him.

"I will check with the doctor to see if we can give you something to ease the pain. You have taken massive trauma to the head so I can imagine it is hurting." Even these words that she spoke to him sounded like they were slamming directly down on his head with full force.

"Please do. I would greatly appreciate it." Jace said rubbing both his eyes with his thumb and pointer finger. The nurse left the room and Jace flipped to his side hoping that a different position mixed with a cooler spot on the pillow would help his head.

It didn't.

Just as he was slipping back to sleep, the tall doctor entered the room again.

"So, I hear you are having some discomfort in your head." Looking in the same folder as the nurse did, Jace began to wonder what was so magical in there that both the nurse and the doctor needed to look at it to give him some medicine to stop a headache?

"Yea, it is killing me Doc. Please, I will take anything." He figured the doctors heard that a lot, but he was not faking it like he assumed some people did.

"I do have something here for you." He had a very small tube of clear liquid. The doctor hooked the tube up to the IV and began to press down so the liquid went in gradually. A sudden rush came over his body starting from the arm where his IV resided and worked its way from one side of his body to the other. This liquid gave him the sensation of floating on a cloud. The doctor was saying something to him, but he didn't care at all. It was as if he was deaf and his voice was background noise that was inaudible. He put his head back and enjoyed the relief that this magic medicine was giving him.

A hospital was never a place that Jace's parents liked to be. Of course, they didn't know anybody who was happy to have to go to the hospital. Having had four children, there were plenty of accidents and trips to the hospital for ailments. Robert had asked his wife to go home and get some rest as Jace was sleeping and he was going to stay with him. His two sisters had already gone home and planned to stop back in the morning. Even though she put up a fight, Marie reluctantly agreed to leave but would only go for a few hours before she came back. The pit in her stomach was going to prevent her from sleeping no matter how tired she was. She couldn't get the fact that Jace couldn't remember anything out of her mind. She had the worst-case scenario running through her mind. That always seems to be the way people think when things go wrong. She couldn't help herself. The doctor had explained that Jace had suffered major trauma to his head and that he had been knocked unconscious. Short term memory loss was a big result of having such a hit on your head. When he hit his head, his brain crashed against his skull and he suffered a severe brain bruise. The doctors seemed optimistic because a lot of times people who suffer similar injuries regain their memories after a period of time. Not all cases were the same and after his parents had seen the wreckage that used to be his dad's car, they knew it was serious.

Marie left Jace's room after giving her sleeping child a kiss on his forehead and embracing her husband. She turned around one last time looking as if she was about to change her mind.

"Marie, you need to go home. Get some rest. He will be fine now. I'm here with him." Robert didn't want to sound mean, but he was very concerned about his wife's wellbeing.

"Alright I'm going. I will be back very soon." As she made her way to the waiting room, a feeling of fear mixed with guilt that she was leaving her son there while he was hurt came over her. She wanted to go back, but she knew Robert wouldn't let her. A small television in the corner of the waiting room had the news scrolling across the screen. There was no sound coming from the television but tiny subtitles that she was not able to read were popping up in little black boxes. Sitting down in a plastic chair in the waiting room that wasn't very busy this time of night, she glanced over at a table which had some well used magazines on it. She reached out to get one, but then remembered that she was in a hospital. She didn't know what kind of sicknesses resided in the pages of those magazines. Slouching down in her uncomfortable seat, she rolled up her jacket and put it behind her head to use for a pillow. Her plan was to just rest her eyes for a few minutes. Not even five minutes later, she was out.

Two large glass doors sat at the hospitals entrance. Lizzie had decided to come back that night because she couldn't sleep and she wanted to be there for her brother and her parents. The glass doors slid open by themselves as she walked up to the entrance. When she had left, Jace was still in emergency and they were waiting to get him a room. The waiting room had only a few people in it yet the line to speak with the front desk had four people in front of her. A horrific smell coming from one of the people in front of her made her casually cover her nose. She instantly felt bad for any nurse that would have to deal with that smell. Fifteen long minutes later, she made it to the front of the line and found out where he was. Just as she stepped out of line, she noticed a woman sleeping in the corner of the waiting room. Her purse had fallen on the floor and she appeared to be uncomfortable even though she was completely asleep. It looked like her mom, but she wasn't sure. Walking up to her she confirmed it was her mom and she gently touched her knee.

"Mom." She whispered trying not to scare her. This startled her mother and she jumped back in her seat.

"Lizzy! Oh my goodness you scared me. I was just resting my eyes for a few minutes." She bent over and picked up her purse and a few items that had slid out of it when it had fallen to the floor.

"You need to go home and get some rest Mom." Her concern was clear by the tone of her voice.

"What about you? What are you doing back at this time?"

"I couldn't sleep so I thought that I would come relieve you and Dad." Her mother touched her cheek and smiled at her.

"Your dad is in there right now. They will only let two visitors back at a time so go on back and see them. I will wait here."

"NO! You need to go home Mom. You may be MY mother, but I still need to look out for you!" Lizzy began to walk away and looked back at her mom one last time.

"You better not be here when I get back." She pointed at her and smiled.

Jace's room was dark except for the many different flashing lights provided by the machines he was hooked up to. Jace appeared to be sleeping and a figure was sitting in the chair across from the bed which she assumed was her dad. Suddenly, the lights popped on and a voice from behind her rang through the air.

"Time to get your vitals." The nurse that came in was almost singing these words. She was very happy for someone who was working the night shift. The nurse moved past Lizzie and flashed her a smile. Their dad looked very tired and Lizzie couldn't tell if he had been sleeping or forcing himself to stay awake. She greeted her father as the nurse gently woke Jace from his sleep.

"How are we feeling today?" Her annoyingly good mood continued.

"Well I was sleeping well until about fifteen seconds ago!" The irritation he felt was as clear as day. He was trying to be as nice as possible to the nurses, but sleep deprivation seemed to be their goal as they were checking his vitals several times throughout the night.

"I will be very quick, I promise. I just need to take some

blood and check your blood pressure and heartbeat."
Reluctantly, Jace obliged as his eyes were still half shut. He held out his arm and she did what she needed to do.

"Alright, we are all set. Before I leave, are you in any pain?" Jace opened his eyes the whole way looking right at her.

"I was just sleeping! If I was in pain I obviously wouldn't have noticed it then!" He snapped at her.

"Hey! You treat her with some respect. She is being nice to you!" His father was not happy with the way he was acting towards everybody.

"It's really okay. He has been through a lot." The nurse said smiling at their father.

"Tell you what, I will go see about getting you something to help you fall back asleep quickly." She turned and left the room.

"Great! They wake me up just so they can give me medicine to help me sleep!" Jace rolled his eyes and put his head back on the pillow.

"Dad, go home for a few hours. I want to stay with Jace."

"Thank you, Lizzy, but I'm alright." She knew that he would say that. He was always 'alright' even when he wasn't. He had been working around the clock at the vineyard and this was the last thing he needed. Thinking of what to say to him to get him to go home and rest, she suddenly had a clever idea.

"Well why don't you go down to the waiting room and wait with Mom."

"What? Your mother went home a while ago."

"Well I just saw her sleeping downstairs in the waiting

room. She is looking as poorly as you are." Robert shook his head and exhaled loudly.

"She must not have gone home. I tell ya, that woman is gonna be the death of me." He grabbed his coat and stood from his chair. He must have been sitting in that chair for a while. When he stood up, he grunted and looked to be stiff. He took a few steps towards his daughter and the thought of Frankenstein entered her mind as he barley was bending his knees.

"Jace, I will be back later. Be nice to these nurses and doctors please." Robert kissed and hugged Lizzy and left the room.

Lizzy pulled the chair her father had been sitting in around the side of the hospital bed and sat down. Jace was still awake and looking out the window. It was a dark night and the sky had no stars. If the moon was out, you could not see it from his room.

"Well I am sure you have been asked this a thousand times already, but how are you feeling?" Lizzy was trying to ask this gently as she saw that her brother was tired and already in a poor mood.

"Well besides the crippling headaches and the fact that no one wants to tell me what happened, I am doing great!" Jace was flailing his arms around wildly trying to get loose. The tubes he was connected to were tangled on the edge of the bed and restricting his range of motion.

"Relax!" Lizzy said jumping up and helping him get untangled. Jace took a deep breath of frustration and adjusted his butt in the bed. The remote to the television had slid onto the floor and you could no longer hear the faint sound of the audio to the late night show that was on.

"Do you know what is going on Liz? I have tried very hard to remember, but all I can think of is leaving the house at night. I was planning on going to New York City and I was sneaking out so everyone would stop fighting about it. A puzzled look came over Lizzy's face.

"That is the last thing you remember?"

"Yes! Why do you sound so surprised?" Lizzy looked towards the door to see if anybody was standing outside. Deciding not to risk it, she stood up and shut the door to his room. She sat back down and looked at Jace with the most serious look he had ever seen her have.

"Jace, you just crashed Dad's car. You flipped over several times and were knocked unconscious. You left home over two years ago!" The look of shock that came over him was palpable.

"Get out of here! I would never drive Dad's car! Nor would he let me." Lizzy smiled and thought it was funny that the car was what he caught out of everything she just told him.

"You did!" Clicking her cell phone on, she pulled up a picture that had their dad's Camaro on a flatbed tow truck. It was demolished.

You could barely even recognize it.

"Oh my God!" Jace took her phone from her and held it closer to his face.

"How did this happen?" His mouth hung open.

"I just told you. Do you remember that you and I were supposed to have dinner the next night?" Jace took a few moments and thought hard about what she had just told him.

"I can't remember that. Like I said, the last thing I remember is Dane standing in the driveway before I left. I know he is probably mad at me for trying to leave. Is that why he hasn't come to see me yet?" Lizzy didn't know exactly how to approach this conversation. How could she tell him what was going on if he couldn't remember anything?

"Dane has been missing since you guys had the fight at the bonfire party." Jace looked at her like she was speaking a different language.

"I have no idea what you are talking about. I have to get out of this hospital. I am going crazy in here." Desperation filled his voice.

"Well I know that you are doing well. Your head is what they are concerned about. They are hoping your memory comes back before they let you go."

"Hmm..." Jace was thinking about what she had just said and how he could figure a way out of the hospital.

"Can you help me? Tell me everything that I have apparently forgotten and I can play it off like I remember." For someone who had just had their brain crash against their skull, Lizzy was surprised that he had come up with this idea and skeptical that it would work. She decided that it couldn't hurt to try and began to tell him everything. She told him about when he left home, working in New York City, returning home after years of being away, Dane's disappearance and she even went into detail about what he was doing when he crashed the car.

"Maybe I should take notes?" Jace said giggling as she explained everything to him. In a weird way, Lizzy was hoping that by hearing these things, he might be able to get his memory back or at least remember a few things. It did not seem to be successful.

Several days had gone by and Jace began to wonder why he wasn't receiving any visitors other than his immediate family. He wondered why Dane and Ally had not come to see him. He knew they were both mad at him, especially for wanting to leave them both, but he figured they would be sympathetic at least for what he was going through. Getting released from the hospital was proving to be more difficult than escaping from prison! Jace wanted everyone from the doctors to his parents to feel comforted, so he pretended that some of his memory was coming back but he still claimed it wasn't all there. What his sister had done for him really helped this cause.

Finally, the day had come where they were releasing him and he couldn't wait to leave. His head was healing but they were unsure if he was going to have a scar or how big it might be. His head was still bandaged and the headaches were actually beginning to get better. The vomiting and nausea were still random and he never had any clue when they would hit him.

Today, Jace felt remarkably good. His energy was coming back and he was excited to get out of the hospital. He was starting to have a little clarity on what had happened as his sister kept talking with him and reminding him of his life. One thing that did help was he kept have a reoccurring dream of him telling everyone that he was going to leave and they always took it the same. The dream always ended with him pulling out of the driveway. Jace figured the reason why it was the last thing he could remember is because he kept dreaming about it over and over again.

"Jace!" McKenzie screamed from the waiting room as his father wheeled him down. He was not sure why the hospital required that he be in a wheelchair and be wheeled to the car. He had taken walks around the floor he was on many times and he was positive he wasn't going to fall. Apparently, the hospital was not allowed to risk it. "How are you feeling? You look good for someone who has just been treated like a rag doll in a washing machine." As she hugged him, Jace couldn't help but wonder where her sister was. Jen stood with McKenzie and tapped him on the shoulder.

"Where is Ally? I feel like it has been forever since I last saw her." He said with a smile.

"Umm, let's get you on home." Lizzy cut in before he started to reveal how much he didn't remember to everyone. McKenzie walked with them to their car and kissed Jace on the cheek.

"I'm so glad you are okay! I have so many questions. Call me later when you get a chance?" Jace nodded his head in agreement and looked at Lizzy confused. Jace got into the back seat of his mother's car and Lizzy sat next to him.

"Why would I call McKenzie later" Jace leaned over and whispered in Lizzy's ear.

"That is one I am not sure of. I guess you guys were spending some time together and she wants to be something more than friends with you."

'Hmm...really? But she is Ally's Sister." Jace questioned her explanation.

"Yea! That is how we all feel too!" She said with a sarcastic chuckle.

The first night home went by quickly. Lizzy stayed at her parent's house instead of going back to her place. She wanted to protect Jace just in case he needed it. She wasn't completely sure of who she was "protecting" him from, but she felt better being there then if she would have left. Happy Gilmore's voice screamed out of their television set as he was swearing at his golf ball for not going into the hole. Adam Sandler was a popular actor in their household growing up and Jace always liked to watch his movies. Even though he had probably seen this one a hundred times!

"Thank you for all you have done Lizzy. You are a good sister." He smiled at her and she couldn't tell if he was being serious, or if he was still hopped up on pain medication.

"You are welcome Jace. You should try to get some rest." He looked tired even though all he had been doing lately was sleeping. She grabbed the plate of noodles and chicken he had been eating and set it on the dresser near his bedroom door. The 'TV Table' which had short legs and was perfect for eating in bed was folded up and set by his dresser as well.

"Sleep well Jace and I will see you in the morning." She flipped off the lights and closed his door leaving it open just a crack. She probably wanted to be able to hear him call if he needed anything. Putting his head on his pillow, he thought about the scenarios his sister had told him were his life. If he had really destroyed his dad's car, how come his dad still had not said anything to him about it? Even though Jace was in the hospital, he figured it would've come up. Plus, he had not seen Dane since before his hospital visit. Jace thought he was going to be at home mad at him for trying to get away in the night. He was not there.

Maybe Lizzy was telling the truth, but who knows. Popping two pain pills in his mouth and taking a big gulp of water, Jace closed his eyes feeling frustrated that he could not remember much of anything. The problem with memory loss is...you don't know what you don't know.

Chapter 14

Morning was refusing to come as the moon appeared to be winning the battle against the sun. Jace lay in bed feeling exhausted yet not able to sleep. Going in and out several times, his head was propped up with pillows so high that his neck was hurting him when he woke up. He proceeded to throw the excess pillows on the floor and try to fall back asleep with just one flattened one.

No luck.

Tossing and turning was going to be his fate for this night. Sitting up in bed, he flipped the television on to see if he could find something good on to relax his mind. He hoped there would be a funny movie that would make him chuckle and feel a little better or even a sappy romance movie that could at least put him to sleep. He grinned at the joke he just made in his head.

No luck on that either.

Leaning over to his night stand, he took another sip of water which had become room temperature by sitting out. He smacked his lips and set the glass back down. The feeling of sadness came over him and he wasn't sure why. Alone in his dark room, he decided to keep the television on and lay back down. The flicker of light that it was providing was soothing for him. National Geographic was having a special documentary on ants. They called them

Siafu ants and supposedly, they were one of the most dangerous predators in Africa. Their legs kicked wildly and there were so many of them, you could only see a sea of movement sliding across the ground. Flashing to a human in Africa, these ants had what looked like pinchers on the front of their bodies. They were latching on to this skinny man and he was pulling on the ant's body but the small creature was refusing to let go. The people that lived near these ants lived in small huts and slept on cots that were about a foot off the floor. Jace was glad that he was not living in those conditions. The narrator had a deep voice and was stressing how dangerous and strong these little creatures are. If the people there are not careful, the ants will cover them in the middle of the night or worse, they will cover their infants. Scared looking children crossed the screen as they were watching a trail of ants pass by what looked to be their hut. Jace laid his head back down on his flat pillow. Folding it in half, this was the most comfortable position he had been in all night. The sound of the ant's legs clicking along mixed with the narrator's voice soon helped him drift to sleep.

A bright flash of light surged violently in his direction. Squinting as if the light were causing him physical pain, his hand came up to protect his face. It was coming right for him. He was powerless to stop it. Taking a deep breath, the light hit him and passed by. Looking around, Jace had a sky view of his parent's house. He was moving through the air with a clear view of sight. He was flying.

Looking down, he could see people moving around, but he

couldn't figure out who they were or what they were doing. A flock of crows flew by making a series of loud caws as they passed.

"How is this possible?" Jace said to himself. He was moving uncontrollably toward the house. Before he knew it, he was heading right for the outside cellar doors. They were painted green but the paint had been chipping away over time. The doors were at an angle leading into the ground right next to the house and each had old handles that had been tied together with a rusty chain and lock. They were heavy old doors and had to be propped up with a piece of wood to stay open. Bracing for impact, he covered his head and closed his eyes. A few seconds went by and he opened his eyes. He was now still and the world around him was motionless. Standing in the basement, he looked back at the doors which were both still shut and did not look like they had been opened.

What was going on?

Jace looked around and saw the old basement which he had never liked to come down to as a child. The partial dirt floor, the old foundation blocks that made up the walls, and the deep darkness that the basement always had, even with the small lightbulbs on, gave him an eerie feeling that always put him on edge. Even at his age now, he knew monsters and ghosts were not going to come out and get him. Yet he had watched too many horror movies and his mind would run wild whether he wanted it to or not. There was an old rundown shelf in the back corner of the basement. He tried to look away but whatever was happening kept making him focus on this shelf. The old wood was breaking and the dust and webs that made their home on the shelf were thick. Jace was getting closer to it but could not see anything odd about it. Looking down at the floor, he noticed a small scratch in the packed down dirt. It looked like one that the bottom of a door would make on a floor it was rubbing on. It led right to the sharp angled corner of the bookshelf. Wanting to see more, Jace tried to move forward.

"NO NO NO!" Jace shouted as he began slowly moving away from the shelving unit. His pleas were to no avail. In one swift motion, he was sucked out of the basement like a piece of dirt gets sucked up into a vacuum. He was again in the air only this time, moving toward the back fields.

"This has to be a dream!" He said but his voice did not accompany his words. Trying to wake himself up, he was unsuccessful. Heading for the trees behind the back field, he again tried to brace himself for the impact of a tree. He was almost positive they were not going to hurt him, but his instinct kicked in and he couldn't help himself. Dodging in and out of trees like a cheetah trying to catch its next meal, Jace was stopped in a random spot in the woods. Having trouble seeing, he looked around to see what he was supposed to be seeing. Suddenly, Dane's face flashed before his eyes. Dane was standing there motionless in the middle of the trees under a branch. His arm was extended out and his finger pointed to the ground. Jace tried to speak to his brother but no words came out.

It was beginning to happen again.

Jace was being pulled back from where his brother stood and he was powerless to stop it. Smaller and smaller, Dane was almost out of sight when his mind kicked in.

"Oh my gosh, the door!" He yelled to no one. The old door he and his brother had found! What was he trying to tell him?

"No! Go back! Please!" Jace shouted. The memories of his brother and the bonfire party were rushing back to him.

"Please go back!" Jace yelled as loud as he could trying to get answers to his questions.

"What does all this mean!? IS SOMEONE TRYING TO SHOW ME SOMETHING!? As loud as he could, Jace mustered up the strength from the pit of his stomach up to his chest. The words came bursting from his throat to his mouth out like lava erupting from a volcano.

Everything went black.

Jace could hear a voice in the distance. The first clear sound he had heard since he saw the flash. At first it sounded muffled. Then, it progressively got louder and louder until the voice could be heard in complete clarity.

"JACE!" The voice yelled to him. Looking around, he couldn't see anyone speaking to him.

"Wake up Jace!" A strong shake jolted him from his deep sleep and back into reality. His eyes were wide like saucers as he looked up at his mother and Lizzy looking down at him.

"You are screaming in your sleep." His mom sat on the side of his bed. She was breathing heavily as if she had just run up the stairs. Confused, Jace sat up trying to assess the situation. He felt what he saw was so real! It made no sense to him. Lizzy slid open his curtains and the bright sun had inevitably won the fight versus the moon for now. The sun was perched high in the sky and Jace figured it couldn't be that early in the morning due to its position. "I was having the weirdest dream! I remember everything that has happened. It's all coming back to me now!" His mother was looking at him puzzled.

"I thought you already remembered? That is why they discharged you from the hospital." Being that he had just woken up and was a little shaken from his dream, he had forgotten that he lied to get out of the hospital. Trying to think on his feet, he came up with what he thought was a clever response for his mom.

"Yes, I do. It is just all getting clearer to me. That's all." His mother raised her eyebrow at him. Jace grabbed his cup of water and before he could take a sip, it was snatched from him.

"Don't drink that, let me get you a fresh glass. Or better yet, would you like some orange juice?"

"Orange juice would be great Ma. Thank you." Jace smiled with appreciation towards his mother. Trying to move to the edge of the bed, his legs were caught up in the tight sheet that he had rolled in while asleep. Finally getting free, he swung his legs to dangle over the edge of the bed and sat erect facing the bedroom door.

"Oh my gosh, the bed is soaked!" Lizzy said pulling the sheets clean off the bed. Looking back, Jace saw a body-shaped dampness where he had just been lying.

"Your shirt is covered too!" Lizzy tug at the corner of his t-shirt.

"Will you knock it off!" Jace said pulling his arm away making his shirt snap out of her fingers.

"It was just warm in here last night that's all. I feel fine." Lizzy looked up as their mother entered the room holding a glass full of orange juice and what looked to be a container of medicine.

"What is the matter? Do you not feel well Jace?" Handing the glass to him, she examined the bed and looked back at her son. "Are you feeling alright?" She proceeded to put the back of her hand on his forehead.

"Will you two relax. I am fine. It was just warm in here that's all."

"I brought you some mild pain medication. The doctor at the hospital gave you a prescription for it if you feel pain. With the way you were screaming, I wasn't sure if you were in discomfort or not.

"Thanks Ma, but I'm not in pain and I don't have a temperature." He said moving her hand away from his head.

"Are you sure it had nothing to do with your dream or maybe what you were screaming at?" Lizzy asked.

Jace glared at her as if she had just told everyone his grand secret.

"No! I am sure it was the heat. I'm going to take a shower and go help Dad today. I want to have a talk with him about everything that has happened." Looking at his mom, her look went to his sister, and then back to him.

"Just get ready and I will make you some breakfast. You still should take it easy. You had severe trauma to your head and I want you to get better not worse!" Both women left the room and Jace indeed went to the bathroom to take his shower.

Jace could not get the dream out of his head. The warm water fell from his hair to his shoulders and down. Even though the water was warm, he could still feel it cooling him down. His relaxing state of mind was disturbed by the sound of voices outside the bathroom door. Heavy footsteps walked loudly down the hall and then back again. Quickly, Jace rinsed the conditioner from his hair and turned off the water. He grabbed a towel and slowly made his way back to his bedroom. Drips of water dropped on the floor as he walked. He went into his bedroom but left the door open to try to hear what the voices were saying.

Unable to understand the voices clearly enough, Jace put on his clothes and headed for the stairs. As he stepped out of his bedroom, something grabbed his attention. A noise began to rumble from the room he just came from. Turning around, he went back to see what it was. His cell phone was lit up and buzzing across his nightstand. McKenzie's name flashed across his screen. Debating whether to answer or not, he decided he would call her back and jammed his phone down into the pocket of his jeans. Peering out the window of his bedroom, there were two police cars in the driveway. Both cars were running but did not have their lights on. Wanting to act casual, Jace walked down the stairs at normal speed even though he wanted to fly down the rail as fast as he could. Covering a yawn with his hand, he stopped at the bottom step as he saw what was going on. The police had his Father in handcuffs by the front door and were talking with him as if they were there for a social call.

"What's going on?" The fake surprise Jace had mustered must have worked. His mom immediately tried to talk the situation down.

"A mistake has been made and they need to speak to your father."

"What kind of mistake? Why is he handcuffed?" Jace's attention went from his mother to officer Harper who was standing next to his father.

"Let's go."

These two simple words that his father muttered were cold and irritated. Robert winked at his Wife before turning around and walking out the door. The house appeared to be empty other than his mom. There were no cars at the store, but the workers cars were parked next to the house and they were presumably already harvesting or taking care of orders.

"Why did they just take Dad? His best friend shouldn't need to handcuff him to simply speak to him." His words were making too much sense and painted his mom in a corner she was not going to be able to talk herself out of.

"They are saying that Dane killed farmer Johnson and that your father had something to do with it." Sitting down in her old chair that she had just reupholstered with dark blue and white fabric, she looked down at her hands which Jace could clearly see were shaking. Walking over to her, he knelt down on both knees and put her hand inside of his. They were as cold as ice and shaking uncontrollably even as his hands tried to stop them.

"Do you know something about that?" Jace asked carefully. Looking up at him, her eyes were holding back what looked to be an oceans worth of tears.

"Your father did not kill anybody. He is an honest and kind man. I don't know what I would do without him."

"Mom, just try to relax. You are speaking as if he is going away and not coming back."

"These are serious accusations Jace. I was with your dad the night that Dane disappeared. I am positive that he didn't do anything." The passion in her words was undeniable. She was clearly positive of her husband's innocence.

"If he did nothing wrong, then they have nothing to convict him of. He should be home by this afternoon." Trying to make his mother feel better, it came off sounding like he was trying to be a wise guy.

"I guess we will see." Marie stood from her chair and quickly wiped the single tear that had broken loose from the dam that was holding them back.

"I will make you some breakfast Jace." She said as she exited the room and made her way to the kitchen. He almost refused but he knew she would make it anyway.

"I am going to go out and see how the guys are doing in the fields. I will be back very soon." Sliding his shoes on, he went outside with other ideas in his head. He made sure to stop and see how the guys were doing with the harvest and talk with them for a few minutes. Several of the men there he had known almost all his life. They worked for his dad every year since he could remember. This year, there were also some new faces who he did not know but introduced himself anyway. After exchanging pleasantries, Jace decided he was going to casually take a walk through the grapes. He wanted to go back to the woods where he had found that door in the ground with his brother, but he didn't want to set off any red flags by going straight for it. Walking down to the water, he ran his fingers through the clear liquid. It was cold, too cold to swim in. It was on par for this time of year though. Gentle ripples moved towards his feet and fizzled out once they hit the land. Jace looked back at his house to see if his mom or anybody was watching him. From where he stood, he could not see anyone and he was unable to see in the kitchen window which faced the back fields and water where he stood. The simple thought ran through his mind to just run to the back woods and search to see if he could find it as fast as he could.

Would he get caught though?

The paranoia he was experiencing was consuming his thoughts. Why was he still thinking that everyone was keeping things from him and that they were out to get him? Shaking his head from side to side, he tried to erase these thoughts as you would erase an Etch A Sketch. That was enough! He decided to just walk back there and look around. Walking back up to the barn, he figured he would need a flashlight and something to dig with if the door was covered with dirt. At first glance, Jace only found a hand-held gardening scoop. Trying not to waste too much time, he decided that was the best tool he could find. Grabbing it, he went for the door and something caught his eye. An old shovel perched in the corner! It was dirty and completely covered in rust, but it would do the trick. Snatching it up, he slid out the barn door and made it back to the woods without anybody noticing him...at least that is what his hope was.

The look on Dane's face in his dream was seared into Jace's mind. It was like he wanted to tell him something but was unable to for some reason. Looking around the trees, Jace tried hard to remember where he had been when they found it but it was turning out to be much more difficult than he had hoped. Every tree looked similar in some way. It had been raining so much the last week that the ground was still marshy. A loud pop from the mud releasing his sneaker caused him to stop. His shoe had come off and the mud had spilled over the top of them. Trying to slide it back on with only two fingers, he wasn't having much luck. Hopping on one leg, he plopped to the ground and forcefully pushed his mud filled shoe back on. Continuing forward, he remembered the cloth in the tree that was near what he was looking for. Another fifteen minutes passed of him searching through the trees and he was about ready to give up for now. He was certain his mom had his breakfast made and was probably wondering where he had gone. Jace looked to his left, and then back to his right. He had forgotten which direction he had come in through. Thinking to himself how stupid he was for not keeping track, he chose a direction and hoped it was the right one.

Stepping over down trees and muddy spots, the shovel and flashlight that he had been carrying began to feel astronomically heavy. Switching his grip on the tools only helped minimally. Coming to a small stream, Jace decided to sit for a minute and wash his shoes. The stream was higher than he imagined it would normally be. Since they were already soaked completely and wet from the mud, he stuck them right in and scrapped the sides with his bare hand. The cold water felt good on his hands that were beginning to hurt from clenching the old metal shovel. Both feet now in the water, Jace leaned back and propped his body up with his elbows.

A jolt of noise moved some fallen leaves that had gathered next to a rock by the stream. Quickly scooping up the shovel, he got to his feet ready to defend himself from whatever was moving. The metal shovel swung through the air and came down on the rock next to the leaves with a loud bang. A tiny chipmunk scurried out and looked around. Jace smiled at the little creature as he thought it was ironic that he was startled by probably one of the smallest and harmless creatures in the woods. Running off, Jace's eyes followed the little chipmunk and to his amazement, the tiny rodent ran right under a big tree with the cloth hanging from its lowest limb! *It's like it was meant to be* Jace thought to himself. If he hadn't stopped to clean his shoes, or if he would have just gone the other way instead of watching the chipmunk, he would have missed what he was looking for.

Jace's heart was racing with excitement. He searched the ground frantically looking for the little metal piece that he had tripped over. Leaves were providing an unwanted challenge for him. Dropping to his hands and knees, he took big swipes with his arms to clear the leaves away so he could find it. Finally, his eyes landed on the top of a piece of metal buried in the ground. Someone had reburied it or maybe the weather had possibly done it. If he didn't know it was here, he would have never tripped over it this time. Digging the shovel in, the metal on metal noise confirmed it was still here. Swiping with the side of the shovel, he cleared a big portion of the door off and stood up.

There was a brand-new lock on it!

He grabbed the lock and looked at it. The door was rusty and mud covered. The lock was still shiny even though it had mud on it as well. Looking around, there was only one option, he had to get it open. Jace didn't want to go all the way back to the barn to try to find a cutter that he was likely not going to be able to find anyway. Grabbing the shovel with both hands, he slammed it down missing the lock. Huffing with irritation, he tried again. Second swing resulted in the same as the first, a miss. One more time, he put extra might into it this time slamming the end of the shovel down and making contact with the lock. Denting it, it did not break. Continuing this for several minutes, his chest went in and out as he tried to catch his breath. Frustration was setting in. The lock was looking pretty beat up but it did not let go. Adrenaline pumping through his veins, he began again. Hit after hit the little lock mocked him. One final ax-like swing and the no longer shiny lock burst open. Ripping it off, he threw it aside with the feeling of great accomplishment. Pulling the door with all his might, it opened and he propped it up with the shovel. The flashlight clicked on and the beam of light showed a dark tunnel going into the earth. One side had little rungs that were clearly meant to be steps. Timidly, with the flashlight in one hand, he set his feet on the rungs and began to descend. Jace felt a rush of fear go through him, but nothing was going to stop his curiosity now. It was getting darker and darker with each step as the sunlight was getting farther away. Pausing for a moment, he flashed the light down to see where he was going.

He could see the bottom! A couple more steps and his foot hit a cement floor. Jace looked up at the tunnel he had just climbed down. He wondered who had built this originally and what it could possibly have been used for? Taking about three steps, Jace lost the little sunlight that was left from the opening above. The walls appeared to be reinforced by cement. This looked like something that had to have taken some time to construct! A few more steps and Jace's flashlight revealed a door. It had no windows and did not look as if it had been opened in while. Pausing quickly, Jace thought he heard something. Putting his ear to the door, he held his breath. He could feel his heartbeat in his ears.

BANG BANG BANG!

Loud pounding came from the other side of the door! Jace flew back and his flashlight crashed against the wall. The batteries shot out from it and the flashlight went out. Frantically looking around, he couldn't see anything. Feeling for the wall, he found it and guided himself back to where he came from. Kicking the flashlight with his foot, he bent down to grab it. Feeling the batteries were gone, the chances he found them in the pitch-black darkness and put them back in the right direction were slim. Looking up to try to see the light, panic started in.

He wanted out of there.

Pressed against the wall, he came to the little rungs he had climbed down. Looking up, there was no light coming through the opening he came down originally. Leaving the flashlight behind, he started up the rungs and did not look back. His shoes must have had some mud left on them as his left foot slid off the rung. Frantically kicking his legs, he was able to hold his body weight with just his arms. Dangling, Jace found the rung with his feet and regained his balance once again. Taking a deep breath, he knew he needed to do this slower. Not knowing how far he had climbed, he also was unsure of how far his fall would have been. The darkness was playing tricks on his strained eyes. Finally, his head hit the metal door letting him know he had made it to the top.

It was closed.

Pushing with one arm, he was trying hard to get it to open without falling back down the tunnel.

It didn't budge.

A Walk Though the Grapes
David Jackson

__Chapter 15__

"You are free to choose, but you are not free from the consequence of your choice." This was the quote hung above the entrance doors at Willowcreek High School. Words that Jace had never forgotten and thought about often.

Clinging to the rungs, Jace could feel his body hurting and the exhaustion that was setting in. Pushing up from this angle on the cold door while trying his best to keep his balance was wearing him down. He had been at it for what he assumed was an hour. In reality, he knew it was only several minutes. Pausing for a minute, Jace tried to regain all his energy for a big push. He wanted to use both hands but was afraid of falling back down. A fall from this height almost guaranteed some sort of broken bones...if not worse.

He needed to get out!

With all his might, he threw caution to the wind, put both hands out and kicked off the rungs. The old door popped open a tiny bit for a split second and Jace jammed his arm in between the door and the ground. Letting out a shriek, he immediately realized this was a bad decision. The heavy door was crushing his arm. Turning his head to the side, his left eye could see out and the shovel which was keeping the door open had fallen. He reached for it with his free arm and tried to wedge it by the door hinges. This worked. It opened the door enough to let his arm free to grab a hunk of grass. Pulling himself up, his knees hit the ground and he pushed the door open completely.

Sitting next to the wide-open hole, Jace didn't know what to do next. Who or what was down there making that noise? Who could he trust with this? He always thought he could trust his parents, but recently, he wasn't so sure. Getting to his feet, he shut the door but decided not to fill it back in. He planned to be back soon so why create more work for himself. As he turned to try to find his way out of the woods, his pocket began to buzz again. He had his cell phone in his pocket the whole time! Pulling it out, he didn't know the number that was calling. The area code was one that he was not familiar with. He waited for the ringing to stop and began to search through his phone. The thoughts of stupidity he had for himself were growing. He could have used the light on his phone in that dark tunnel. He could have even used it to navigate the woods so he wouldn't have been so lost. It had a map and a compass. Using this logic, he easily found his way out and back to the fields.

Trying to come up with an excuse for his mom was not going to be easy. He was covered in mud and had been gone for a while now. Upon entering the house, nothing seemed awry. It was quiet and the noise of running water from the upstairs shower filled the walls. Walking into the kitchen, there was a lonely plate sitting at the kitchen table. It has filled up with two over easy eggs, toast, bacon and what looked to be small cut up home fries. Jace was starving and it looked very tasty. Ripping off his shirt, pants, and socks, he ran down the basement stairs and tossed them in the dirty clothes hamper. He mixed them in with other clothes that were already waiting to be cleaned so it didn't look so obvious. Running back up the stairs in his underwear, he still heard the shower which he took to mean that he was safe. Sitting down at the table, he grabbed a fork and began to eat. The food had gotten cold. There was no sign of warmth in anything that he put in his mouth. Wanting to microwave it, the plate was too big to be able to spin in their microwave. He couldn't not eat it though. Especially since his stomach was feeling discomfort from hunger. Taking big bites, Jace managed to finish almost everything that resided on his plate. Moving the last few potatoes around with his fork, he tried chewing as best he could, but his cheeks were stuffed full of food resembling a squirrel that was gathering nuts for the winter.

The sound of keys clanking on the garage door alerted him that somebody was home. Before he could move out of his chair, Jen stepped in. Taking one look at her brother, she stopped dead in her tracks. Sitting at the kitchen table in his underwear with his mouth stuffed full of food, Jace gave a whimpering smile.

"How are you doing?" Jace mumbled rolling food between his cheeks.

"What did you say?" His sister grumbled.

Swallowing whatever he could, he tried again.

"How have you been? I haven't seen you in a while." His sister turned away from him and opened the fridge.

"I'm fine. Better than YOU have been lately." The cold

answer his sister gave him made the situation even more uncomfortable. One last movement of the food in his mouth, he swallowed as fast as he could.

"Well I am glad things are fine with you." Trying to sidestep her comment, Jace was trying hard to be nice to his sister. The last thing he wanted to do was argue with her or anybody for that matter. Pulling an iced tea out of the fridge, Jen plopped down in the chair next to his.

"You know, you are causing a lot of trouble for everyone here. I thought you coming back would be a good thing. Lately, I am not so sure." Her voice was serious and even though her words were mean, she was not being her usual snarky self. Pausing for a moment, he began to answer before she cut him off.

"Why are you sitting here in your boxers?" She asked tugging on the corner of them.

"It's hot in here! I'm not used to these high temperatures anymore since I moved out." Jace was pleased at the cleverness of this answer. Raising an eyebrow, Jen stood up and walked to the thermostat.

"It's only seventy-two degrees in here!" She snapped back at him.

"Well I am hot okay! What's with the accusations?" Just as he responded, the shower shut off.

"What are you doing here at this time of day anyway Jen? Sitting back down again, she took a sip of her iced tea and pulled her cell phone out of her pocket.

"Mom asked me to come home. She said she wanted to talk." Jen's phone began playing annoying music accompanied by loud beeps and crashing sounds.

"What did she want to talk about? Did she tell you? Why didn't she ask me I wonder?" Jace's voice sounded hurt with his question.

"No, she didn't tell me what it is about. And maybe she didn't ask you because she can't trust you at all to do anything right! Or maybe she didn't ask you because you already live here and have nowhere else to go!"

"That is enough! Why do you always have to be like this?! What did I do to you that is so bad that you treat me like crap all the time?" Jace pounded the table with his fist making her phone jump.

"Relax killer. We wouldn't want to make the golden child angry, now would we?"

Standing up from his chair, "Why don't you just shut up and mind your own business!?" He yelled at her. Still only having his boxers on, it was hard to take his anger seriously.

"And one more thing, if you think that..."

"THAT IS ENOUGH!" Jace was cut off by his mother standing in the hallway with her towel around her and hair dripping.

"Why is it that I need to run down here right out of the shower dripping wet because my two ADULT children can't seem to get along!?" Their mother's voice was raised and the look she gave cautioned them that she meant business. Both looking down, neither responded to her.

"Now I'm going to go up and finish getting ready. Please do not keep arguing and be civil to each other." About to turn around, she flashed Jace one last look.

"I don't know what is going on but put some clothes on

Jace!" With those words, she was up the stairs and out of sight.

"You got in trouble." Jen mocked him as if they were both in kindergarten.

"Shut up Jen. What are you five years old?" Frustrated with her, he went to his room to get some clean clothes.

After getting ready and throwing her hair up in a towel, Marie sat in her living room in front of the big television screen that was blank. She could see her reflection in the dark screen. A few moments later, she was joined by her two children. First Jen went in and fell onto the couch. Jace soon followed and parked himself in their dad's chair away from his sister.

"I want to talk to you both about what is going on. Jace you saw a little bit of it already, but they have arrested your dad on suspicion of murder...well, I believe it is manslaughter. As you both know, Farmer Johnson was killed, and they have not been able to find who did it. They have found paint on one of the pieces to the vehicle that hit and killed him. It matched your father's truck." Breathing deeply, she continued.

"They also want to know where Dane is, and they want to get a close look at your dad's truck."

"So why don't they come and look at it then?" Jace asked.

"It has been stolen. I thought your father told you that?"

"No. He never told me anything like that. In fact, I saw his truck in the small garage where he normally keeps the Camaro."

Jen scoffed under her breath at the mention of the car he had demolished. Looking at her with anger, Jace's attention was quickly grabbed by his mother to prevent further arguments between her two children.

"Where did you see it and when was this?"

"Not that long ago! Just the other day. Come on, I will take you to see it!" Grabbing his mother's hand, he pulled her towards the door.

"Well I guess I'll come then too." Jen remarked wisely.

"Nah, just stay here, we've had enough of you to last a lifetime."

"Stop it Jace! I'm not going to tell either one of you again! Now get your shoes on and let's go." Complying with their mom's request, they headed towards the garage. Arriving at the side door, it was not locked. Turning the knob, Jace pushed the door open to reveal what was inside.

Empty.

There was nothing in this garage whatsoever. Stepping in and frantically looking around, Jen laughed at her brother, but he completely ignored her.

"It was right here! I'm telling you the truth! It was pulled in and the front end was smashed up! I saw it with my own two eyes!" Jace was pleading with his mother to agree with him.

"Maybe things are still a little foggy for you Jace."

"NO! It was here! It must have been moved!"

"Yea, it was stolen. Right from the driveway!" He could tell by his mother's tone that she did not believe him at all.

"Plus, your father only uses...well...used this garage for his car."

"That's it. I am going back inside." Jen spun around shaking her head and walked back up and into the house. Looking defeated once again, Jace walked out of the garage and shut the door behind him.

"I don't know what is going on, but I am not crazy! Things seem to keep happening that I can't explain." His mother put her arm around him.

"Everything will be alright don't you even worry about it." Her confidence was surprising for a woman whose husband was just taken away in handcuffs.

Sitting back down in the living room, Jen was once again on her phone.

"Jen, I need you to run down to the police station and pick up your father when they are done questioning him."

"Wait, I thought you just said they were accusing him of murder? Do you really think they will just let him go?" Her question was valid and Jace wasn't positive on how his mom would answer it.

"Just do it please. Call me if you need anything or have any more information. Thank you, Jen,"

Jen obliged with her mother's request and left out the front door.

"I want to talk to you about something Mom." Jace said looking out the window to confirm his sister was driving away.

"I stumbled upon something in the back woods. It's hard to explain but it is an old tunnel that goes beneath the ground. It was locked, and I was just wondering if you knew anything about it?" His mother looked up quickly, her eyes wide as if she had just heard some bad news.

"I'm not positive on what is back there Jace. I know that there is an old wine cellar back there that hasn't been used in a very long time. Maybe that is what you found?" Looking confident in her answer, she picked up a book from the coffee table and pulled it open to where the bookmark sat.

"Yea but I..." Pausing to think about how to tell her what he had heard, the right words were not coming to his mind. Jace had to be careful after the missing truck stunt that he just pulled.

"But you... what Jace?" Not looking up from her book, she seemed to be losing interest in this conversation.

"I was just curious about it, that's all. It looked pretty old and fascinating. Like it could be a passageway to buried treasure or something." He said this with a joking tone and a half-hearted grin. Deciding to keep what he had done and heard to himself, he did not press the subject any further.

"I'm going to head out for a bit Mom." These words finally made her look up.

"Listen, you need to be careful! Drive slowly. Your father was able to pull your truck out and it is by the barn."

"Thanks Ma." With those words, he was off.

Stepping into his truck, the old familiar smell that greeted him gave him a strong feeling of contentment. Even something as small as a smell told him that it was his truck and he was comfortable and safe inside it. Having more questions than answers on his mind, he wanted to talk to someone but there was only one person he could think of...Ally.

He was almost positive that she wouldn't want anything to do with him after her outburst at the store about her sister and him. Jace had to try though. She was always one of the most level-headed people he knew. Thinking about her throwing the corks at his head made him question how level-headed she still was. Driving slowly like his mother requested, cars were passing him over the striped yellow lines at higher rates of speed than his own. His mother wasn't the only deterrent that was making him drive extra cautiously. The vague memories of his crash were still meandering through his mind. Finally, Jace pulled onto her street and into her driveway. Secretly, he was hoping that McKenzie wasn't home and he could just talk with Ally.

His wish was granted.

As he stood at the front door, Ally answered the door. Her nose was bright red and her hair was as messy as he had ever seen it. Still in her pajamas and an oversized t-shirt, she held a crumpled-up tissue and a bottle of water.

"What can I do for you Jace?" She sniffled at him wiping her nose with the only dry spot left on the tissue.

"What's wrong? Not feeling well?" In the back of his mind he was kicking himself for such a stupid question. Like she always walked around with a red nose and sniffles when she was feeling healthy.

"I am a little under the weather...I will be fine though." She finished her sentence with a cough and one more wipe of her nose for good measure.

"I want to talk to you. Are you up for it?" Looking at him, the answer she wanted to give was NO, but she invited him inside anyway. Her house was very clean except for the couch was littered with used tissues and the table was full of drinks and different types of medicines. There was even a cup of what Jace assumed was hot tea from the steam coming out of the green and yellow cup.

Ally sat down on the couch and grabbed the remote for the television. Pausing the television, Jace could tell that she was watching a Disney movie. She had always loved Disney movies and wanted Jace to take her to Disney World someday when they could afford to. Those dreams they once had together now seemed like a distant memory a million years in the past.

"Are you home all by yourself Al?

"Yes. Everybody else is at work, but I called in sick today." Jace smiled as he was happy that she was alone.

"You think me being sick is amusing?" Caught off guard, he quickly responded.

"Gosh no! I'm just happy to see you." Not knowing how to explain his ill-timed smile, this was the best excuse he could muster up at that precise moment.

"What's going on Jace? I heard about the accident you had with your dad's car." A look of surprise as this caught him off-guard once again!

"I didn't think you would find out about that." Embarrassed, Jace broke eye contact from her.

"My dad is a cop, remember? You look like you are recovering from it well." The kindness in her voice was much appreciated by Jace who felt like everyone else in his life was kicking him around or calling him crazy.

"Yup, I am feeling better. I did want to talk to you about something that has been going on. Can I trust you? Can we talk like we used to before I left?" A faint smile came to her face. We can always talk Jace. I never broke your trust before. What makes you think I would now?" This was a valid point that she made. When it came to being a good girlfriend, she had it down to a science! Besides, he was the one who left her. It's not as if she had ever broken his trust the way he had hers.

"Things have been going on at my parent's house. Dane is still missing as I am sure you know. I feel like I am seeing things and then I turn around and they are gone. Something is happening and I can't seem to stop it!" His voice was growing louder and filled with emotion. He wasn't sure where to begin and he wasn't even positive how to explain to her what he wanted to say. Jace sat down in a chair next to the couch she was currently sitting on. Her feet were up on the couch next to her and she had pulled a blanket over her bottom half.

"Wait, that was a lot of information at once. Are you sure that you are feeling okay and fully recovered from the accident?" If one more person asked him that he was going to flip out!

"I am sure! Trust me, I feel fine. I just need a friend to talk to who doesn't hate me! I don't know why I chose you because I know you hate me for what I did to you." A tear was welling up in his eye and his voice was becoming shaky. The overload of emotions he was feeling was catching up to him. A look of shock was on Ally's face. She could not even remember a time when Jace cried in front of her.

"Come over here." She said patting the sofa cushion next

to her. He did as she said and sat beside her. He could feel the warmth coming off her like a furnace gives off heat. She reached out and pushed down on her hand sanitizer. Rubbing her hands together, the sanitizer soon wore in. She grabbed his hand and looked right into his tear-filled eyes.

"I don't hate you Jace. The love I felt for you when we were together is stronger than any love I had felt before or since. I was and am still mad at how badly you hurt me, but I don't hate you! If I truly hated you, it would have been easy getting over you and I can promise that was the hardest thing I have ever had to do in my life! Honestly, I still haven't." Rubbing her hand with his thumb, she literally and figuratively was giving him a sense of warmth and comfort that he was looking for. Looking back at her, he couldn't believe that he had let this woman go. She was sitting there with what he assumed was a fever, runny nose and chills. Plus, he was the man who had broken her heart and left her, and she was still, after all this time, trying to help make HIM feel better.

"I know I have told you this many times Al, but from the bottom of my heart, I am truly sorry for leaving you. If it makes you feel any better, I can promise you that I have hurt myself more by losing you than I could even put into words." Sincerity filled his voice and the puppy dog smile he had brought back good memories for Ally of the time they had been together. Reaching out her arms to hug Jace, he turned and reciprocated. Hugging her tightly, he couldn't have cared less that she was sick. Her arms pulled him tightly and the warmth of her body strangely felt good on his.

Suddenly, the screen door opened and Tyler stepped in with his hands full of bags. Stopping abruptly in his place, he took a moment to process what he was looking at. Ally let go of Jace and readjusted herself on the couch.

"Hey Babe." She said in a voice that sounded sicker than the one she had been talking to him with.

"What the hell is going on here?" Stepping forward, Tyler threw the bags on the chair Jace had just been sitting in.

"Wait, it's not what it looks like." Ally said. A look of guilt draped over her face like she had done something wrong.

"You tell me not to come over because you don't want me to get sick. So, I decide to go out, buy you your favorite soup, crackers and some cold medicine to surprise you and help you feel better, and you invite him here to hug and kiss you and god knows what else!" Jace could tell he was in trouble as Tyler's voice was not getting any calmer.

"We did not kiss at all…"

"Just shut up man!" Tyler yelled in Jace's direction, but his eyes stayed glued to Ally's.

"He just stopped by for a minute to talk to me about something. That's all I swear!" Ally was stern hoping that her confidence would help ease the situation.

It didn't.

"Are you kidding me right now?! This idiot you still love comes over and you guys are hugging and touching each other, and you expect me to think that nothing is going on?" How was Jace going to be able to explain this to her boyfriend?

"Listen man, she is telling the truth. Nothing happened! We were just talking." Tyler turned around and reached for the bags he had brought. Looking through them, he was searching for something specific.

"Tyler, what are you doing?" Ally could sense that nothing good was about to happen. Turning around, Tyler was holding a bowl full of soup.

"See, I told you that I got your favorite kind." Popping the top off and tilting the bowl ever so slightly, she saw that indeed it was the kind she enjoyed the most.

"Thank you, Tyler. That was very nice of you." An odd tension filled the air. Trying to defuse the situation was the goal for both Ally and Jace.

"You made me out to look like a fool going behind my back Ally!" Getting closer to her, Jace began to stand up to stop whatever Tyler was about to do to her.

"Just back off okay?" Jace said trying to get his attention off her. It worked as Tyler looked at him and screamed...

"I TOLD YOU TO SHUT UP!"

The next thing Jace knew, hot soup was flying at him and hit him right in the stomach and crotch. Jace flew up off the couch with a loud scream and shoved Tyler back as the scalding water was burning the skin beneath his clothes.

"Oh my God! Tyler, you are so stupid! Why did you do that!?" Ally screamed looking at Jace who was ripping his clothes off in a panic. First his shirt came off and he frantically tried to unbutton his belt to let his wet pants free of his body. Standing there in his boxers, his lower stomach had a giant red mark that Jace was rubbing.

"You need to leave Tyler before my dad gets home!" Ally

yelled at him.

"Fine, screw you. You can have each other. We are done." Turning around, he stormed out the front door.

"Tyler, wait!" She pleaded. She wanted him to leave but did not expect him to break up with her!

"Well, I see that he is not a hot head whatsoever." Jace said sarcastically as he carefully opened the top of his boxers and looked to see if everything was alright inside them. His stomach had taken the worst of it and his jeans protected everything that was in them. Ally went over to Jace who once again was standing in his boxers, only this time, he had a pretty good burn on his stomach.

"I'm so sorry Jace. It's all my fault." Ally's concern for his burnt stomach was surprising to him.

"Let me go get some cream for it, I'll be right back." Maybe she was telling the truth. Her concern was great enough for him to tell that she did not hate him. For a brief moment, the thought that Tyler may have been right and she did still care for him made him forget about the pain. This thought made him shake his head and realize how stupid these thoughts were. Picking his clothes up and setting them on the coffee table, he was about to sit down when Ally came back in the room holding a white tube.

"This is ointment to help ease the pain." She clicked open the tube and squirted the cream on her hands. As she began to rub the affected area, an awful thing began to happen. Her hands were so soft and she was being so gentle with him, he could feel an uncontrollable erection beginning to happen. He had to stop this immediately! Standing in his thin cotton boxers, she was sure to notice!

~ 214 ~

"Ouch! Hold on a minute!" He grabbed his stomach to play it off like the cream was hurting him.

"Move your hands! Just let me finish this." Clearly unaware of what she was doing to him, she persisted and swatted his hands away herself. Not knowing what to do, he tried to subtly lean back to stop it from being so blatantly obvious.

"Okay! I'm good. Thank you." Spinning around away from her, he grabbed himself praying the blood flow would calm down and he could go back to being normal.

"I should get some of your waistline too. I see how red it is there. Turn back around. It will only take a second."

"No!" Jace could feel himself getting warmer and he figured his face was flush with awkwardness.

"Will you stop that! Just turn around already!" Before he could step away, Ally grabbed his shoulder and spun him around to face her straight on. She got a clear glimpse of what he had been trying to hide. Jace was afraid of what she would say. He did not want this to happen...it just did.

"Well thank you for the compliment Jace." She said with a devious smile.

"What are you talking about? I didn't say anything."

"Haven't you ever heard that actions can speak louder than words? And I would say that your bodies actions are speaking pretty clearly to me." Raising her eyebrows and looking up at him, her smile was still planted on her face.

"Listen, I didn't..."

"Just stop. I am kidding with you. I'm not sure why you are so shy about yourself now? It's not like I haven't seen it before! Many times before. Honestly, you have a very nice penis." Shrugging her shoulder, she was clearly not embarrassed about what was happening. Dropping to one knee, she pulled his waistband down ever so slightly. She moved her hand back and forth until the whole undersection of his stomach was smooth and polished with cream. Wanting to say something, Jace was at a loss for words. He felt very vulnerable standing there in his boxers in front of his ex with his penis making a pop-up tent out of his boxers.

"There, all done." She patted his stomach and began rubbing her hands together to get the remaining cream to soak in.

Looking up at him one last time, both their heads simultaneously shot towards a noise coming once again from the front door. Panic seared through Jace's body. The thought of Tyler coming back for round two as he stood there in his boxers was the last scenario Jace needed right now. Unfortunately for Jace, he was mistaken.

There was a worse scenario.

Standing there just inside the door was McKenzie with a look of shock on her face. Not one second later, the door opened again and their dad, officer Harper, walked in holding what looked to be a full duffle bag. He paused next to his daughter and looked in to his living room. Standing there in his boxers, Jace looked down at Ally. Rising to her feet slowly, her expression was palpable. It was the exact look of terror that he was himself experiencing inside!

A Walk Though the Grapes
David Jackson

Chapter 16

"My death will probably be caused by being in the wrong place at the wrong time." As this thought trickled through Jace's head, it was the first time in his life that he truly feared what was about to happen to him. Unsure of what the reactions were about to be, he grabbed his jeans that were thrown over the chair and held them in front of him to shield his semi-nakedness. If he were to die today, he hoped he would have more dignity in death than to die with no clothes on.

"Hey Kinz, what are you guys doing home already?" Ally broke the silence with a question that actually made them sound guiltier than they already looked! Not her intention, she realized this once it was too late.
"Not expecting anyone to be home huh?" McKenzie entered the room and sidestepped the chair without her head moving whatsoever. She moved like a ghost floating on gentle air currents.
"No! Of course not!" Looking at her clearly angry sister, the line of questioning paired with the answers she gave confused herself and McKenzie.
"Of course not what? You were not expecting to get caught?"
"No! We weren't doing anything to get caught from! Jace just came over to talk with me about a few things."
Clarifying her answer, she knew she had to explain in more

detail. Before she was able to, her sister interjected.

"Yea, I always love to have long conversations with my ex boyfriends when they are in their underwear!" What McKenzie was implying *looked* to be true even though it wasn't. The girl's father still stood in the front corridor taking off his shoes and assessing the situation.

"Tyler came over and saw us talking and flipped out. You know what a hot head he is."

"Yes, we know. We saw Tyler flying down the street and he stopped to tell us that you were here cheating on him with Jace! His words not mine." These were the first words uttered by their dad.

"Your sister and I were going to go to lunch, but we had to stop here to see if it was true. I told him that his accusations couldn't possibly be accurate but then I get here and see this!" His voice was beginning to escalate.

"Tyler threw hot soup on Jace and burned him. Did he tell you that? Why else would Jace be in his underwear in our living room?" Ally fired back at both of them.

"Well I can think of *SEVERAL* reasons why!" McKenzie's look of accusal was directed towards Jace.

"Let's just stop and calm down here for a minute." Jace finally decided to chime in.

"She is telling the truth! Just look at this burn!" Moving the jeans that he held down to reveal his red mark, he pointed with his free hand at the large cream covered burn that resided on his lower stomach.

"I think you should leave now before I get really upset!" The calmness in their father's voice was laced with fury. Jace did not want any part of this large police officer especially when it came to his daughters. He could see that it didn't matter the reason he was standing in his living room in his underwear with his daughter, there was no excuse that would be acceptable to him.

"I have called you multiple times and you never answer me! You never even call me back! For someone who wants to talk so badly, I am pretty sure I had made it clear that I wanted to talk to you!" McKenzie was making a little too much sense for comfort. How could Jace tell her that he felt more comfortable with her sister. He was in a very uncomfortable place that he now wished he would have never gotten himself into with both women. He knew that getting involved with his ex-girlfriend's sister could have potentially negative ramifications, he was just shocked that they had happened so quickly. The sad part was, in the back of his mind, he knew he could never feel about McKenzie what he did for Ally. This situation was a perfect example of his actions speaking for his true feelings.

"I am sorry." Jace pulled his still wet jeans back on each leg and clumsily buckled them leaving his belt unfastened. His shirt took the worst of the soup attack and was still too wet for him to want to put back on. Moving towards the door carefully, he had to pass McKenzie from where she stood. Her hands reached out and shoved him backwards.

"Yea, I'll bet you're really sorry *NOW*!" Losing his balance, Jace was able to catch himself with one hand on the edge of the couch.

"Stop it!" Ally shouted as her dad grabbed her arm.

"The Hell with you Jace!" Fire spewed from her eyes as she turned and took the stairs two at a time.

"You really need to calm your life down and try to get it back on track. Now, I don't know where your brother is, but if you have information about anything that is going on, you had better tell me and soon!" The officer's finger pointed right at his face almost touching the tip of his nose. Thinking about what he had just heard, he couldn't tell him what he knew without incriminating himself and probably his family. Not wanting to continue the conversation about his brother or what he was doing in the officer's house with his daughter, Jace did what he thought was the smart thing and agreed.

"Yes sir, I understand." Grunting at this answer, their dad 'helped' him out of his house and closed the door with a little extra muscle than normal. He stood on their porch for a minute and heard the exchange between Ally and her father. It certainly was not a pleasant one as the tone Ally was using was one he was very familiar with. For her not feeling well, she was still able to raise her voice to a pitch that Jace thought would hurt his own throat and he wasn't even ill. Taking several steps away from the house, the sound of a window sliding open from the second story caught his attention.

"HEY! Here is your toy back!" With a heave of her arm, his watch came flying through the air in his direction. Ducking out of the way, her throw was nowhere close to him. As the small watch flew over his head, he caught a fast glimpse as it smashed against the side of his truck. Looking back up at the window, his anger was building and he took a deep breath preparing himself to verbally fire back at her. Instead, all Jace could hear was inaudible words which

he assumed were curse words, and the sound of the window slamming shut. Picking up the pieces to his now broken watch, he rubbed the side of his truck to make sure no damage was done. Tossing the watch in the bed of his truck, he hopped in the cab and tried to focus his attention away from McKenzie's immature behavior.

Jace's mind was racing faster than the wheels on his truck were turning. Nothing was seeming to go his way. He needed to try and stop to clear his head. Instead of going home, he decided to take a drive. Finn lake was peaceful today and not a breath of wind disturbed the calm water. There was a spot that he and his family went to fish. An old dock that was put in the lake each year still hung over the surface of the water. Parking his truck, he strolled down by the water contemplating if he should just leave town again. His return clearly was not adjusting well with anyone around him. Looking down into the clear seaweed filled water, Jace could see all different types of fish. Their sizes were as varied as their colors. How come all these fish can get along and live in the same place and he couldn't seem to do that with people he loved? Sitting down on the old rusted metal dock, he kicked the water with his shoe making the fish scatter in all directions. "That's more like life." Jace said to himself.

Pulling up next to his truck was a white car that he did not recognize. It was very small and sounded like it had had better days! If his foot hadn't scared off the fish, he was quite sure this old contraption would have. A man and woman stepped out of the car holding fishing gear. The bearded man opened the back door of the car and out popped a skinny little kid with a camouflage trucker hat on his little head. He hopped around kicking the stones with excitement that he was about to go fishing. It was funny how kids were so excited for the little things in life. Jace suddenly wished that he could be as excited and happy about anything as much as this kid was about fishing.

The family came down to the side of the water and the kid jumped on the metal dock making a loud noise. He continued to jump around making the dock move up and down with loud crashes until the man spoke to him. "Look here boy! How do you expect to catch any fish when you are scaring them all away!?" This guy had a small cooler that he had thrown over his shoulder. Reaching in, he inevitably pulled out a can of beer and cracked it open. The boy listened to the man who Jace presumed was his father by the way he spoke to him. Finally getting their hooks in the water, the little boy plopped next to the woman who looked to be trying to get some sun. This family unit was refreshing to see. No matter what problems they may have had in their lives, it all stopped when they went fishing together.

Deciding it was time to get home, Jace stood up and tried to step lightly down the dock to not scare the fish that they were trying to get.

"Jace?" The male voice directed towards him. Jace stopped in his tracks and turned cautiously to the voice that had just said his name.

"Do I know you?" Jace responded curiously. The man raised the brim of his hat revealing his face completely. Jace could not put a name to this face.

"You don't remember me, do you?" The man said with a smile.

"I can't recall your name, I'm sorry." Pretending that he recognized him, he didn't want to hurt the man's feelings.

"It's Will. I have been friends with your brother...well...it feels like forever now." He chuckled at this statement he made.

"This is my wife, Nicole." Pointing to the woman beside her, she looked back at him shading the sun with one hand and waving at Jace with the other.

"I remember you. You and Dane would always get drunk and try to wrestle each other down until you could pin the other or make them say you were the best." Will laughed at this flashback.

"I haven't thought about that in years! We did some stupid stuff when we were younger!" Looking down at his side, the little boy was tugging at his shirt.

"This is my little boy Garrett." Will rubbed the boys head almost knocking him off his feet.

"It's nice to meet you Garrett." Jace said kneeling so he was eye to eye with the little boy. He held out his hand for a handshake, but Garrett hid behind his father.

"It's okay ya goof." Will tried to step aside but the boy stepped with him.

"He is a little bashful sometimes." He whispered to Jace.

"Go keep fishing with your mother. You need to catch us dinner if you want to eat tonight boy." He steered his son in the direction of Nicole. The last thing she appeared to be doing was fishing. Her arms were out and she was strategically rotating them so each part of her skin would get equal sun.

"You have a very cute son." Jace complimented him.

"He is not really my son." Will leaned to whisper in his ear. "Garrett is Nicole's son. But I have been there since before he could walk. So, he is my boy now for sure!" He winked at Jace proudly.

"Good for you man! You have a great family." Will reached down to the ground to pick up his open can. Taking a big gulp of beer, he smacked his lips with satisfaction.

"Where are my manners? Would you like a cold one Jace?" Will held out his already open can and pointed to the cooler. I have five more on ice and another six pack in the car...Just in case I'm still thirsty." Will whispered this with a smile and a wink.

"No, I'm good...but thanks for offering." Jace appreciated his kind offer, but alcohol was the last thing on his mind right now.

"You are looking very well Jace. The last time we saw you was at the bonfire party your brother threw." A look of surprise engulfed Jace's face.

"You were at that party?" For some reason these words sounded excited.

"Yea, just me and Nicole though. Little man doesn't drink yet if ya know what I mean?" He said nudging Jace's arm and laughing.

"It was a great party. Good drinks and I even won some money playing cards that night! All in all, a good time." Nodding his head, he made it sound better than Jace remembered it.

"I do remember you guys getting a little wasted yourselves

and you and your brother getting into a little tussle!" This confirmed that he was there and knew what he was talking about.

"Yea, just a misunderstanding. You know how siblings can be sometimes."

"Oh hell yea! I've got six siblings of my own. Four brothers and two sisters! They can be a pain in the ass sometimes, but I love em' no matter what." Raising his beer in the air after making his point, he sipped once again.

"Will, I brought some snacks for you." Nicole tossed a bag of shelled peanuts onto the empty chair that he had been sitting in.

"Okay babe. Thanks." He looked back at Jace.

"Would you like to join us? We are just doing some fishing and catching a little buzz. She brought snacks if you are hungry?"

"Thank you very much for the kind offer, but I have got to get going. Maybe next time?" Patting Will on the shoulder, Jace waved at Nicole and Garrett and said his goodbyes.

"I am glad to see you are feeling better and I hope to see you around." Jace stopped walking towards his truck and turned back around.

"Feeling better?" Jace asked.

"What was wrong with me exactly?" His curiosity was spiked.

"Well, you were in the accident." Will's obvious tone was surprising to Jace.

"You knew about my accident? How did you find out?" Stepping down to where Will was next to the water, his jovial tune turned serious.

"I was there, don't you remember?" Will was beginning to look confused himself.

"You were there? How is that possible? I crashed right outside of town. Did you hear about it from someone? I am sure rumors have gone around because I was driving my father's Camaro." Nicole stood up and made her way over to the boys.

"I am not sure what you are talking about, but I had no idea you crashed your father's *CAR*." She said surprised.

"Neither did I!" Will chimed in. Garrett was still sitting in his small camp chair sipping on a juice box. Animal crackers had fallen on the ground next to his feet that he was kicking around playfully.

"I am not sure what accident you are talking about Jace. We were there when you crashed your dad's truck into the ditch." A stunned look came to Jace's face.

"What the Hell are you talking about?"

"The night of the party, you and your brother got into the fight and he sped off after we tried to stop him because he had been drinking. You were drinking very heavily as well and decided to take the keys to your dad's truck and chase him down." Nicole's explanation of what happened did not ring a bell to him whatsoever.

"You are saying that I was wasted, took his truck, and tried to run down my brother who was also wasted?" His eyes could not have been wider.

"I'm not sure what your intentions were. But Ally was bringing you into the house to lay you down as you were confessing that you still loved her..." The thought of him doing this while he was drunk made him feel smaller than

~ 226 ~

he ever had before.

"...and she got you into bed and came back out to the fire. Next thing we knew, you were running out the door with keys in your hand. You got into your dad's truck and peeled away. So, I assumed you were going after him." What Nicole was telling him made his jaw drop open. He was having a difficult time processing what he had just heard. Nothing was making any sense. Was this true what she had said?

"So, you are saying that I took off after him and no one tried to stop me?"

"YES! We all ran towards the truck, but you were gone so fast that we couldn't get to you. Your dad came running out of the house as well and he asked us if we knew where you were going. Ally told him about the fight you and your brother had and he went after you guys in a car." Shaking his head, now things were starting to make sense. That is how his mother knew that he had gotten into a fight and been punched that morning when she told him that 'mothers know everything.' Jace grabbed Will's arm getting closer to him than he normally would have.

"How do you know I crashed the truck? Are you just guessing that is what happened?" The couple looked at each other for a moment and then focused their attention back to Jace.

"No, we are not just guessing. Your father brought you back home that night and you were laying in the back seat of the car looking to be passed out. He told us that everything was alright and that you ended up in a ditch. That is all we know." Nicole nodded to confirm what Will just told him.

"We didn't ask any questions beyond that. It was not our place. You don't remember any of this?" The way he was responding to this news made Nicole feel uncomfortable like she had just pulled the pin of a grenade and was awaiting the explosion.

"No, I don't remember any of this! Do you guys know where Dane is?" His question was bold and forceful. These two appeared to have lots of information and Jace wanted to drain them of it so he could learn what was going on himself.

"I would assume he is either at Macie's apartment or at your parent's house."

"Would you stop assuming things!" Jace snapped at Will. "Whoa man, I am just telling you what I know." Instantly feeling bad, Jace apologized for snapping at them how he had.

"Is Dane missing or something? Why wouldn't he be at home?" The sincere question confirmed that Will did not know where Dane was or that he was even gone.

"Never mind. It was very nice to see you two again." Jace turned around and was about to go for his truck when his arm was caught.

"Wait Jace. What is going on? Can we help in any way?" Will had grabbed his arm and stopped him from moving any farther away.

"No, I thank you, but I am really okay. I have to go now." Grabbing Will's hand off his arm, he shook his hand and ran to his truck. He wanted to get home and talk to his mother about what he had just learned. Was she lying to him all along? Why would his parents keep this from him? He wanted answers and he wanted them now. The fear of driving that he had before quickly left his body and the gas pedal touched the floorboard. His truck wheels spun violently as he peeled away from the lake. Not sure at what he was going to say to his mom, he contemplated his words as the truck sped back towards his house.

The driveway entrance snuck up on Jace. Slamming on his brakes, the truck slid right by the driveway. The shriek of the wheels on the pavement made a loud uncomfortable noise. With the smell of burnt rubber surrounding his truck, he turned the wheel, he hit the gas hard and the truck did a tailspin until it was pointed in the right direction. There were cars next to the store but Jace could not even see them. He had tunnel vision. The house was in his sights and he wanted to get there as fast as possible. Parking his truck next to the garage, he tried to calm himself down, but he was having no success. The excited anger he was feeling was strange. It wasn't like him to yell at his parents, but he could feel inside that he was about to.

Pushing the front door open, lights were on in the living room and the kitchen. Jace called out for his mom and she quickly answered. Her voice sounded muzzled like she had her head in the refrigerator. Walking down the hallway, Jace couldn't help himself, he began his rant of planned questions before he even entered the room she was in.

"I had the most interesting conversation a few minutes ago. Would you like to tell me what happened to dad's truck...?"

Cutting off the end of his sentence, he entered the kitchen and to his surprise, realized she was not the only one there. At the kitchen table sat his father, officer Harper, and a younger looking man who was also a police officer. All three men were looking at him intently. They had gotten quiet waiting for him to finish his question.

"Go on Jace, tell me what you think happened to your dad's truck." The officer's cunning words struck fear through his bones. He glanced at his father whose eyes were piercing his. If he could communicate with him without having to speak, this would be the time he would do it. The movie "The Shinning" flashed through his mind and he wished he could 'shine' with his dad right now! Looking back at his mom, she was cleaning the countertop with a cloth and appeared disinterested in this conversation even though Jace was unsure how she couldn't be interested or at least be subtly listening to what they were saying.

"Well...I ugh..." Stammering like a child learning how to speak, he was waiting for someone to step in to save him. No one did.

Desperately trying to think of something to say, the last person he wanted to tell what he had heard was the police. Even though the officer was his dad's friend, he had just made a big scene with both of his daughters and Jace was quite sure that he wouldn't mind getting him into trouble. Plus, he didn't know the other officer, so he held no "get out of jail free" card with him either. Pushing out a chair, the officer invited him to sit at the table.

"It's alright, just take your time and let's hear what that *interesting conversation* was all about." Jace looked at the ground and then back at his father. Not knowing where to look next, Jace closed his eyes and wished he could morph back into bed to start this day all over again!

Chapter 17

Has it ever crossed your mind which would be worse? Saying something and wishing you hadn't, or, saying nothing and wishing you had. Jace sat there with his eyes clenched tightly shut, not knowing what to say or even where to begin. A female voice came from the officer's radio and he quickly lowered the volume. Tension sat on the air making it hard for Jace to breath.

"I have had a headache all day today. I haven't had a day where I have felt like my normal self since going to the hospital." He figured leaning on this excuse would prevent further questioning.

It didn't.

"Just take a moment and try to tell us what you know." The young officer asked politely.

"I think I need to rest. Could I possibly call you guys or stop by the station tomorrow maybe?"

"You do understand the severity of this situation, don't you?" Officer Harper's stern response made it clear they wanted answers now. Looking back at his father, then to the officers, they were both looking down clearly distracted by something on their cell phones. Officer Harper stood up and gave a subtle nod to his partner signaling to him that they needed to leave.

"We're not done here. There is a situation that needs our attention. We will be back. Thank you, Marie, for your kind hospitality." Setting the coffee cups down that they had been drinking from, both officers made their way down the hallway and out of the house. His father had still not said anything and the silence was deafening. Jace stood up and went to the front door to make sure both officers were gone. Their car was just pulling out of the end of the driveway.

"I can get you some medicine for your head if you need some Jace?" His mom was going to take care of him no matter what he had done or how badly he screwed up in life.

"It's fine Ma. I just didn't want to speak to the police until I had my story straight." His father had stood up from the table and grabbed a bottle of water out of the refrigerator.

"Can you both please tell me what is going on here? Where is Dane and did we have something to do with Farmer Johnson's death?" Frustration was building and Jace could feel himself ready to explode. He could feel the pulse of his heartbeat pushing on the back of his eyeballs. His parents looked at one another silently debating what they should tell him.

"Listen Jace, why don't you have a seat." His mother said pointing to the table he had just been sitting at with the officers.

"We have known where your brother is all along. He is completely safe and you don't need to worry about him..." His mother paused.

"Well, where is he? Why did he just disappear?"

"He didn't just disappear..." His father's deep voice finally chimed in.

"We found him on the side of the road in his truck the night of the party. He was at the site of the accident that killed the farmer."

"Robert...please..." His mother pleaded with her husband.

"He needs to hear this! We can't keep shielding him from the reality of the situation." Robert sounded angry as he responded to his wife's pleas. Taking another sip of water, he screwed the cap back on and sat across the table from Jace. His mother had sat at the counter on a small barstool that was hardly used.

"Are you saying that he killed the farmer?" Jace asked this carefully in an exaggerated whisper.

"No. DANE did not kill anybody." His dad's eyes glared into his own. Looking back at his mother who was now looking down, he met his father's eyes once again.

"I'm not sure what you are saying to me." Confusion filled his voice. The grandfather clock had just begun to ring, and it caught all their attentions as the beautiful sound filled the house.

"You don't remember that night at all?" Robert asked.

"I do remember a lot of it. We had a fight and he went storming off. I was upset with the whole situation, so I drank pretty much anything that was in front of me." The fatherly look he was getting followed by the disapproving head shake, gave Jace the feeling of shame that he hated so much.

"You don't remember stealing my truck keys and going after him?" Upon hearing this, Jace's eyes opened wide with amazement.

"That is what I was just told! I can't believe it's true!" His upbeat tone almost sounded happy that he was getting this news.

"Who told you?"

"I was at the pier on the lake and Dane's friend Will was fishing there. He recognized me and told me the exact same thing!" Jace answered his mother's question.

"Wait, so if Dane was at the scene of the accident and wasn't involved, why was he there?" A long pause from both his parents filled the room with silence once again. Jace swallowed hard as he literally felt a lump in his throat.

"He stopped there because he saw my truck smashed up. It was very late and dark that night. He stopped to see what had happened around the same time I got there."

"You were at the scene of the accident too?" Jace asked surprised even though he recalled the story he had just been told at the lake.

"Yes, I was there. I was trying to catch up to you when I saw that you had crashed my truck. You were passed out in the front seat and the farmer and his son were lying by the side of the road." These haunting words sent a shiver through Jace's body.

"There is no way that can be true!" Panic suddenly filled his thoughts.

"You are saying I killed someone?" His question was not answered by either of them. A long tense-filled silence scared Jace.

"TELL ME!" Jace shouted.

"Take it easy. You need to stay calm."

"You are lying!" Jace yelled at his father. A sudden grin came to Robert's face.

"Boy, you really have no clue about anything in life, do you?"

"Dane did it, didn't he? That is why he is hiding... God only knows where!"

"I sent your brother to a safe place until this blows over. You already know that he has been in trouble with the law before and I felt we couldn't risk getting another strike against him."

"If he did nothing wrong, then why would he get another strike?" Jace's question made a lot of sense.

"When he stopped at the crash, he went to check on the farmer and his son. His footprints and fingerprints were all over the eventual crime scene. I pulled you out of my truck and took you back home as fast as I could. Dane helped me get my truck out of the accident and back home. He ditched his truck in a field that you unfortunately found." This whole story was hitting Jace like a tidal wave. He couldn't even find the words to formulate a sentence.

"A parent's number one job is to protect your kids and we felt like that is what we had to do." His mom held back tears as she said this in a shaky voice.

"It's not as if we had this all planned out. It's the situation that fell into our laps and we did what we thought was best for our family. A split-second decision was made to save you." His mom justification only made sense from the perspective of the family.

"So, you are telling me that I killed someone?" After a long moment of tense silence, Jace's question was answered by a small nod from his mother confirming that was in fact the truth. Sitting back in his chair, he could not digest what he had done. The magnitude of the situation was too high for him to fully comprehend.

"You are saying the police are looking for me? I murdered someone and I can't remember doing it?" A quick thought flew through his mind. Would his parents be lying to him? Would they be trying to get him to accept blame for something that happened so *they* didn't get caught? Jace couldn't wrap his mind around the fact that this could be true and he couldn't remember doing it.

"The police have suspicions. We are trying to lead them off the trail, but we are not having much success. They brought me in to question me but had no evidence to keep me detained." His father said.

"Everything will be alright. You just can't go around trying to figure everything out. You are going to blow the cover that we are desperately trying to keep."

"I can't believe what I am hearing! Does anybody else know about this?"

"Your sisters know. We needed their help and no matter what you think of Jen, they CAN be trusted." Marie was trying to instill whatever little confidence she had left to her son.

"What about that strange tunnel in the back woods? I went down it and there is something living down there!" Desperately grasping at straws, Jace changed the subject faster than a blink of an eye.

"Wait...what?" His father's genuine confusion surprised him.

"What are you talking about Jace?"

"Dane and I found a door in the woods and I opened it and

went down the tunnel. I heard noises coming from what I can only guess is some kind of a hidden room or bunker."

"Are you sure you are feeling okay sweetie?"

"YES! I'm fine Mom! I heard it for myself! It sounded like banging on the other side of the door."

"I told you that I believe there is an old wine cellar back there." His mom said.

"Then why was there something living down there?" His father looked uneasy with Jace's building frustration.

"I think you are letting your mind run away with you. We haven't even been down there since we bought this house."

"Mom I'm not mistaken. I know what I heard!"

"Alright that is enough. I can't take any more problems from you Jace! Don't you see what a mess you have put this whole family in? A man lost his life and we could lose you too and a lot more because of your poor choices!" His father had finally snapped.

"Now I don't want to hear another word about your fantasies about strange tunnels and noises from wherever!"

"Where is Dane? Tell me now! I need to talk to him." He clearly was not going to get anywhere with his father. How much could he expect his parents to endure before frustration and anger consumed them both?

"You don't need to worry about that."

"Please. I really need to speak with my brother." Trying a new 'nice' approach did not work either.

"No Jace. You will see him when the time is right."

Standing up from the table, his father finished the

conversation and walked out of the room.

Jace looked at his mom who still looked saddened by this whole conversation.

Who could blame her?

Pausing for a moment, Jace sat with a blank stare as if his thoughts were so deep, he couldn't even see what was right in front of him. Jumping up from the table, he ran towards the door.

"Where are you going Jace?" His mother stood as well.

"Macie" He replied.

"No wait…" His mother's words were lost in the distance as he bolted out the door and into his truck. He was sure that his best shot may be with Dane's girlfriend. Tearing out of the driveway, the sun had begun to set and the air was once again cool. A shiver ran up his spine as he reached for the temperature knob on his dashboard and turned it all the way up. His engine roared as he ordered more speed from the gas pedal. He was not sure if he would find Macie in her apartment or if she was at work. He remembered that Dane had said she worked all the time and wished that they could spend more time together. A flashback of Dane kicking down her door made him chuckle at his stupidity. This was the first time in a while he could remember laughing about anything! Before he knew it, he was standing outside her apartment complex. Unsure of what he was going to say, he was hoping she would be more willing to share information with him then his family was. Jace wasn't positive, but he saw a car that resembled that of Macie's and a confident feeling that she was home washed over him. Several knocks later, her door sung open.

"Jace! What a surprise." She said in a surprised tone.

"Hi Macie. Can I talk to you for a few minutes?" She was barefoot and wearing pajamas with little ducks on them. Her shirt matched the color of the ducks.

"Yea, come on in." Her welcoming tone was odd to Jace. How could she be so chipper if she thought her boyfriend was missing?

She must know where he is!

"Thank you, Macie. I see you even match your shirt and pajamas huh?" Sounding impressed, he wanted to compliment her to warm her up for some questioning.

"No. Just a happy coincidence I guess." She smiled at him. "Come and sit. Would you like something to drink? I have beer, water and I believe some wine." Declining her hospitality, she pulled her refrigerator door open and only pulled out one bottle of water for herself. Plopping on the couch, she was clearly still comfortable with him even though she had only seen him twice in the last few years.

"So, what's up Jace?" She said happily reaching for the remote control. Pointing it at the television, she pushed the buttons hard as her desired outcome was clearly not being met. Holding the remote in one hand, she banged it on her other hand.

"Damn stupid thing." She mumbled under her breath. Trying once more, again she was unsuccessful. She tossed the remote to the other end of the couch and stood up to manually turn the television down from its side.

"I just changed those damn batteries too! Something must need to be fixed." She let out an exaggerated sigh as she fell back down on the couch.

"I'm not sure about how much you know, but, I really want to know where Dane is. I know that you probably know. I won't tell anybody that you told me where he is." Looking over at him with her lips attached to the opening of her water bottle, she slowly brought the bottle back down and the water inside slushed to the bottom again. Pulling it away from her lips, she wiped her chin with the neck of her shirt.

"You think I know where your brother is?"

"Don't do that. Don't respond to my question with a question. By you deflecting like that shows me that you do know something!" Macie smiled from the corner of her mouth.

"Even if I did know, what incentive do I have to tell you?" She felt as though she was being attacked and she wanted to fight back.

"We both love him, right? I need his help with some trouble that I'm in."

"I'm not sure if you know this or not, but Dane is not exactly the right person to lean on when you are in trouble. Especially considering that is where he spends most of his life. In trouble with something or somebody." Jace stood up slowly and sat next to her. Grabbing her hand with his, he looked deep into her eyes. She had some of the most beautiful eyes he had ever seen. They were the perfect size, color, and even had a glassy twinkle to them.

"I need my brother. I know everyone else in this world thinks I am crazy...even my parents. Dane knows me the best and will believe me, no matter what. Feeling a surprising shock of sympathy for Jace, she squeezed his hand and hugged him.

"I don't work until the afternoon tomorrow. Come back in the morning around 9:30 and I will take you to him."

He had a mixture of feelings about what he was just told. He had broken through finally and gotten somebody to agree to tell him where he was. The problem was he didn't want to wait until the morning. He felt very anxious and wanted to go now!

"That sounds good. Thank you, Macie..." Even though he wasn't sure how he was going to make it through the night, he did not want to be pushy and cause her to change her mind. She placed a gentle kiss on his cheek and squeezed his hand one last time before letting go.

"Try not to worry. Everything will be just fine." Good lord was he sick of people telling him not to worry. It always made him feel that he had no control over his own life and that he would just have to depend on others for his own outcomes.

"I'll try not to." He responded with a smile. Walking to her front door with him, he thanked her once again for helping him and wished her a good night. Walking away from her apartment, the sky was filled with bright stars that lit up the darkness. It was a gorgeous night.

Sitting in his truck, he did not leave the apartment complex. He watched as cars would roll by at many different speeds. He assumed that the slow cars were driven by older people who could barely see over the steering wheel. And the fast cars were driven by irresponsible kids who were just begging to get a speeding ticket. Taking a minute to just sit there and relax in the silence felt strangely good. He had nothing in particular to feel good about but watching other people's busy lives drive by as he sat there still gave him a brief sense of calm. It did not last long as a police car drove by and Jace immediately tensed up. Was this what his life was going to be like now? Was he a criminal? Constantly looking over his shoulder and trying to run from the law to keep his freedom. Was he now an outlaw...a fugitive...a public enemy? Shaking his head at these thoughts, the police car drove right on by causing Jace to feel stupid for letting his thoughts scare him like that.

Once home, Jace knew he was not going to be able to sleep. The house was quiet and he successfully made it to his room without causing a stir. With his head on the pillow, his eyes could not have been more awake. Thinking about trying to count sheep just sounded like an irritating waste of time. He couldn't figure out why his body was treating him like he had just drank twelve cups of coffee! Whipping his sheets off the bed, Jace lay there feeling warm and agitated. Flicking through television stations was not helping either. Jace tried to find a show about animals again but was having no luck. Closing his eyes tightly for several minutes, they finally shot open as a thought entered his mind.

The shelving unit in the basement!

The bookcase-looking wood shelving in the basement from his dream. He had forgotten about it! He was so busy with the hole and trying to find out what was in it that he had forgotten about that part of his dream. That was the one part of the dream that he did not quite understand. What was the meaning of it and why was it shown to him? Maybe in meant nothing, but, at this point, Jace was willing to investigate anything that was presented to him. Poking his head ever so slightly out of his bedroom door, the faint sounds of snoring filled the bedrooms. Grabbing his phone and turning on the light, he made it down the steps and away from the people he did not want to wake. The basement door was situated off of the kitchen. It was a solid metal door which was different from the other doors that had been replaced periodically throughout the house. Making his way into the stairwell, he closed the basement door behind him and flicked the switch for the basement lights. The lights always had a buzzing sound to them like you would hear in an old scary movie. The rickety handrail that led to the basement was kind of pointless. If you applied any amount of pressure on it, the rail would bend and presumably break if the pressure did not stop. Frantically wiping his face, Jace had walked into cobwebs which were abundant in this basement. He hated spiders with a passion. Not completely sure why, they just grossed him out and he even had trouble killing them. People would ask him why he was so afraid…he never had a good response. It was just one of those things that he could not explain. Luckily, he wasn't the only person in his family that was afraid of them. Both sisters and his mom didn't care for them either.

"They are more afraid of you than you are of them. They are more afraid of you than you are of them." Walking through the basement, he kept repeating this to himself even though he did not believe it whatsoever. How could they be more afraid than he was when he couldn't even look at them without beginning to panic? Jace moved slowly through the low ceiling basement. He kept the light of his phone on to reach the dark parts of the cellar that the big lights did not touch. Sidestepping several cardboard boxes that sat on a wooden skid in the middle of the floor, his curiosity got the best of him. Kneeling, Jace pulled the flap on one of the boxes revealing bottles full of what he assumed to be wine. This was not where his dad kept wine normally. He didn't want to put any more on his plate then he already had so ignoring the oddity of the wine was his best option.

Being by himself meant that he could be scared and didn't have to act tough and brave in front of anyone. He was, in fact, nervous as he thought every dark corner of the basement had eyes watching him. The freezer's motor kicked on and made a soft humming sound. The old sump pump that resided in the large pit at the lowest point of the basement appeared to be in rough shape. It was still working though as he could see stale water at the bottom of the pit. Having the lake right next to their property gave them an amazing view and great soil for the grapes, but it also gave them something else that was less desirable...a flooding basement. When he was younger, Jace and his father had put in a second pump on the opposite side of the basement. This ensured that if one stopped working, the other could pick up the slack so there wasn't knee high water collecting down there. It even got so bad that

Robert had hooked a generator outside the house to connect it to the pumps so if they lost power, the basement would stay dry.

A loud bang prompted Jace to whip his phone around pointing his light to see the cause of the disturbance. With another click, he heard the blower from the furnace kick on. Taking a deep breath, he tried to shake off all these noises and webs. The old shelving unit stood weakly in the back of the room. It looked different than he had remembered in his dream. Stepping up to it, the wood had a smell of rot to it. The shelves appeared so weak that they would come apart just by pulling on them. Trying to be as careful as he could to not make any noise, he grabbed the shelf in front of his face and pulled gently. The wood was rough on his hands. If he were to rub it, chances are he would have gotten several splinters. The structure didn't budge at all. Looking at the floor, nothing appeared to be awry with the dirt pattern like he recalled. Maybe he was being crazy. This old thing was nothing but junk. Moving the light up and down from shelf to shelf revealed nothing but empty shelves and more webs. Feeling discouraged, Jace was about to give up when his light revealed something shiny that caught his eye. Moving closer, there was a metal band around the outside of the bookcase shelves. It looked new and was clearly holding the wood together. Grabbing the band, he yanked it away from the wall. The top portion flexed out but the bottom stayed in place. The unit was attached to the wall somehow. When it was pulled away, a portion of the wall came with it. Kicking at the dirt trying to create space for it to move, he tried again. With a big pop, the shelving unit jolted forward revealing it to be a door! A hidden door that was not meant to be found. The space between was very small as he couldn't open it very much. Excitement filled Jace as he had found something! Nervous that he had made noise, he paused for a moment to listen to the silence in the air. If anybody was moving around the house, the squeaky wood floors would alert him of it. Chuckling, Jace thought to himself that this was the first time that the noisy floors were helping him instead of trying to get him caught. Satisfied that the house was quiet, Jace stuck his arm all the way in the hole that was behind the shelving unit. His head followed as the cell phone in his hand was not providing enough light to see much further than his eyes could. Retracting his body, he decided he had to try to squeeze his whole body into the opening to get a better look. Turning sideways, his left leg went in first. Then the top half of his body followed. With one last pull, the right leg was in as well. Dusting himself off, everything had gone dark as his phone's light had gone off. Pushing the buttons, Jace frantically tried to get it to come back on. His breathing was accelerated. The small phone appeared to be freezing up. Finally, after a few seconds had passed, the light reluctantly came back on.

He was standing in a passage way that had dirt walls. Every couple of feet that he moved, there were wooden poles on each side of him clearly put in place to help keep the structural integrity of the passage way. The air was very thick. Jace shined his light from side to side as he moved forward slowly. What was this used for? Harriet

Tubman and the underground railroad floated through his mind. This would have been an ideal place to hide people from the outside world. A pile of rubble and dirt sat on one side of the tunnel. A piece of the wall had fallen off. Realizing the situation Jace had put himself in, he suddenly felt nervous. If these walls were to cave in, chances are nobody would be able to find him in time. He couldn't give up now though. He had to keep going.

"Is this ever going to end?" Jace muttered to himself. He had been walking very slowly for a while now and his nerves were causing exhaustion. Between the short half steps that he was taking and his stopping to look around every couple of steps, this made the tunnel seem much longer than it probably was. Stopping for a minute, he turned off the light on his phone. The small device was getting very hot from constant use and he wanted to give it a break. Being that he was dependent on this phone's light, he could not afford to have it quit working on him now! Jace had gone so far that he couldn't possibly still be under the house. This long tunnel had to lead out under the fields. It couldn't go towards the lake as he would have hit water by now. A quick squeak caught his ear. It sounded like the noise a small critter would make. Fumbling to turn the light back on, he searched around him to see if he had company. Not finding anything, he decided to proceed. His phone was searching for service. This made it clear to him that he was in fact all alone and he could not even reach out to anybody if something were to go wrong. Walking a straight line next to the wall, Jace came upon a metal pipe sticking out of the wall. The end was open and there was nothing in it and nothing coming out of it. Not sure what the purpose of this pipe was, he began to think about who had dug this tunnel. How long ago was it built and for what purpose? A big puddle lay before him that the light just caught before he stepped in the water. Jace could see the other side and decided to jump. Landing on one knee, his pants soaked in the wet muddy dirt that made up the floor. Getting to his feet, he looked up to see a wall before him. This appeared to be where the passageway stopped. The wall was different than the rest of the tunnel. It was made from grey cement and looked to be much sturdier. A door nestled in the wall was made from the same material. It had a small dark window that sat about eye level to Jace. The handle to the door was very small and accompanied by a large lock. Hoping that this was not the end of his exploration, Jace pulled on the door to see if on the off chance it may have been unlocked.

It wasn't.

Peering through the window, he could not see anything through the tiny glass. Even flashing his light did not help the darkness that was on the other side of the door. Taking a step back, he looked around to make sure that he was not missing anything. This was exactly like what he had found in the back woods. Was it the same thing only with two entrances? His swirling thoughts were not helping him make sense of things. Not finding anything else helpful to him, he held his light up to the window one last time before turning back. Suddenly, a pair of dark brown eyes came into his light from the other side of the door. Jace jumped back from fright letting his phone slip out of his hand and splash into the big puddle. Frantically moving the water around, he found his phone. The light had gone off and so did the phone. Pushing the 'on' but several times, it was unresponsive. Quickly getting back to the door, he pressed his eyes against the glass to try and see the eyes that were looking back at him. Without the light, he could not see anything at all. Frustrated with himself, he pounded on the door and screamed to the eyes on the other side. He heard nothing in return. He could not see if the person was trying to communicate with him and did not hear anything either. Stunned, Jace dropped to his knees.

Who was in there?

He needed to find out! No choice but to walk back in the pitch-black darkness, he put his hand on the wall and used it to guide him out of the tunnel. He must have been moving quicker than he had been before because he reached the basement faster than he expected to. At this point, his hands were dirty, pants were soaked with mud, and his shirt had a hole tore in it from getting caught on the shelving unit when he squeezed through it the first time. Once he was back in the basement, he was pleased to find that there was no sign of life anywhere and that he had not been discovered by his family. Pushing the hidden door closed, he tried the best he could to fix it to look like it had not been tampered with. Jace even moved the dirt around with his hands to eliminate any footprints he may have left behind.

Getting to his room was proving to be more

difficult than what he had just gone through! Jace stood at the top of the basement stairs. Again, he made sure everything was silent.

It was.

Grabbing a paper towel off the counter, he opened the fridge looking to get a drink. He did not want to touch anything with his muddy hands. He figured that if he was going to get caught, he could use the excuse that he was thirsty and came down for a drink. He wasn't sure how to explain the dirt, but he was looking at one problem at a time. His orange soda waited for him on the middle shelf. Snatching the bottle, he closed the refrigerator softly and made his way to the top of the stairs. He could still hear snoring which was a good sign. Almost to his bedroom door, Jace froze in place. The door to Jen's room opened and his sister stepped out yawning. She was clearly still half asleep as she stumbled towards him.

"Hey." She said in a groggy voice.

"Hey." Jace responded back. She stepped into the bathroom and shut the door behind her not noticing or even caring one bit that Jace was standing in the middle of the hall completely dirty. Breathing a deep sigh of relief, Jace entered his bedroom. Slowly shutting his door, he stripped off his clothes and got back into bed. He needed to figure out who was down there, and he was determined to find out as soon as possible! Strangely, he was finally feeling tired. His escapade underground really seemed to wear him out. His brain was mentally tired too as his head was starting to ache with soreness. Not even ten minutes later, he was asleep.

Chapter 18

As Eleanor Roosevelt once said, "With the new day comes new strength and new thoughts." This was half true for Jace. Waking up feeling rejuvenated was a wonderful way to start the day. His thoughts on the other hand had not changed one bit. The eyes that he saw on the other side of the door were the first thing that entered his mind that morning. The prospect of finding his brother was the next. He knew that Dane could help him figure everything out. Grabbing for his cell phone, it once again did not turn on. The water must have gotten inside of it and damaged it for good now. Just what he needed, to lose his way of contacting people. He had heard a rumor that if your phone gets wet, put it in a bowl of rice and it should be fixed. Not having the time to go find rice, Jace tossed the phone on his nightstand vowing to deal with it later. Pulling on new pants and a faded blue shirt, he couldn't wait to get to Macie's place. Brushing his teeth, he heard a loud knocking followed by familiar voices downstairs. Looking out his bedroom window, a police car sat in the driveway surely waiting for him. Spitting toothpaste out back into the sink, Jace set the toothbrush back gently trying not to make any extra noise. He could not go down and talk to them now! He had too much else on his mind. Quickly trying to come up with a plan, he needed to get out of the house without being seen. His bedroom windows were a straight drop down from the second floor to the ground. His sister's room was situated above the porch where he could drop down onto the overhanging roof.

That is what he did.

Escaping through her window out to the roof, Jace made sure nobody could see him and jumped off aiming for the bushes next to the house. Landing in them, he took a piece of wood to the side and scratches up and down his arms. Pulling the small stick out of his skin as fast as he could, his lips tightened with pain. Regretting his decision instantly to land in the bushes, Jace pressed his hand hard against the spot that was wounded. It was not bleeding as bad as he anticipated it would. The pressure must have helped. Looking around, a sense of relief came over him that nobody had seen or heard him. Once he started his truck, he knew that would alert them of his presence. This meant he would have to move quickly. As Jace carefully opened the door and slid up into the driver's seat, a better idea came to his mind. Being that the front end of the truck was already pointing in the direction of the road, Jace popped it in neutral and pushed with one leg half out the door until he was far enough away from the house. Knowing the inherent risk of this, he had no other choice. Looking back at his house, he was in the clear. Turning the small key, the engine growled to a start and he took off. A shot of pain in his left arm made Jace grimace as he peered down. He was bleeding. Touching the outside of his arm, the blood was coming from the deep scratches. The bush that he fell into must have cut his arms worse than he had originally thought. Wiping the blood with his other hand, he flexed the muscles in his arm to see if any more blood was going to drain out. The pain was strange because it was certainly a cut from the branches, yet it felt like he had been dragged across a carpet and got a rug burn.

Pulling into the apartment complex, a beat-up old car pulled out from its parking space right in front of him. Slamming on his brakes, he didn't blow his horn in fear that it may be someone Macie knew and he didn't want to cause a scene. With his heart racing, he came very close to signaling something to her out of anger. Instead, he smiled at the driver of the car who had almost backed her car into the front of his truck. She responded to his kind gesture by throwing him the finger. She was an older woman who looked like she hadn't taken a shower in months. A cigarette dangled from her lips as she was shouting something at Jace. Her arms were flying around uncontrollably as she apparently thought Jace had been in the wrong. Waiting for her performance to be over, she hit the gas and flew by him. His smile grew as the only thing he could do is shake his head.

"Some people really live their lives like a Jerry Springer episode." He mumbled to himself. Not knowing if there were assigned parking spaces, Jace found it perfectly justified to take the angry woman's spot so that if she was to come back, she would need to park further away. Walking up the steps to get to her apartment door appeared to be an adventure as well! A medium sized dog was stretched to the end of its leash. Unfortunately, the dog was able to reach both sides of the stairwell and was barking ferociously. Staying motionless in one spot, he was still safe standing about two arm lengths away from the wild k9. His shirt had soaked up much of the blood and he wondered if the dog was smelling it. The dog's behavior showed that he may like the smell of blood. Perched at the top of the stairs stood Macie with a big grin on her face. "Well? Come on tough guy, come on up here." The dog paused barking for a moment to look back at the voice he had just heard. It didn't last long as the dog turned back and once again began to bark at him.

"Whose dog is this and why is his leash so long? What is the point of a leash that can reach the whole walkway?" Irritable sarcasm filled his tone.

"Just come on up. Fluffy is fine. He won't hurt you…at least I think he won't." Winking at Jace, she turned around and went back into her apartment.

"Ugh, are you kidding me!" Jace mumbled inching closer to the dog. Holding his hand out, the dog sniffed his hand cautiously. Jace was ready to retract it fast if the dog were to have other ideas.

"Just let me by boy. You're a good dog." Jace said patting his head and sliding by him. The dog followed him up the stairs sniffing his shoes like a police dog that was looking for hidden drugs. Macie had left her door open for him. Feeling a little uncomfortable, Jace stood by the door waiting for her to appear. She was not in the kitchen or living room, both which could be seen from the front door. Stepping out from the hallway, a toothbrush sat in her mouth as she was using both her hands to fumble with her hair.

"So Jace…" As she began to speak, she took a big gasp to catch the toothpaste that was coming out of her mouth. Her hands flew down to catch any dribbles that might have come out. Her hair which she had been trying to put up flopped down as well. She stuck her pointer finger up at Jace indicating for him to hold on a minute and she ran back into the bathroom. A moment later, she was back out with her arms in her hair again. This time, no toothbrush. "Sorry about that. So, you want to go see your brother huh?" Her jovial tone confused Jace a bit. Didn't she realize the severity of the situation he was in? How could she if she didn't know everything. At this point though, Jace wasn't sure who knew what or how much they knew. Deciding not to say anything, Jace just smiled and nodded at her.

"Well, let's get going then. Would you like something to eat? I think I have granola bars."

"No thank you. I appreciate the offer though." Jace in fact was hungry but he did not want to be slowed down any more, so his stomach was going to have to take a back seat to everything else. Jace was purposely hiding his arm that was all scratched up. She didn't notice the blood on his shirt either as the brown color hid the blood well. Boy was he glad he'd worn this color shirt!

"Alright, let's go then." Snagging her purse and flipping the light switch, they both made their way out. The dog was now laying down. His head lifted as they stepped out and his ears were pointed straight up at attention. Jace was relieved that the dog did not move this time as he went down the stairs unbothered.

"Do you want to take my truck?"

"No, we will take my car. Come on, hop in." She walked to the driver's side and motioned for him to follow her. Before he got in, he could see her scrambling around through the window. Once he opened the door, he could see what she was doing. Her car was a complete mess. She was grabbing handful after handful of papers, and shoes, and old coffee cups, and makeup. It appeared like she could have lived out of her car no problem.

"Sorry about the mess. Working at the hospital, I have odd hours and always seem to be on the go."

"No need to apologize. I am sure you see the way Dane kept his truck. He was always messy and had no excuse for it...just laziness." He smiled at her and sat down on a semi-clean seat. She began to tug at something that was wrapped around the shifter.

"Do you need me to help? What is that?" Jace inquired.

"It's my damn phone cord. It is so long and always gets caught up in everything." Stating this like a fact, Jace tried to help her pull it off the shifter but no luck. Finally, she was able to get it to break free. Letting out a big moan of frustration, she tossed the charger in the back seat and started the car.

This girl is a hot mess! Jace thought to himself not daring to say anything like that to her. Once the car was in gear, they took off like a rocket. This woman definitely had a heavy foot! The small engine in the car whined as Jace was positive the corner they had just taken was on two wheels. Grabbing for the handle above his head, Macie laughed at him and smacked his stomach. Jace groaned loudly cradling his stomach looking like she had shot him with a bullet. Macie had playfully hit the spot that had the piece of wood cut through his skin. It was still very tender and Jace was not expecting to have to protect it.

"Come on! I'm not that bad of a driver. You are being dramatic just like your brother."

'Just like my brother' Those words bounced around Jace's mind for several minutes after she said them.

"That is funny. Most people who know both of us well would say that we are night and day." Jace replied strangely happy that she had compared him to his brother. They were heading out of town and towards the north end of the lake. The lake itself had a very funny layout. One side of the lake had small to medium sized homes. This was the "working class" side of the lake as people would say. The other side had the large homes that were clearly owned by wealthy individuals. Jace always thought that it would be nice to own ANY home on the beautiful water regardless of which side it was on.

The air was damp this morning and the cloud cover which was rolling in quickly looked threatening. These were not white fluffy clouds that you see in the movies where happy people sit under them and try to figure out what animal each cloud looks like. They were much darker, the kind you would see in a horror film right before Michael Meyers jumps out with a knife and kills someone. Movies always had the perfect weather that was needed for any occasion.

Not realistic whatsoever.

"How far are we going? We are going to get rained on soon." Masking the question he wanted answered the most with a statement about the weather, he couldn't help his curiosity was bubbling over.

"It's not too far, we will be there in ten minutes. I don't mind getting wet. Do you?" She said with a gentle smile on her face.

"Nope." Jace replied looking back out his window. About five minutes later, drops of water began to splash their windshield. Raindrops plopped into the lake splashing up like little cannon balls. This part of the lake was an area that Jace had never spent much time. It was a little further away from any restaurants or arcades. The car began to slow down as they came upon a line of large Arborvitae trees. They were clearly planted in a straight line and were perfect for privacy as you could not see through them. A small break in the trees revealed a dirt driveway. A puddle was beginning to form at the end of the driveway as the rain was coming down harder now. The car began to turn indicating that they had reached their destination...or at least that was Jace's hope. Each pothole the tires sunk into caused the car to jerk hard. Water splashed up from the tires. Macie flipped the windshield wipers to their highest speed. Slapping frantically back and forth, they were having trouble keeping up with the rain. Trees lined both sides of the dirt road. Several of their limbs hung low enough that the car brushed them as it drove by.

"You don't happen to have an umbrella in here somewhere do you?" Jace asked.

"Maybe somewhere in the back. Go ahead and look. She

responded to Jace without taking her eyes off the road. Between the potholes and rain, she was fighting to keep the car moving.

"This driveway never used to be this bad. It needs some repairs!" She said frustrated after another pothole slammed her car. Unbuckling his seatbelt, Jace fumbled around pushing lots of her things in the back seat from side to side. So many of her clothes were back there, it was hard to see what was on the floor. Another bump sent Jace off balance and his elbow flew into the side of Macie's head. Collecting himself, he apologized to her as she rubbed the spot of impact.

A sharp pain from the twisting rose through his side. "Looks like we are just going to get wet." Jace said plopping himself back into his seat. He could have looked more but the discomfort he was feeling was not worth it.

Coming to the end of the dirt path, they finally hit pavement. The lines of trees ended as the car slowed to a stop. Moving his face closer to the window, Jace's eyelids squinted as he desperately tried to see where they were. The rain was making that impossible.

"Let's run. Follow me up to the house." Macie said. Before Jace could protest running through the rain, her door swung open and she was out. Pulling his door handle, Jace was right behind her. Fierce rain drops pelted his face as gusts of winds blew through the trees angerly. A loud clap of thunder rang through the sky. Macie had disappeared into the rain. Having no other choice, Jace followed the direction that she went. Coming to a tall structure, Macie's figure reappeared under the protection of overhanging awning eaves. Running up to her, he pressed his back up against the brick wall to get himself out of the rain as well. "I thought I lost you there." Macie said with a smirk. Jace was breathing hard after his short burst of running. Water was dripping down off his bangs and onto his face but he didn't care. They were both soaked.

"Where are we? Can we get inside out of the rain?"

"We are out of the rain." Macie replied sarcastically raising her hands above her head to indicate no falling water.

"You know what I mean." He said ringing out the bottom of his shirt. Pale red water was coming from his shirt as the rain must have been washing some of his blood remanence off. Standing still for another minute, it appeared Macie was trying to wait for the rain to die down.

No such luck.

Mother nature appeared to be angry about something today and her wrath was not letting up. Grabbing his hand, she was off again. Turning a sharp corner at the end of the brick wall, a beautiful house came into focus. One last push through the storm and both were standing on a beautifully large porch that was overlooking the water.

"Where are we?" Jace asked again noticing that his question was still unanswered. Macie smiled pulling keys out of her pocket and turned towards the front door.

"Come on! Just tell me!" His anxiety was building and his patience for secrets was quickly running out. Ignoring his demands, the door creaked opened and she stepped in. This was an absolutely gorgeous home. It was situated right along the lake and had from what Jace could see a very nice sized yard. Trying to ring water out of his clothes one last time, he entered behind her. A grand chandelier's lights glistened as Macie continued through the house flipping switches.

"This is my parent's summer home on the lake." She said from a different room.

"I didn't know they had so much money!" Envy filled his statement. He could hear Macie chuckle at him.

"They are not rich. My mom is a Registered Nurse at the same hospital where I work. I thought you already knew that?" Turning the corner and coming back into sight, she had a puzzled look on her face. Jace still stood by the front entryway looking around.

"I must have forgotten. It seems like I am forgetful a lot more often lately." Slipping out of his wet shoes, he put them neatly next to each other on the mat next to the door.

"What about your dad?"

"He is a lawyer. He has a small practice several towns over. He used to have an office in Willowcreek, but better opportunities caused him to move his office. He just has to commute a little bit farther now."

"A lawyer and a RN? So, I guess they are rich then." He said matter-of-factly. Not responding to him, her confusion appeared to be growing.

"Is Dane here? I assume that is why you brought me here."

"Yes, this is where he has been staying. Your parents asked me to keep it a secret from everyone...including you."

"Well isn't that nice! I don't know what is going on with them lately!"

Moving through the house at an increasing speed, Macie almost looked to be in a state of panic.

"Is something wrong?" Jace asked in a calm tone.

"No, everything is fine. Just stay here for a minute okay?" Before he had a chance to answer, she left the main foyer and headed to what Jace assumed was the back of the house. A door opened and shut quickly and he could hear footsteps going down stairs. The sound was getting fainter. She must have been heading to the basement. Deciding not to listen to her, Jace began to look around searching for any clues that would alert him of his brother. The floor didn't creak like at his parent's house, that made sneaking around much less difficult. The vaulted ceilings were massively high and you could tell the furniture that resided in this house was not from a discount store. A large buck hung over a wood burning fire place. Large windows would let in lots of natural light if not for the storm. Jace looked at end tables and around all the furniture. He was even looking for any stacks of papers that might be laying around.

Nothing.

This house could have been photographed for a magazine it was so clean. Certainly not a place where his brother could live without messing it up or breaking something. Jace made his way into the small dining room which was attached to the kitchen and living area. Looking around the corner, he saw what appeared to be a hospital bed with two poles on wheels that were used for medicine bags. The bed was neatly made and tucked away in a corner. Stopping for a minute, Jace could hear a voice beneath him. Dropping to his knees, he pressed his ear against the wood flooring. Macie's voice was calling out for his brother. She must not know where he is if she is looking for him!

Jace had begun to debate if he should just go down there with her and see if he could assist. About five minutes later, he heard footsteps climbing the stairs. This time the sound was growing louder. The basement door opened and Macie stepped out.

"We might have a problem."

Those five words were ones that Jace could not stand to hear any longer. He did not want any more problems!

"What's the matter? I assume you can't find Dane." His lips tightened as he tried to control his frustration. This emotional roller coaster that his life had become was a ride he was ready to get off of!

"He's not supposed to leave here! That's what we agreed on."

"Who is 'WE'?" Jace inquired.

"Your parents and me. He is safe here for the time being." She flipped the lights off and charged towards the door. Jace reached out and grabbed her arm.

"I need to know what is going on here!"

"Ouch. Jace you are hurting my arm." He was squeezing it harder than he realized. Loosening his grip yet not letting go, he apologized.

"Dane is in trouble and we just need some time to sort things out. So, he was staying here away from town."

"What kind of trouble is he in? Please tell me!"

"You should ask your parents."

"I have asked them. I don't think they are telling me the truth. Please Macie, tell me what you know."

"I can't. I need to find him and fast before your parents find out he is gone. They trusted me with taking care of him and keeping him safe." She pulled away from his loosened grip and slid her wet shoes back on.

"We need to go now!" She said in a hurry. Jace pulled the big front door open. As Macie looked up, she let out a loud shriek and both hands flew up covering her open-gasping mouth. Startling him, Jace jumped from the loud noise. Macie was frozen in place. Her hands stayed glued to her face.

"What's the matter?" Jace asked looking at her.

She did not move.

He turned his attention from her to what her eyes were fixated on. Standing at the front door were two dark figures dripping wet...his mother and father.

A Walk Though the Grapes
David Jackson

Chapter 19

Sometimes, a divine intervention wouldn't be such a bad thing. In Jace's case, he was praying for one! A miracle that could help him or guide him in his decision making. Heaven knows he was not good at making his own decisions.

All four people stood there frozen in place staring at one another. Two still in the house and two on the porch. Jace waited uneasily to hear who was going to break the silence first. Before he knew it, HE was speaking. "Come in out of the rain." He slid his body to the side opening a path for them to enter. Motioning his hand as if to invite them in, they did not move.

"What are you guys doing here?" Macie finally broke the thick air which was inadvertently suffocating Jace.

"We are very disappointed in you Macie. I thought we could trust you!" His mother laid on her all-too familiar guilt only this time, it wasn't directed at him.

"Wait, what the hell did I do? Where is Dane?" The fight in her voice impressed Jace.

"I asked you not to tell anyone that he was here. ANYONE Macie." His father bellowed these words as he stepped into the light. His tall figure mixed with his deep voice was intimidating.

"This is your SON! I didn't think that it mattered because he is your family."

"We already spoke about this in some detail!" His mother said.

"We told you specifically not to tell Jace where he was. Don't you remember having this conversation?" Both of his parents' eyes were wide open, clearly filled with disbelief.

"Yes...but I just..."

"Why are you keeping this from me!" Jace cut her off quickly.

"What have I done to be kept as an outsider in this family?" Turning towards his son, Robert's cold stare pierced his eyes.

"What have you done?... WHAT HAVE YOU DONE?" His voice was growing with each question.

"Take it easy." His mother whispered grabbing Robert's arm. Taking a step back, he looked back at Macie.

"You are willing to risk everything that we have done? And for what?" Macie looked down upon hearing these words.

"You are as involved in this as any of us are...probably more." Marie chimed in.

"I know I am. I'm sorry." Robert grunted at these words. He either didn't believe what she said, or he was subtly telling his wife 'I told you so'.

"WHAT THE HELL IS GOING ON HERE!" Jace screamed. Macie grabbed an umbrella which was resting in an umbrella stand by the front door.

"Excuse me." She said sliding between his parents and out the front door. Her words sounded as if she was about to cry. Watching her run through the rain, ironically, she didn't even take the time to open the umbrella. She just wanted to leave and fast.

"Let's go Jace." His dad said starting to walk away. His mother followed.

"NOW!" He shouted back at his son. He didn't even turn around to see that Jace hadn't moved an inch. The rain was finally letting up a little, but the sky still gave no indication that it would be clear anytime soon. Obediently following his dad's instructions, he made his way to their car. Macie was already long gone. She must not have wanted to stick around to see anymore family drama. His foot stepped down into a large puddle that he didn't even notice. He caught himself before he fell and pulled his now wet foot out of the water. He didn't care that he stepped in a puddle. He didn't care that it was raining. A thought ran through his head wondering if he cared about anything at all anymore.

Opening the back door to the car, he slid in not concerning himself that the seat or anything in the car would get wet. As soon as he got in, he wished that he hadn't.

"I can't believe my own damn eyes that you are here! Is it impossible for you to stay out of trouble?" His father had finally had enough. He lost it. Yelling at his son from the front seat made Jace feel like a small child again. His mother tried several times to interject but with no success. His voice was magnified by the small cars size that they all were trapped in. His father went on and on as the car moved slowly down the driveway. Jace just looked out the window figuring the best way he could respond was to just be quiet.

"I haven't even touched on the fact that you smashed my car because you are such an idiot!" This was it. A bridge can only hold so much weight before it collapses. And his father's bridge was collapsing. Jace didn't think it was possible, but his dad's voice seemed to actually be getting louder and stronger as the outburst continued.

"I have given you so many opportunities with our company as well! A simple task of just meeting with potential buyers and making a good impression was apparently too much for you to handle! Everything that your mother and I have built is all set for you to take over and run it yourself. All you had to do is sit there and let this opportunity come to you. You don't seem to have any interest or ability to run anything...including your own life! People would kill for an opportunity to step into a successful company and make a good living for themselves. I don't know what it's going to take to get you on the right track!"

For a brief moment, Jace began to say something but the booming voice from the front seat would not let him interject. To make things worse, Jace had a clear view of the rear-view mirror which Robert's eyes were looking back at him. They were filled with fire and fury. He didn't even recognize them as he wasn't sure he had ever seen his father this mad before. At one point, Robert cocked his fist in the air and slammed it on the dashboard in anger. Both Marie and Jace jumped from surprise.

"That is enough!" Marie cried out to Robert grabbing the arm that had just punched the dashboard.

"We will figure this out. We always do." How could his mom always remain so calm and level headed? Jace was sure that she was upset about everything as well, she just tried not to show it. For the rest of the ride home, silence filled the air. It was the calm after the storm. The questions floating around his head would have to remain unanswered for now. This was not the time, or for that matter, the place to potentially make anyone angrier with questions they didn't want to answer.

The rain had all but stopped now. His dad flipped the windshield wipers off so hard he thought he was going to snap the lever right off.

"I think maybe I should talk with him alone darling." His mother said carefully to the angry man.

"You need to relax a little and check on the workers anyway, don't you?" Trying to change the subject was her best defense in this situation. Not answering her, Robert just kept driving. She was holding his hand with one hand, and the other was rubbing the top of his hand which was clearly red.

"How did your arm get all cut up Jace?" She asked. He looked down at his arm to see how bad it looked. He was still trying to be inconspicuous about it, but it clearly was not working with his mother.

"Yes, I did notice. You have tried to hide things from me your whole life. Has it ever worked out for you Jace?" She said with a cunning smile.

"Not the way that I plan them, no." He responded relaxing his arm and looking defeated. His father was still quiet but the look upon his face was one of severe unhappiness. His mind must still be in turmoil.

"Can we please stop at the store for a minute. I have to

grab a couple things for dinner tonight that I forgot to get when I went shopping yesterday." Marie's voice was delicate and fragile carefully asking her beloved husband to stop for groceries.

"No! I need to get back and make sure everything is going smoothly with the harvest. You know I don't like leaving them alone for too long. You shouldn't have forgotten them when you went yesterday." Robert fired these harsh words at her as he pulled his hand out of hers and placed it back on the steering wheel. A look of shock and bewilderment blanketed Marie's face. Being in the back seat, Jace had a perfect view of both of their looks and expressions. Robert must have been truly angry as he would never talk to his wife this way. The look of hurt on her face almost made Jace say something but he didn't want to make things worse. Plus, it's never a good idea to make the person who is driving and in control of your life upset. Slouching back in her chair, Marie adjusted her shoulder seat belt strap and didn't respond to him.

Several minutes passed and Jace noticed his father had pulled onto a street that was leading away from their house and towards main street...where the store was. The truck pulled in to the grocery store's parking lot and Marie unfastened her seatbelt and leaned over to give her husband a peck on the cheek.

"You gonna stay in the truck Jace or come in the store with me?" This was not a hard question for him to answer. The choice was go with her to safety, or, stay in a confined place with a man who was very upset with him. The shear fact that it would be unimaginably awkward silence waiting for her in the truck made his choice easy.

"I will help you carry your bags Ma." Jace said following her out of the truck. He never wanted to go into any stores before, so he figured this was a justifiable reason to go with her.

"Let's hurry. I don't want to make your dad wait any longer than he has to." Marie said speed walking into the store. Half jogging, Jace caught up to her. Tearing a piece of paper in half, she handed him what appeared to be a list. It only had two things on it...heavy cream and a dozen eggs. He could see her half of the list had several more items than his did. As soon as her feet hit the inside of the store, she snatched a basket and was off leaving her son to fend for himself.

Doing as instructed, Jace walked through the big store searching for the dairy aisle. He had been in this store many times before but it had been totally remodeled since the last time he shopped there. He checked where the refrigerated items used to be but apparently, they had been moved as well. Trying to move quickly, the pressure was on to beat his mother to the cash registers. Stopping a store clerk who was walking by with a cart full of packaged meat, Jace asked where his two items were located and the clerk pointed him in the right direction. Plucking both the eggs and the heavy whipping cream from their refrigerated shelves, he headed for the front of the store. Wanting to run, he decided better of it as people may think there was a problem or that he was trying to steal something. Of course, why would you run through the entire store just to steal items that cost less than ten dollars? These thoughts ran through his head, yet he still decided not to move any quicker than he was.

With the front of the store in sight, Jace turned the last corner to the registers when someone caught his eye. Taking a few steps back, he gazed through an end cap full of bags of chips. Trying to be inconspicuous, the person was getting closer and closer until he had a clear view of who it was.

"Jace?" The female voice said. The person he had been watching had stopped and now appeared to be looking right at him.

"Are you trying to hide from me?" Coming around the rack of chips, Jace quickly dropped to his knees to tie his sneakers... which were not untied. Setting the eggs down, he quickly pulled at his laces until he felt a hand touch his shoulder.

"Hey Ally!" He said giving one last tug on his shoelaces and coming to his feet.

"You were hiding from me, weren't you?" Ally repeated her question.

"No, no, not at all." He said unconvincingly. Grinning at him with a raised eyebrow, she accepted his denial even though she was pretty sure it was not true.

"I know that last time we saw each other it was awkward with my sister and Tyler. There is no need to avoid me if that is what you were doing." Ally winked at him and smiled.

"Trust me...I wasn't hiding from you. I thought that I saw you from a distance, but I wasn't sure. How did you see me so clearly through all of the chips?"

"Well, I could just sense that it was you" Clearly kidding, she nudged him with her elbow.

"Plus, I ran into your mom and she told me you were here."

"Oh okay." He said thinking that he was certainly going to beat his mother to the registers now that he knew she had stopped to talk with Ally.

"How are you feeling? Any better than the last time I saw you?"

"Yes. A lot better. It felt like I had the flu, but the doctor told me it was just a very bad cold."

"Well that is good. I hope things are better with you and Tyler." He didn't want to know about her relationship with Tyler at all but wanted to be polite. Strangely, he hoped that it did not work out.

"Things have been better. He called it off and won't hardly talk to me anymore. He thinks that I cheated on more than one occasion and for someone who has never done anything like that, it can get very exhausting being accused all the time." This made Jace think about their relationship and that he had accused her of things in the past.

"I hope you two work it out." Jace replied. If he was Pinocchio, his nose would be stretching across the store by now.

"Do you really hope that?" Ally asked as her smile faded.

"Well...I uh..." Stammering, Jace couldn't find the right words to say to the woman he still had strong feelings for.

"That's what I thought." Ally's smile began to return.

"I have to go now. As you know I'm with my parents and we are kind of in a hurry. It was good to see you...like

always." He touched her shoulder and reached back down to pick up his carton full of eggs.

"Maybe we could do dinner sometime?" Ally asked as he began to walk away. Stopping in his tracks, he spun back around to face her. Suddenly, his being in a hurry took a back seat.

"Dinner? Are you asking me to go on a date with you? The same girl who was mad that I was talking to her sister. And threw wine corks at my head? And whose boyfriend poured scalding hot soup on my crotch."

Laughing at this, she nodded.

"It's just dinner, not a marriage proposal." Ally said. This was a bad choice of words mentioning marriage as they both looked down feeling sad about their past.

"Anyway, call me sometime soon?" She asked in a flirtatious tone. Jace was not sure what had all of a sudden changed with her and now she was interested in him again?

"My phone is broken right now. I don't have access to your number because it won't turn on. Looking at him curiously, she reached into her purse and pulled a pen out. Scribbling her number on a scrap piece of paper, she held it out to him. Accepting the number, Jace stuffed it into his pocket.

"See ya." She said pushing her cart by him and into the next aisle over. Standing there in a bit of shock, Jace watched as she walked away. She still looked as good as ever. She had grown into an amazing woman. The thought of what he had done to her and that she was able to forgive without holding a grudge towards him was something he wasn't sure he himself could have done.

Marie had just gotten to the registers when Jace walked up.

"Did you see that Ally is here?" Her voice sounded hopeful that he had.

"Yes Ma, I did."

"And...?"

"And what Ma? We talked for a minute, that is it. Can we just pay for our stuff and get going?" Jace never liked discussing women with his mother. It was a well-known fact that she was desperately wanting one of her children to give her grandchildren.

"Okay. Don't bite my head off." She said loading the conveyor belt. She paid for the items and made their way to the parking lot. It had turned very muggy out and it felt like a hundred degrees now even though it was probably nowhere close to that. Parking the basket at the front of the store, Jace grabbed the majority of the plastic bags and headed towards their truck. Waiting to cross the small roadway before the parking lot, Jace saw another familiar face that he knew walking from the parking lot towards the store. This one was not smiling, and her body language clearly showed that she wanted nothing to do or say to him.

It was McKenzie.

Jace wondered what she was doing here. She must have been meeting her sister. Or maybe it was completely random...but what were the chances of that? Trying to make eye contact with her, he kept his eyes glued to her as he moved across the parking lot. She did not look at him once. He was almost positive that she knew it was him as she was not the type of woman to walk around with a scowl on her face.

"Jace!" His mother screamed at him. Looking quickly at her, he took one more step and began to topple over. Trying to put his hands out to catch himself, the bags he was holding weighed them down. As he fell, he tried to get the bags out from underneath him but had no such luck. Smacking down on the pavement, he sat up looking at the curb he had just tripped over. Shooting one more glance back at McKenzie, she was entering the store looking back at him with an evil smile. She clearly had seen him fall and approved of it. Marie put her bags in the truck and came over to where Jace was sitting. Scared to look in the bags, he handed them to his mother as he got to his feet.

"Don't worry, I don't think I bought anything breakable." She said trying to heal his bruised ego.

"Oh no." She said putting her hand in a bag and looking up at Jace.

"What's the matter?" He had no idea what he had squished. Pulling her hand from the bag, it was covered in clear and yellow goo. As she stuck her hand back in, she pulled out a little white shell.

"You fell on the eggs." A disappointed look on her face, she tried to wipe the egg off her hands in the grass nearby.

"I'm sorry Mom. Let me run in and get another one. It will only take a second." Starting to run towards the store, Marie yelled to him.

"NO! We don't have time. There are a couple that didn't break. I'll use those ones. Just get in the truck. Your dad has been patiently waiting for long enough." Doing what he was told, he returned to the car. His dad was right, he couldn't do anything right...even buying a carton of eggs proved to be too difficult of a task.

"What happened?" His father's voice asked.

"He just tripped over a curb, that's all. No big deal." Marie said clearly protecting her son from another scolding.

"I just got a call from John. They need another part from the damn store again. I swear all they do is break stuff!" His father put the car in gear and they took off.

"See! It was a good thing that we went to the grocery store. I just saved you from having to make a trip back here again later." Marie said with a smile.

"You should always listen to your wife. She knows what is best. Haven't I proven that to you after all these years together?" Speaking in the third person, Marie was clearly still trying to get her husband to come around by playfully joking with him.

"Yea yea. When do I not listen to you? Happy wife happy life...I know the motto."

A minute later they were at the hardware store.

"I'll be just a minute." Robert said slamming his door shut. Watching his dad walk into the store, Jace saw an opportunity to speak to his mom. They were finally completely alone, and now, they were trapped in the car together. No distractions and no place for his mother to go.

"Can we please talk about what is going on now?" Jace pleaded to his mom.

"We already told you what happened. We are not trying to trick you Jace. Your father and I are doing our best to protect this family."

"What does that mean? And how is Macie involved?"

"We needed a favor from her...a big favor. She came through for us...well... up until now at least."

"What was the favor?" Marie turned back to look out the front windshield watching a young woman pushing a baby stroller.

"I miss when you kids were young. Those were probably some of the best times of my life." She sounded sad.

"Please mom, just tell me!"

Marie paused for a long while before she responded to her son.

"We will tell you everything once we sort it all out. I promise you Jace." Making eye contact with him, he could tell she was not going to tell him anymore than she already had. Slouching back in his chair, he felt frustrated. Giving up for the time being, they sat there in complete silence waiting for Robert to emerge from the store. A police car pulled up and parked three spots down from their truck. The officer that stepped out was not one that Jace recognized. He was carrying a small brown paper bag that looked like it could be a bag lunch or something like that. He disappeared into the store as well.

The minutes felt like hours waiting. The car was starting to get warm inside and they did not have the key to turn the air conditioning on or even open the windows.

"What is taking him so long?" Jace whined.

"He has been in there over a half an hour. I thought he just had to run in to get something?" His complaining was making him feel even warmer.

"I know as much as you do Jace. Your dad wants to get home just as much as we do."

It was getting to be late in the day and Jace had still not eaten anything. He was starting to feel the effects of this as his stomach was aching from the inside.

"What are we having for dinner tonight?"

"I'm planning on making breaded chicken with mashed potatoes and corn if we ever get back home today." The first glimpse of frustration his mother showed made him happy. He wasn't the only one being tortured.

"Can you call your sisters and let them know we will have to push dinner back tonight?" Reaching down for his pocket, he remembered he didn't have his phone. It was broken. He couldn't tell his mother that or she would ask questions about why it was broken.

"I left my phone at home." He said.

"What? You never go anywhere without it." A puzzled look on his mother's face subtly told him that she either didn't believe him or that he was up to something.

"I don't know. I was in a hurry this morning and just left it." That was kind of true.

"I will try to find mine then." She said fumbling through her purse. Pulling it out, she dialed the numbers and put the phone to her ear. Both numbers she called didn't answer so she ended up leaving messages.

Another ten minutes passed before Robert finally stepped out with a plastic bag in his hand.

"Don't say anything to him about how long he took. Understand?" The firmness of his mother's warning made it clear she was not kidding.

"Obviously I won't. I'm not stupid you know!" Jace said rolling his eyes.

Setting the bag in the middle next to his wife, Robert started the car and they were off once again.

"Did everything go okay in there? Find what you needed?" Marie asked.

"Yup. They had to research what I needed but we found it. My phone was going crazy in there. Could you check it for me?" Robert reached into his pocket, pulled out his phone, and handed it to Marie without taking his eyes off the road.

"Oh my gosh!" She exclaimed looking at the phone's small screen.

"You have eleven missed calls! Why didn't you answer any of them?"

"I was talking to the guy behind the counter. We were doing some research on the internet about the right part that I needed. My phone always rings in my pocket and when I'm with people or doing something, I just plan to call whoever it is back." Robert shrugged his shoulder as if to say, 'what was I supposed to do?'

"Eight of them are from John and the other three are from Tommy. I wonder what they wanted. Maybe something is wrong with the harvest?" Marie sounded concerned.

"Well we are almost home now. Don't bother calling them back. I will just talk to them when I get there."

Shutting the old flip phone with one hand, Marie handed it back to him. Stuffing it in his pocket, the car turned onto their street. Jace and his mother both had their windows open to let the fresh air cool them down. Suddenly, a funny smell poured through the open window.

"What's that smell?" Marie asked her husband.

"I don't know. It smells like burning rubber or plastic." Rolling his window down, the air whipped from side to side through the car. The sun was still fairly high in the sky, but it was certainly on its way down soon. The clouds had thinned out and you could vaguely see blue sky hiding between them.

Turning into their driveway, the stones clicked beneath the car's tires as they rolled over them. Getting beyond the trees that lined the driveway to where their view opened up, the sight that was there to be seen was a horrific one!

Black smoke was billowing out of the windows.

Their house was on fire!

As Marie shrieked with panic and horror, Robert hit the gas hard as the car jolted forward. Slamming on the brakes a second later, he jumped out. Jace couldn't process what he was seeing. Instant tears from his mother crippled him. He jumped out of the car as well to follow his father. Robert had already made it up to the house but was now standing completely still in front of the burning house. You could not see any flames, but the smoke promised that they were not far behind. Running up behind him, Jace finally saw what had made him stop in his tracks. There was a body lying on the front porch!

Taking a closer look, Jace could not see who it was. Robert moved closer and pulled a wicker chair up off the body. In one swift motion, he lifted the chair and threw it off the porch revealing the man's face.

It was Dane!

In complete shock, Jace stood there frozen. It had been so long since he had seen his brother he almost didn't recognize him. Dane's face and head was now covered in black soot and as Jace looked closer, it looked as if Dane was bald. Robert dropped to his knees by his son's side. Blood covered his right pant leg and he appeared to be unresponsive. Grabbing his ankles, Robert screamed to Jace.

"Help me move him!"

Jace looked down at his hands and they were shaking. He needed to help save his brother, but he was in shock. He finally mustered the courage to move and jumped up the porch's steps. Grabbing Dane's shoulders, he moved his brother as quickly as he could. Once down the stairs, they laid him down flat in the grass. He was not unconscious, but he didn't look good. Dane's eyes were still looking around and he moved his arms ever so slightly. Jace looked into his brother's eyes and Dane looked back at him. If two people could communicate without speaking, this was it. The sadness that filled Jace's eyes was offset by the relief that filled Dane's. Robert looked his son up and down. Tugging at his jeans, he looked to see how badly his leg was injured.

His father froze.

His head slowly began to rise up as his eyes met Jace's. Robert's eyes were wide open. The look on his face was one that Jace had never seen on his father…fear.

"What's wrong Dad? We need to call an ambulance!" Jace screamed to him. Fire began to pulsate out of the windows. His father waited a long time before he finally spoke.

"This wound is NOT from the fire...It's a gunshot."

Chapter 20

The wind whipped intensely through the narrow trees picking up flurries of snow and gently laying them back down. Snow was piled up to the roofs of the cars parked along the street. Some were completely buried and couldn't be seen at all. The big plow trucks worked tirelessly through the night and into the early morning battling the worst storm Colorado had seen in some time...and that is saying something! Dane and Jace tried with all their might to move through the thick snow, but, at eight and nine years old, they were no match for it. Marie stood with Lizzie outside the old lodge holding a camcorder. She smiled watching her boys stumble and play in the aftermath of the snowstorm. Robert carried little Jen on his shoulders. He too was having a hard time moving through the snow.

"Run Dad!" Jen giggled and screamed to him. Moving his legs as fast as he could, he toppled over setting Jen down in a snowbank and giving her a face full of soft snow. Her wide smile filled with snow as Robert tickled her. High pitch laughter burst out of her lungs in random spurts. The boys wrestled around throwing snowballs at each other diving from snowbank to snowbank for protection.

The laughter that filled the air and the good memories of one of their best vacations were ones that Marie cherished. She had this video transferred to a DVD so she could save it.

Time seem to stand still as the thought of Jace and his brother whipping snow at each other when they were younger filled his mind. Easier times in life when they had no responsibilities or cares in the world. Looking down at his brother lying flat in the grass, he couldn't help but wonder how they had gotten to this point.

"A gunshot? Are you sure?" Jace questioned his father.

"YES!" Robert yelled back at his son tearing Dane's jeans even farther apart exposing the wound. Looking behind him, Jace noticed his mother standing about ten feet away. Her hands covered her mouth. Her eyes were red and full of tears.

"Do you know where your sisters are?" Robert asked Jace.

"No. We tried to call them earlier, but they didn't answer." Running up behind them, Marie fell to the ground next to her son.

"He is still breathing but appears to have inhaled a lot of smoke." Robert said. Jace wasn't sure if he was trying to make them feel better or warn them that he didn't look good.

"Where are all the workers?" Marie asked.

"I don't know. Maybe they are around back?" Robert stood up and looked around.

"We need to get help. Where is your cell phone?" He asked his wife.

"It's in the car. I'll get it." She said running back towards the truck.

Suddenly, a loud gunshot rang out through the air. Both

Robert and Jace dropped down frantically looking around.
"That came from inside the house Dad!"
"I know! Keep your voice down." He said calmly. Marie must have heard it as well because she stopped looking for her phone and looked back towards the house.
"What's going on?" Jace whispered to his dad. Shrugging his shoulders, Robert didn't have an answer either. Jace looked down at his brother. His eyes were glistening and his chest was going up and down with quick breaths.

The grass was still wet from the rain that had passed through. Jace's knees were muddy but he didn't care.
"How would the fire have started in the rain?" Jace asked his father.
"I don't know Jace!" He said clearly annoyed by all his questions. He had no more answers about what was happening than Jace did. Marie ran back to her husband and gave him the phone. He quickly gave it back to her.
"Call someone. Quickly!" He said.
Her hands were shaking. She was clearly traumatized by what was going on. Her phone fell to the grass as she frantically bent down to get it.
"Just give it here." Jace said reaching out his hand. She reluctantly gave him the phone.
"Call the hospital Jace, not the police." His father told him.
"What? Why? I don't know the hospital's phone number." He said as his panic was growing as well. Looking back at his dad, he was no longer paying attention to Dane or him. Jace looked to his mother and her stare was fixated on the same thing Robert's was. A figure now stood on the front

porch looking out at them. Standing completely still, the eerie figure looked to be assessing the situation.

"Well look what we have here." A young man's voice said. Taking a few steps forward, he held his shirt in one hand and a rifle in the other.

"Oliver?" Jace asked in disbelief.

"Well how 'bout that? You're not as dumb as people say you are Jace." He said sarcastically. The fire was growing rapidly and was now consuming what appeared to be the living room and the main entrance of the house.

"Put the gun down Oliver!" Robert yelled to him.

"Shut up old man!" He screamed back slowly moving down the front porch stairs. He acted as if he had not a care in the world. His movements were slow, and the fierce flames did not seem to faze him one bit.

Jace slowly put his mom's cell phone in his pocket. He wanted to call someone...anyone now, but he didn't want to risk getting shot.

"What's going on? Why did you do this?" Jace asked him in a calm voice pointing down to his brother.

Oliver smiled back at him.

"It wasn't bad enough that your idiot brother went and killed my dad and ALMOST killed me too, but then, I wake up here in some room, locked up like a dog."

Jace's mind was racing.

Oliver moved towards where they were kneeling and motioned for them to get up. He appeared to have some sort of device around one of his ankles that still had two chain links dangling from it.

"I was finally able to get loose and I took Dane down

~ 288 ~

pretty easily actually. I knew when you would usually bring food down to me, so I waited until the exact right time and it just so happened to be Dane that walked in. First time I had seen him since he killed my dad." Jace was trying to process what he had just heard as fast as he could.

"Are my daughters in there?" Marie squeaked between tears.

"I didn't see them, but if they are, I'd say they are probably well done by now." Oliver chuckled at himself.

"Just give me the gun Oliver. No one needs to die here today." Robert was trying hard to calmly talk him down.

"Didn't I tell you to shut up?" He snapped back at him pointing the rifle at him with one arm. Robert's hands went back into the air.

At this point, the workers would have to see the smoke coming from the house and hopefully call 911. Jace could not be sure of this and needed to take this situation into his own hands.

A quick idea popped into his head. His father might not have liked it, but at this precise moment, he couldn't exactly run it by him. Reaching into his pocket, he grabbed the phone and waited for Oliver to turn his attention away from him. Oliver was talking loudly at his father and was not focused on Jace or Marie. As fast as he could, he dialed 911 and stuck the phone back in his pocket. He figured that the police would respond even if he didn't say anything over the phone. They would see where the call was coming from and hopefully come there. This meant he needed to keep Oliver talking as long as possible, so he didn't hurt anybody else.

Waiting for a break in Oliver's angry words, Jace found an opening.

"So, what was your plan here? You just burned down the house for no reason?" Smiling back at Jace, he walked over to where he was standing. He jabbed Jace in the stomach with the butt end of the rifle. Keeling over in pain, he dropped to his knees once again gasping for air.

"None of this was for no reason! Your family kept me locked up to protect that piece of crap!" He pointed the rifle at Dane.

"Now he is getting what he deserves. You all are!" He said turning back around.

"I was planning on burning the house down with Dane in it. I broke into the gun cabinet and shot him, so he couldn't get away. I didn't want to kill him though. I want him to burn and suffer the way that me and my family have!" Oliver's voice was crackling from all the screaming.

"Now you're all here and I have to kill all of you." His voice calmed back down. Jace wondered if his call had worked and what their response time would be if it had.

"Please. Let's talk about this for a minute." His mother had composed herself and was continuing to plead with him.

"Enough!" Oliver said in frustration. Walking over to where Dane was still lying, he stood over him looking down deeply into his flickering eyes.

"This can't really be happening" Jace said under his breathe. Frantically trying to think of what to do, his mind was blank. He looked around to see if there was anything on the ground to use as a weapon, but all he saw was grass. Before he could move, suddenly, a loud shriek came from inside the burning house. It sounded like that of a young woman. Robert shot a look at his wife and she looked back at him through her tears. His next glance was to Jace. His eyes squinted at his son trying his best to communicate with him without speaking. Just as Oliver looked back towards the scream, Robert made a quick move to his feet and ran as fast as he could towards his house.

"Hey! I told you not to move!" Oliver screamed as he raised the rifle aiming at Robert. Jace dug his foot into the ground and leapt forward. Taking three steps, he dove over his brother's body toward where Oliver was standing. He wasn't going to make it. With one last ditch effort, Jace reached his arm out as far as he could and clipped Oliver's elbow. As the gun fired, a loud clap rang through the air. A small cloud of smoke emitted from the rifle. Jace turned his head to see the shot go through the front window and his Father disappear into the smoking house. Hitting his elbow was just enough to knock Oliver off balance and in doing so, the gun itself too. Looking back at Jace with hatred in his eyes, he was furious that he had missed Robert. And it was Jace's fault. Time froze that very minute as Oliver got to his feet and took a few steps back. Cocking the gun against his shoulder, he pointed it towards Jace, and fired.

Lightning shot from the barrel of the gun as Jace was powerless to stop the bullet coming right for him. He heard his Mother moan with grief.

It happened so fast.

His body contorted from the mighty power of the weapon.

Jace's head slammed to the ground as grass poked him in the eye. He lay motionless unable to move. His thoughts were fuzzy. His eyes were small slits trying desperately to see anything. His mother's eyes were staring into his. He could see her lips moving but couldn't make out any words.

As Marie lay between her two sons, she wept uncontrollably. Jace had gone into shock. His extremities had begun twitching involuntarily. Holding her son tight, she didn't want to see where he had been shot as she feared the worst. Oliver said nothing more and was slowly retreating back to the house. Marie knew he was going after her husband, but she felt numb. She didn't try to stop him. She didn't say anything between gasps of air and tears. Her body lay motionless as she had reached out and was touching both of her sons. Dane's hand moved over hers gently squeezing her fingers. Finally, she mustered up enough energy to turn her head to see if Oliver was still in sight.

He was not.

Tugging at Jace's shirt, her hand was covered with his blood. She turned him over onto his back and he did not move. His body was limp. She couldn't tell where he had been shot as his shirt was all twisted and soaked with blood. Pulling as hard as she could, she finally got his shirt up under his neck. The sight of her son covered in blood was horrifying. Jace gasped a sudden shock of air as his left eye opened ever so slightly. He whispered something to his mother. Trying hard to hold back the sound of her own sobbing, she quickly put her ear next to his mouth.

Desperate to hear what he had said, he didn't repeat it. She knew what he was trying to say. Softly spoken words to tell his mother he loved her. This was the last thought he had before everything went black. Marie dropped from her knees to a sitting position. The view of her beloved house that she had raised a family in was disintegrating fast and there was nothing or no one there to stop it. Even worse were her two sons that lay in the front yard struggling to hang onto life. She wiped the tears from her face and closed her eyes hard. Her prayers were laced with helplessness. Every precious second that passed by, the glimmer of hope that she desperately clung to was deteriorating rapidly.

Chapter 21

The deep sound of the church bells rang through the cold day's air. On normal days, the old bell was used to signify time. Today, the loud ring gave off an ominous sound. The sky was dark, and the morning dew still sat atop the blades of grass. The smell of dampness was all around. Small drips of water were trickling from the old church's downspout. Cars pulled into the parking lot slowly being careful not to hit others walking towards the entrance. Everyone dressed in black.

The small town's people being such a tight knit community, always showed their support for a family going through tragedy. People herded through the front doors and found any available pew they could. Marie moved slowly down the aisle towards the altar. The black dress she wore was accompanied by a small hat that covered her eyes when she looked down. She was not the type of woman who liked to show emotion, especially in front of everyone she knew. Yet that was not going to be entirely possible today. Her outfit was one that she had never worn before. Stopping at the front pew, she looked around at all the candles that were lite. The flicker of the small flames provided minimal light. They instead, cast eerie shadows near the dark corners where they were placed. The stained-glass windows which would normally be letting beautiful rays of sun in were dark. It was as if they felt her pain. Elizabeth and Jen met her where she stood. Both of their eyes were red and wounded from their tears. Reaching out to grab her hand, Elizabeth hugged her mom tightly trying as hard as she could to hold in her sobs. She was trying to be strong for her mother but was not able to. Like a damn breaking, the tears flooded down her face. She put her head on Marie's shoulder as both women's tears uncontrollably filled their embrace. Jen stood behind them wiping tears from her own eyes. She kept her eyes down and tried very hard to avoid making eye contact with anyone who was around her. Elizabeth's tight hug loosened, and she slid into her seat. Jen hugged her mother next, but their embrace was much shorter. Jen held out her hand to direct her mother to her seat. Marie obliged and sat down. Out of town relatives had shown to pay their respects. Friends and family came up to Marie and gently shook her hand offering their condolences. She tried her best to thank everyone and give them as much of a smile as she could muster up.

Several more minutes went by until the church was packed full of people. The church had not been this full in a long time. As much as the priest would encourage people to come every Sunday, the many rows of pews would remain half empty. The big entrance doors shut tightly. Elizabeth and Jen held their mother's hand, one on each side of her. A long moment of silence filled the room. A baby in the back of the church was making small noises. Marie looked up at the bench in front of her. It held a Bible and the book of songs you could follow along with. Father DiPiazza, who had been the head of their church since

Marie could remember, walked slowly towards the alter. He stopped where Marie and her daughters were sitting and touched each one of their hands. Stepping up to his podium where he had given countless sermons every Sunday, he stood silent. A moment later, he raised his arms asking everyone to please rise. The large doors where everyone entered slowly creaked open. Six men stood next to a shiny wood casket. Each man stepped slowly to keep the rhythm with the man next to him. They were all dressed in sharp looking black suits. The four men that were bringing up the rear of the casket all were looking up. The two in the front were both looking down. As they made their way down the center aisle of the church, everyone's sad eyes looked at the casket containing a life that had ended. Setting the casket down, the pallbearers stood at attention facing Father DiPiazza. The priest stepped down to where the men were standing. He reached out his hand to shake the man's hand who stood directly in front of him.

"I am very sorry for your loss Robert." He said in a gentle voice. Marie's husband stood there with a blank stare on his face. He did not respond to the priest. Taking several steps towards the other man who had been in front as well, he offered his hand again. Reluctantly, he shook the priest's hand.

"I am sorry for your loss Dane." Speaking these words, Dane wiped a tear from his already red eyes.

"Thank you, father." He said in a crackling voice. Both men went and joined the rest of their family. The funeral service proceeded with several readings and songs which made many people in the church cry. Dane was asked before if he had wanted to say some words. After thinking long and hard about if he wanted to, he ultimately decided he would be remiss if he didn't. Standing slowly, he went up to the podium and adjusted the microphone to his desired height.

"I'm not sure where to begin. Jace was, and still is, my best friend. He was my brother and I am lucky to have had the privilege of growing up with him." Sniffling, Dane wiped his nose with a well-used tissue.

"This is probably the hardest thing that I have ever had to experience in my lifetime. I will miss him. And not a day will go by that I won't think about him and all of the fun that we used to have." Dane began to cry hard and he took a step back from the microphone. Father DiPiazza stepped up to him and put his hand on Dane's shoulder whispering something into his ear. Breathing deeply, Dane tried hard to compose himself. Robert and Marie watched as their son broke down talking about the memories of his brother. Jen had moved next to her sister in the pew so her parents could sit next to each other and console one another as best they could. Robert's arm tightened around his wife as she cried harder. His eyes were full of tears and were running down his cheek slowly. Dane stepped back to the microphone.

"I'm sorry." He apologized to everyone at the church.

"I'm not going to say much more. I loved him, I will never stop loving him, and my heart will always be broken. Brother is not a strong enough word for our relationship and how I felt about him. Rest easy Jace." His tears began again as he stepped down for good this time. Dane stopped at the casket, ran his hand over where his head would be underneath and kissed it.

Several others spoke briefly about Jace. Some had funny stories trying to make people laugh and remember the good times with Jace. His mother and father did not speak, nor did his sisters. The last person to speak was a surprise to everyone. Ally had sat in the back of the church with her family. She had not spoken with any of Jace's family since he had passed. As she walked towards the front of the church, she made eye contact with Marie. Surprisingly, Ally had not appeared to have cried yet. Her eyes were sad but were not bloodshot or red in any way. She gave a half smile to his mom and sisters. Dane was sitting on the end but was looking down trying to bring himself back from his tears. Once at the podium, she unfolded a small piece of paper from her pocket, set it down and flattened it out with her hand. Looking out at the sea of people who were attending Jace's funeral, everyone sat quiet in anticipation of her voice. Ally took several deep breaths before she began.

"This is an unimaginably sad day for me." She began glancing down at her notes. She did not read them. She used them as a prop almost for when she needed to look away from all of the people starring back at her.

"I don't want to talk about Jace as a person, I want to talk about Jace as a partner, as that is what he was to me for a big part of our lives. I loved him so much, even to this day, I can't seem to recover from that kind of love. A love as strong as I believe we had, cripples you in a way. When it is unimaginably difficult to see yourself without that other person in your life, that is real love. And what can I say...he was my first, true...boyfriend I guess you would call it." She said with a small giggle and air quotes.

"In the time we spent together, he made my life so much better. He was everything a girl could ask for. Everybody knows that he left to pursue a dream of his, and looking back now, I never stopped having feelings for him. Even when he was hundreds of miles away. I don't harbor negative feelings towards him for leaving me. When he finally came back home, the first time I saw him, I wanted to cry. It was like Christmas morning when you run down the stairs to get your gifts. That excitement ran through my body just from the sight of him. I was still upset with him but honestly, when it is true love, like I know we had, anger does not last very long in my opinion." Ally kept a smile on her face as she spoke about her time with Jace. The fun things they had done in high school and all the nice things he had done for her. She finally started to get choked up.

"Ugh, I promised myself I would try hard not to cry." She told everyone as she too took a step back and rubbed her eyes. She nervously pulled a strand of hair behind her ear trying to pull herself together.

"I love you Jace. I hope that our short time together meant as much to you as it did to me. There will never be another like you as long as I live!" Moving away from the podium, she had begun to cry harder. As she went back to her seat, Dane stood up from his seat and gave her a hug.

"He loved you too Ally. You were the perfect woman for

him and he knew that all his life." Resting her head on Dane's shoulder, her tears were so genuine and the pain she felt was clear to everyone. Father DiPiazza had a few final comments and one more song before he called for the pallbearers to stand and take their places next to Dane's body. As everyone in the church began to sing along with the priest, they slowly lifted the casket and made their way towards the doors which he came in from. Elizabeth and Jen had stood up and were talking with some of their friends. Marie stayed seated by herself. No longer did she cry.

She sat motionless starring down at her folded hands. She was in a state of shock and disbelief. The last thing she wanted to do now was to go to the cemetery to lower one of her children into the ground. Father DiPiazza came to her side and helped her to her feet. She walked with him down the aisle until she was out of the church. Robert's hand met hers as they slid the casket into the hearse.

The ride to the cemetery was very short. The small piece of land sat next to the river that ran through town. The funeral procession of cars was very long. Going over the red covered bridge brought good memories to his family. The hearse that led the procession turned into the small dirt road that ran through the cemetery. Robert wondered where all of the cars were going to park but that was something he did not care about at this precise moment. Stepping out of their car, the Grazer family all took their spots. Robert and Dane stood by the hearse waiting for the others. Marie and her daughters stood near the freshly dug hole in the ground that was to be

Jace's final resting place. A small green tent covered the hole protecting it from the elements. The sun still hadn't come out from behind the clouds but luckily, it wasn't raining. People began to gather around and a gentleman from the funeral home was passing out flowers. A small row of chairs was placed directly in front of where Jace would be laid to rest. This was obviously for relatives and close friends who felt they couldn't stand for this. Jace's mother and two sisters sat on three of the chairs at the end of the row. A gentle wind caused the tent to wiggle. The men brought the casket under the tent and set it on the bars to hold it there before it went down. Jen squeezed her mother's hand again trying to give any strength she had left to her mother. For some reason, this part was harder than the church was. Marie just kept thinking to herself that she didn't want her son to go underground and she didn't want to just leave him here. She couldn't explain how she was feeling. It was almost a panic. Robert and Dane came and stood behind the chairs where the ladies sat. The priest said one final prayer before closing his book and standing back. One by one, everybody who was there took their flower and laid it on top of his casket. Ally and McKenzie each put their flower down. Robert and Marie's friends took their turns as well. Every person who was there slowly came up to pay their final respects and leave their flower. Marie sat there with her flower clinched tightly between her fingers. She did not want to do this. She watched as her other children and her husband all lay their flowers down. Now, it was her turn. Everybody waited patiently as she sat there crippled with grief. Robert helped his wife to her feet and she gently tossed it on the bed of roses that everyone else had made with theirs. Spinning around quickly, she buried her head into Robert's shoulder. She could not keep her composure any longer. As people began to leave, they shook Robert and Dane's hand and hugged Jace's sisters. Marie sat back down by her son's casket all by herself. What seemed like hours went by before everyone else was gone. The kids went back home, and Robert went to sit with his wife.

"I can't believe this is happening." Her voice squeaked as her whole body hurt. Her chest hurt, her eyes hurt, her voice hurt. She was numb inside yet still felt the pain outside.

"We need to go home darling. I need you to get some rest." Robert said softly to her. She hadn't had a good night sleep since it had happened.

"I can't leave him here." She said. She knew it made no sense, but she didn't care.

"We can come back tomorrow darling, I promise."

"No!" Marie snapped at him. Reaching out to her, she began to swat his arms.

"I said NO!" She screamed.

Forcing his arms around her, she burst into tears again. Letting her cry into his shoulder, her body felt weak. She had no strength left.

"Okay. I'm sorry." She told her husband between gasps of breath. Standing up, she looked at the casket for a long time before she began to walk away. The whole way to the car she kept looking back. As they pulled away, she could

no longer sense Jace with her anymore and the emptiness
she felt was unbearable.

Chapter 22

The world now seemed to be filled with darkness. Looking around, it was pitch-black. You couldn't even see a foot in front of your face. Silence filled the dark air. Several minutes went by. Your body limp and unable to move. The air content was diminishing rapidly. Struggling to breathe, the small amount of oxygen was not filling the lungs to full capacity.

Trapped.

There is a moment when you want to just give up and close your eyes, but you know if you do, there is no one there to save you. If you don't muster the courage to save yourself, you are out of luck.

Suddenly, a loud beeping sound followed by a sharp flash of strong light filled the air. Jace's eyes shot open. Gasping for breath, his body was covered in sweat. The nurse who had turned the lights on ran to his side to comfort him.

"Oh sweetie, you are burning up." She said touching his forehead with the back of her hand. She spun around to get an ice pack out of the small fridge.

"Where am I?" Jace yelled to her.

"You are at the hospital Jace." She said in an overly calm voice. Plopping his head back on the pillow, he could feel that it was wet from his own uncontrollable sweating. His lungs were pumping as he tried to catch his breathe.

"I can't believe it! I just had a dream that I died! Everyone was at my funeral! And at the end, I swear I was in a box underground!" His panicked voice mixed with his genuinely scared look had the nurse concerned.

"It was just a dream. Trust me, you haven't left this hospital." She tried her best to calm him down.

"It was so dark! I couldn't move at all." A sense of relief came over him that he was in fact alive and not buried six feet under. Jace licked his lips multiple times. His tongue felt like sandpaper against his rough lips.

"Could I have a sip of water please?" Jace asked still breathing abnormally fast.

"My mouth is so dry." He said licking his lips once again to show the nurse how dry they were.

"Yes. I will get that for you in one moment. I just came in to get your vitals." The nurse said with a smile. She did what she had to do and left the room. Jace sat quietly looking around at his empty hospital room. The small whiteboard that hung across from his bed had the names of his nurse and doctor on them. The dry erase marker appeared that it was on its last leg as he could barely read what had been written. Jace could hear shuffling outside of his door but no one entered. The nurse must have forgotten about his water. Looking down at himself, his arm was in a sling and he had several tubes connecting him to the machines around him. He felt strange as he could not feel his arm, or any discomfort for that matter. Whatever medicine they had him on must have been doing its job well. Then, as if someone flipped a switch in his brain, he remembered.

"The fire!" He said out loud to an empty room. All the memories of what happened came rushing back to him. How had he gotten here? What had happened to his family?

Before he could answer any of these questions, his door creaked open slowly and a man in a white coat came walking in looking down at a clipboard.

"You are awake!" The man said happily as if Jace had done something good. Jace didn't respond, he just smiled and looked up at the tall man.

"I am Doctor Woodruff. I will be monitoring your recovery Jace." The doctor still seemed to be preoccupied with whatever he was reading.

"It's nice to meet you." Jace said.

"I am just checking on your pain level and if you are in need of anything today." The doctor dropped his clipboard to his side and gave Jace his full attention.

"I was shot." Jace looked confused after saying this.

"Are you asking me or telling me?" Doctor Woodruff almost sounded jovial.

"How am I still here if I was shot in the chest?"

"You are a very lucky young man. The bullet didn't hit any major organs. You did need surgery as we needed to remove the bullet." The doctor told Jace.

"How did everything go? I mean, am I going to be alright?" The doctor smiled down at him.

"In time, you will heal up completely. It's just going to be a long road to recovery and managing your pain will be crucial." Laying back after hearing this, he couldn't believe that he had actually gotten shot...and lived!

"Could I get a cup of water doc? I am so thirsty." The doctor made his way to the door.

"I will send a nurse right in for you." With those words, he was gone.

I just had a nurse and am still thirsty! Jace thought to himself as he rolled his eyes. His eyes felt heavy, but he did not want to go back to sleep. Lucky for him, he wasn't alone for much longer. Ten minutes later, the door opened slowly again. A head poked in looking over the room. The next thing Jace knew, the woman ran over to him and had her arms around him. It was his mother.

"I can't believe you are finally awake! How long have you been up for?" She could not have sounded more excited and relieved. She kissed his cheek and made a point to be extra careful around his sling.

"Not that long." Jace responded as her arms were still tightly around his neck.

"I told those damn doctors to let us know when you woke up!" Her excitement briefly turned to aggravation. When she finally pulled away from him, she looked into his eyes. She was clearly happy that Jace was still with her.

"Who else is here? I have no memory of what happened after I got shot." Jace tried not to sound frustrated but he was. A loud cry from down the hall caused his mother to jump.

"Ugh, I hate hospitals." She said trying to shake off her sudden fear. Pulling up a chair, she sat right next to her son grabbing the hand that was not in a sling. Her eyes had welled up with tears. Wiping them frantically, Jace instantly felt uneasy.

"What's the matter mom?" He asked concerned.

"Nothing darling. I am just very happy to see you again." She squeezed his hand tightly and pulled a small tissue from the half empty box on the stand next to where he lay.

"Who else is here mom? You said to have the doctors let "us" know when I woke up." Jace asked this beginning to feel impatient. Her tears made him worry.

"Your sisters were here earlier and spent some time with you. I sent them home as they both desperately needed some sleep." Jace looked at his mother after she said this, and he realized she did not look well either. Her eyes were tired, she did not have her usual makeup on, and her overall demeanor was one of exhaustion.

"It looks like you need some sleep too!" Jace told his mother as he ran his thumb over the outside of her hand.

"I'm fine Jace." She said sniffling. There was an obvious question that Jace was scared to ask but he could no longer hold his tongue.

"Where is Dane? And Dad? Are they both here?" Jace sat there for a minute waiting for his mother to answer. He silently prayed that they had the same good fortune that he did...if you could call getting shot good fortune. But at least he had made it through now and was recovering. Looking up at him, she stared into his eyes for the longest time before she finally spoke.

"Dane is at a different hospital." She whispered to him. Jace looked at her confused.

"What? Why wouldn't they just bring him here? We have always come here when we have needed to." Marie looked back down at her lap twirling her tissue between her fingers. Seeing this, Jace closed his eyes as this was exactly how he had envisioned her in his dream attending his funeral.

"Mom. What's going on?" Jace tugged gently at his mother's lifeless hand that he was still holding.

"I guess there is no point in keeping this from you any longer." Marie took a deep breath and looked up at her son.

"There is something I need to tell you." She paused again and then continued.

"This is going to be one of the hardest things that I will ever have to say…" Jace tried to brace himself but was not remotely prepared for what was coming.

"We have lost your father."

Marie's bottom lip began to quiver as the tears began to fill her eyes again. Jace sat lifeless looking back at her. He was immediately in a state of disbelief. What looked like slow motion, Jace fell back in his bed. Marie had begun to cry harder. This was an unimaginable situation for them both.

"That can't be true. I just saw him right before I was shot." Jace sounded like he was pleading with his mother to tell him that it wasn't true, as if she had any control over it.

"It's true." Marie responded quietly.

"He ran back into the burning house to save the young voice that had screamed." She was a total mess now. Between the tear flowing from her eyes and her nose running, she had lost all composure.

"He thought it may have been one of your sisters. He was

such a good man and tried his hardest to always protect this family. And now, he ended up dying trying to protect us." Her voice was shakier than Jace had ever heard it before. She was gasping for air between sobs.

Jace felt paralyzed.

This couldn't have been true. His father was invincible. Jace had no reaction because his brain could not believe what his ears had just heard.

"Did he end up saving one of them?" Jace asked staring up at the ceiling.

"Neither of your sisters were in the burning house." Marie said pulling another tissue out of the box.

"Who was that screaming then?"

"The rescue people found two bodies from the wreckage. Both were burnt very badly and couldn't be identified there at the scene. The house caved in while they were still inside of it. The gasoline he had spread caused the house to burn extra fast and weakened it severely. I knew one of the bodies was your father. I didn't know who the other was. The coroner got back to us several days ago with the result of the second body that was found. According to a DNA test, the second body was that of Macie's." Just as she said that, a nurse came in that Jace had not seen before. She set a cup of water down in front of him and walked back out of the room without saying a word.

"Dane's Macie? Jace asked wide eyed.

"Yes." Marie responded.

"What was she doing there?"

"Remember we found you two at her parent's lake house?

After she left in such a hurry, she went back to our house to find Dane. She figured that is where we would have moved him, and she was right." Marie stood up for a moment to toss her well used tissues in the trash can. "Why did you go through all of that mess? Where is Dane and why did the three of you keep him in hiding?" Jace was no longer scared of what he might hear going forward. What else could she tell him that would be worse than what had already happened?

Marie was now at the sink washing her hands. She played with her hair in the mirror but was not pleased with the way she looked. Jace sat back up in his bed looking his mother's way. As she sat back down, she sighed. Her look was one of giving up. She was throwing in the towel.

"Your brother has cancer. He found out about six months before you came back." Marie shook her head as she told Jace the sad news.

"What kind of cancer?" Jace asked sharply.

"Lung." Marie answered. Suddenly, the bad dream he had about himself dying didn't seem so bad to him. He would have traded his life for his brother and father to keep on living.

"That is why he is not at this hospital. He is at a specialist. All of that smoke intake was one of the worst things that could have happened to him." Jace didn't know what to say. His voice was pulled out from him. His whole family tried to protect him from finding out.

"We hid him because we knew that Oliver had seen him at the scene of the crash and would blame him. He doesn't have much time left to live. The doctors projected that he would have twelve to eighteen months with treatment, which he has been getting. We didn't want his last few months to be spent in a jail cell. Your father sadly knew that you were our only chance to carry on the vineyard after him and I were gone. He wanted you to take over, that is why he gave you so many opportunities. Your sisters told him many times that they had no interest and would probably sell the vineyard. And that was not what your father had wanted."

It was all coming together. Jace had not seen what they had been trying to do. The sadness he felt made him go numb.

"So...I did kill Farmer Johnson?" Jace whispered to his mother. She did not respond right away. A subtle nod confirmed that he had killed the man and injured his son badly.

"I can't believe this." Jace said in a quiet voice. He wanted to get out of bed, but he was connected to so many machines, he didn't know how to get free.

"I could not have made things any worse." Jace mumbled under his breath.

"Our plan was to let Jace live out his life in privacy and if they blamed him for the accident, he sadly would not be here to punish. We didn't know what else to do. We didn't want to lose both of our sons. After all, it was Dane's idea. He wanted to protect you just like we did." A small grin came to her face and she reached for Jace's hand again.

"I don't deserve any of this. I should not have even come home." Jace said sulking to himself.

"Your brother loves you and did not want your mistake to

end your life as well. He wanted his death to clear you, so you could keep on living. He also accepted some of the blame for that night. He knew that the accident wouldn't have happened if you hadn't been trying to chase him down." Even though she was trying, this did not make Jace feel any better about it.

"We kept everything from you because we knew that you would try to fight us on it. Dane told us to try our best to not let you know about him or what he had done for you until he was gone. He knew his death would be hard on you, but watching him suffer through cancer was not a burden he wanted on your shoulders. He always tried to protect you." Jace couldn't believe that so many secrets had been kept just for his benefit. Trying to process everything, he had another question that he desperately wanted the answer to.

"How did Oliver get into our house? Into that hidden room in the basement?" Jace finally revealed that he knew about the secret room. He figured at this point, it didn't matter anymore. Not fazed by this at all, Marie answered.

"Macie was his nurse at the hospital after the accident. He was in a coma for a long time before he came out of it. When he was starting to remember what happened, we didn't know what to do. So Macie was able to devise a plan to move him from the hospital to our house without anyone seeing her. Having an inside person at the hospital really helped us. She continued to take care of him from that room. It was a waiting game until the inevitable happened with your brother."

"I didn't even know that room existed until I found it on

my own!" Jace said feeling like an outcast because his family had not let him in on the secret room.

"It really used to be an old wine cellar. I wasn't lying to you when I told you that is what it might be when you asked me about it before. We just made some improvements so it was safe and secure to hold someone there." Her explanation made this whole situation sound way too normal.

Then, a terrible thought came to his mind.

"Ma, you said that they found two bodies from the burned down house? What about Oliver? What happened to him after he did all of this?" Rage filled anger laced his voice. Marie looked back at her son with a blank stare.

"We don't know Jace. His body was not found, and he has not been seen since it happened." Marie felt like she had failed. She was unable to stop Oliver from doing this to her family, and now, she had let him get away with it.

Whether her feelings had any validity or not, it was how she felt.

"Have the police been looking for him at least?" Jace pleaded.

"Yes. I have given them my account of what happened, and your brother has as well...when he is able to muster up the energy anyway." Jace clenched his fists tightly and punched the bed.

"This is not fair! Any of this!" Jace raised his voice loud enough that Marie thought a nurse might come in to check on him.

"Just try to relax Jace. There is nothing you can do right now anyway accept try to get better." Marie stood up from her chair and ran her fingers through his hair. She always did this when he was younger, and it used to help put him right to sleep.

"Why don't you get some rest sweetie? You need strength to get through this. I promise I won't leave your side." Marie leaned over and kissed Jace on the forehead. Sliding down in bed, Jace turned away from his mother. The emptiness inside that he felt was overpowering.

"I'm so sorry for everything I have done." Jace whimpered and the tears began flowing out.

"I love you Jace."

"I love you too mom." And with that brief exchange of words, both mother and son wept over the loss of their beloved family member, and the loss of the life that they both had as it was now over as they once knew it.

Chapter 23

7 Months, 13 Days Later

The bright sunshine smiled down upon the small town of Willowcreek. Jace rode in the third car next to his mother. His black suit had been dry cleaned and the seams were fresh and crisp. He wore a black and white striped tie that matched his dress shirt. The shoes he wore were shiny black and came to a point at the end of them. Holding his mother's hand tight, it had been a tough day for them. The hearse was leading the way with the priest in the car in front of them.

Dane had lost his battle with cancer.

This was especially difficult because only seven months prior, the family had buried their father and husband. The cars formed a slow train with all their four-way flashers flashing. The police escort flew by on a motorcycle to stop the traffic at the only intersection in town. As they pulled into the cemetery, Jace stepped out first holding out his hand to help his mother. Both of his sisters had gotten out of the front seats on their own. Walking over to the site where Dane would be laid to rest was a gut-wrenching journey.

Death is too final.

The priest always told everyone that they would see their loved ones again someday. Jace always thought that "someday" was too vague of an answer. Plus, he was always a logical thinker and had a hard time believing in theories that had no hard-concrete evidence.

"Watch your step Ma." Jace grabbed her arm as they walked up a small slope covered in grass. This incline made it hard for some of the older people to make it to the cemetery without the assistance of others.

The burial process was short. Tears were shed at a life that was unfairly cut too short. It is a sad tragedy when a parent outlives a child. Ally had stood in the back with her Dad. She wanted to be with Jace but knew that he needed to comfort his mother and sisters.

The gravesite prayer was brief. Even though the family knew it was going to happen, that fact did not make it any easier. As the family began walking away from Dane's gravesite, Ally went up to them to give her condolences. She had been crying as well when she kissed the cheek of her boyfriend's mother. She grabbed Jace's hand and walked back down to their cars together.

Marie had been staying with one of her friends now that she was without a home. Jen had moved in with Elizabeth for the time being and Jace was bouncing from place to place. There was a small get together at the town hall. They had an extra room there that could fit a large amount of people. Food was provided, and memories of Dane's life were shared by anybody who knew him. Jace had an uneasy feeling in the pit of his stomach all day. He had lost two of the most important people in his life in a short amount of time.

"I'm going to head out Mom." Jace whispered into his

mother's ear.

"You are leaving already?" She sounded surprised.

"I need to take a drive or something to just get away from everything. I need to clear my head." He couldn't fully explain how he was feeling but being with a room full of people who wanted to talk to him was the last place he wanted to be.

"Please be safe Jace. You are the only man I have left in my life now." Her words were sad and her face was puffy from all of her emotions that day, and many days before.

"I will Ma. I love you." And with a kiss on the cheek, he was out the door and into his truck.

"Wait!" A voice yelled out to him. He rolled down his window as Ally came running over to speak to him.

"Where are you going?" She asked concerned.

"I just need to get away from here. I can't handle this sadness anymore." He shifted his truck into reverse and it slowly began to roll backwards.

"WAIT!" Ally screamed grabbing onto his side mirror like she was trying to stop the truck.

"If you are leaving then I'm going with you. You shouldn't be alone right now." Her words were forceful and direct.

"Please Al..."

"You don't have a choice, if you need to go for a quiet ride, then I am going to sit there in silence with you. You don't have a choice." She said walking around the back of the truck to make sure he didn't pull away without her getting in first. She figured that he wouldn't run her over no matter how upset he was. As she climbed in, the door slammed shut behind her. Leaning over, she pecked his cheek and got back into her seat and fastened the seatbelt.

Jace froze for a minute looking at her.

He thought how lucky he was that she had taken him back. He was determined not to let anything tear them apart again. He was thankful that he had had his dream about his own funeral. That was the single thing that gave him the courage to try to get Ally back. The truck rolled backwards as she smiled at him not saying a word as she had promised.

They drove around together for about an hour. The radio was on low and was providing just enough sound that their silence was not uncomfortable. Every so often, Ally reached out her hand to touch his. The warmth and support that she was giving him was much needed. Jace pulled his truck onto Stillwater road where his parent's house used to stand. He was planning to drive by it, but he decided not to. Pulling the truck into their stone driveway, the view of the trees lining the driveway was exactly the same. The sign that their father had custom made was still standing proud in their front yard. As the trees opened up, they revealed a sad scene. The house had been cleaned up for the most part but there were still some remnants left. The hole that was their basement was still open with yellow tape around it. Water from the lake was crashing against the rocks making a familiar sound. Nature did not seem to care what happened with all of the humans, it just kept on moving forward.

"Let's go for a walk." Jace said.

Nodding her head, both slid out of the truck and began to

walk towards the spot where the house used to sit. Ally grabbed his hand and put her fingers in between each one of his. They both looked around at the morbid sight. The barn was still standing. The store which was no longer operating looked dark and forgotten about. The driveway had no cars accept for his own. Ally looked at the store's door and remembered throwing the corks at Jace's head. She smiled to herself but didn't bring it up to Jace. It just wasn't the right time. They made their way to the back fields where all of the trees and vines were. The grapes had not been completely harvested the year before and they were not taken care of now. Jace grabbed an old vine and looked at its lifelessness in his hands. The sadness he felt because his father's dream of keeping the vineyard operational and in the family was going by the wayside. "I can't believe this happened." Jace whispered under his breath. Ally stood behind him and wrapped her arms around his chest.

"I'm sorry Jace." She said genuinely sad for his loss. Turning around, Jace hugged her back and put his head on top of hers. He kissed the top of her head and squeezed her tighter. Looking over the big fields of the vineyard, Jace couldn't help but feel lucky. His family had a plan for him and somehow, their plan had worked. The part that was lacking was on his end. The vineyard was still in the family, he just wasn't running it. As he stood there, his woman in his arms, he made a deal with his father and brother. He was going to get their family business going again no matter what it took. They sacrificed everything for him, and it was his turn to return the favor. He promised that wherever they were, he would not let Grazier's Grapes Vineyard die.

Ally and Jace walked up and down each aisle of trees. The more Jace thought about his plan, the more determined he felt. He told Ally what he wanted to do, and she knew that was going to be his plan eventually. She just wasn't sure when he would come to that realization on his own. They strolled by the lake looking out at the boats off in the distance.

"It really is a beautiful sight." Ally said watching a pair of hawks gliding on the wind over the water looking for their next meal.

"It truly is beautiful here." Jace agreed with her.

"There is nothing like small town living. Trust me on that!" Jace said with a half-smile. This made Ally very happy as it confirmed to her that Jace was not going anywhere and hopefully, their future together was looking bright!

As they walked down the last row, the tall trees from the woods resided on their left side. An uncomfortable feeling came over Jace as he remembered the opening to the secret room was not far from where they were standing. They moved closer and closer to the opening that led to that spot.

Jace did not want to see it.

He wanted to ignore that fact that it even existed. Walking by the spot, he kept his eyes forward and they both turned to go back towards the truck. A sound from in the woods made Jace stop walking. As he turned around, he squinted his eyes to look deep into the woods. He saw the tree that was marked right about where the opening was.

His heart sank.

A man stepped out from behind the tree. He was standing right where the door in the ground was. The man took one step forward into the light revealing his face.

It was Oliver!

An evil smile covered his face and his dark eyes were fixated on Jace.

Jace swallowed hard and a rush of panic filled his whole body.

"What's the matter Jace?" Ally asked innocently.

Jace closed his eyes as tight as he could. He kept them closed until Ally grabbed his shoulder.

"What is it?" She asked again. His eyes opened slowly and his vision restored. He again looked into the woods to confirm what he saw.

Oliver was gone.

Looking around frantically, he could not see him anywhere. Shaking his head, he hoped that what he had seen was just a figment of his imagination.

"I thought I saw something, but I was mistaken." Jace said with a smile trying his best to comfort and not alarm her. His heartbeat had risen, and a warm dampness covered his arms. An attack of paranoia was just what he didn't need.

"Are you sure you are okay?" She asked one more time not fully believing his previous answer.

"Yes. Trust me I am fine." He replied, and they again started towards the truck. Hearing the same noise come from the woods again, this time, he did not turn around. The pace at which he was walking increased as he did not want to investigate what he thought he had heard or seen.

Ally did a quick hop step to catch up with him.

"What's your hurry?" She shouted to him as he was putting distance between them and the woods. He didn't answer her right away. Opening her truck door, he hurried her in and jogged to his side. Jumping in, she was smiling at him.

"You are acting so strange all of a sudden." She said hoping he would explain why. Spinning the back tires, the truck was backing down and out of the driveway.

"I have just had enough of walking through the grapes for a while." He said. Shifting into gear, they pulled away. Ally looked at him confused but didn't say anything.

"This is my family's home. This is my home. We will be back." Jace stated in a strong threatening-like voice.

As they drove by the front of the house, Jace grabbed Ally's hand and squeezed it tight. Tears began to fill Jace's eyes as he drove away from the only place he had ever called home.

The End

A novel by David Jackson

Made in the USA
Middletown, DE
10 August 2020